Return items to **any** Swindon library by closing time on or before the date stamped. Only books and Audio Books can be renewed - phone your library or visit our website.

www.swindon.gov.uk/libraries

Moredon &
Rodbourne Cheney
Library 7\13
Tel: 01793 618230

26·9·13

9\1\14

20·2·14·

Wrough

WITHDRAWN
From S...

D0715949

...d. ...saw a heartbeat ... ...e's—one that had become ... ...an any other. She could feel the warm... ...is breath on her face, smell the fresh citrus scent of his soap as he drew closer. In that moment they were totally alone in that deserted theatre. No one else was there…only the two of them.

'Joanna,' he whispered.

His head bent towards hers, his lips drawing closer, and she closed her eyes and reality slipped away…

6 774 364 000

AUTHOR NOTE

Welcome back to the colourful world of Regency theatre and the complicated lives of the Bretton family, who made their first appearance in NO OCCUPATION FOR A LADY.

The second book in this series focuses on Laurence Bretton, Victoria's older brother, a quiet, scholarly man who shocks everyone—including his family—by standing up and claiming to be Valentine Lawe, the celebrated playwright. While his family know that Valentine Lawe is actually Victoria's pseudonym, and that Laurence only assumed the role in order to protect her reputation, he ends up bringing the character to full and glorious life when, overnight, he is thrust into the glittering spotlight that is London society.

But real life isn't a scripted play and, once launched upon the deception, Laurence finds there's no easy way of turning back—something he wishes he *could* do when he meets the beautiful Lady Joanna Northrup. Lady Joanna isn't interested in the flamboyant playwright who takes centre stage at elegant soirées. She's drawn to the amusing, scholarly man she met in a bookshop while browsing for books about ancient Egypt, a subject near and dear to her heart.

Unfortunately the truth comes at a cost, and as one lie follows another Laurence sees the woman he loves slipping away. His only chance is to take off the mask and step out of the role. But shedding a public face doesn't come without painful repercussions...

Enjoy!

NO ROLE FOR
A GENTLEMAN

Gail Whitiker

MILLS &
BOON

All the characters in this book have no existence outside the imagination of the author, and have no relation whatsoever to anyone bearing the same name or names. They are not even distantly inspired by any individual known or unknown to the author, and all the incidents are pure invention.

All Rights Reserved including the right of reproduction in whole or in part in any form. This edition is published by arrangement with Harlequin Enterprises II BV/S.à.r.l. The text of this publication or any part thereof may not be reproduced or transmitted in any form or by any means, electronic or mechanical, including photocopying, recording, storage in an information retrieval system, or otherwise, without the written permission of the publisher.

This book is sold subject to the condition that it shall not, by way of trade or otherwise, be lent, resold, hired out or otherwise circulated without the prior consent of the publisher in any form of binding or cover other than that in which it is published and without a similar condition including this condition being imposed on the subsequent purchaser.

® and TM are trademarks owned and used by the trademark owner and/or its licensee. Trademarks marked with ® are registered with the United Kingdom Patent Office and/or the Office for Harmonisation in the Internal Market and in other countries.

First published in Great Britain 2013
by Mills & Boon, an imprint of Harlequin (UK) Limited.
Harlequin (UK) Limited, Eton House, 18-24 Paradise Road,
Richmond, Surrey TW9 1SR

© Gail Whitiker 2013

ISBN: 978 0 263 89839 2

Harlequin (UK) policy is to use papers that are natural, renewable and recyclable products and made from wood grown in sustainable forests. The logging and manufacturing process conform to the legal environmental regulations of the country of origin.

Printed and bound in Spain
by Blackprint CPI, Barcelona

Gail Whitiker was born on the west coast of Wales and moved to Canada at an early age. Though she grew up reading everything from John Wyndham to Victoria Holt, frequent trips back to Wales inspired a fascination with castles and history, so it wasn't surprising that her first published book was set in Regency England. Now an award-winning author of both historical and contemporary novels, Gail lives on Vancouver Island, where she continues to indulge her fascination with the past as well as enjoying travel, music and spectacular scenery. Visit Gail at www.gailwhitiker.com

Previous novels by this author:

A MOST IMPROPER PROPOSAL*
THE GUARDIAN'S DILEMMA*
A SCANDALOUS COURTSHIP
A MOST UNSUITABLE BRIDE
A PROMISE TO RETURN
COURTING MISS VALLOIS
BRUSHED BY SCANDAL
IMPROPER MISS DARLING
NO OCCUPATION FOR A LADY

*part of *The Steepwood Scandal* mini-series

NO ROLE FOR A GENTLEMAN
features characters you will have met in
NO OCCUPATION FOR A LADY

**Did you know that some of these novels
are also available as eBooks?
Visit www.millsandboon.co.uk**

To my dear friends and fellow Pen Warriors
Bonnie Edwards, Vanessa Grant, E.C. Sheedy and
Laura Tobias, with whom I brainstormed the idea for this
series during one of our memorable Red Door weekends.
I am so grateful for their remarkable creativity and
never-ending enthusiasm. And, of course, for the laughter
that invariably results from five women
being locked up in a house together for three days.

Chapter One

It was in the Temple of the Muses that Laurence Bretton first saw her—a slender, dark-haired young woman standing by the far side of the circular counter, her features partially hidden by the wide brim of a fashionable bonnet. She was engaged in conversation with a clerk whose eagerness to assist was all too evident, but whose frequent blushes and stammering replies seemed to indicate a greater interest in the lady than in whatever she was attempting to buy.

'We do carry...an extensive selection of books dealing with the Ottoman Empire,' Laurence heard the young man say. 'Many of which I've read and can recommend myself. Reynier's *State of Egypt after the Battle of Heliopolis* was most informative and I have...a very good copy of that in stock.'

'As it happens, so do I,' the lady replied in a brisk though not unkind manner. 'And while I found Mr Reynier's perspectives entertaining, they were not detailed enough for my liking. Have you a copy of Volney's *Travels through Syria and Egypt*? The second volume?'

Volney? Laurence knew that name. Constantin François de Chassebœuf, Comte de Volney, was a French philosopher and historian who had spent several months in Egypt and Greater Syria, and who had written his *Voyage en Egypte et en Syrie* upon his return to France in 1785. Even to a scholar it was relatively dry reading and as such, hardly seemed the type of book a flower of English womanhood would be enquiring after.

Curious, he moved closer, in time to hear the clerk say, 'Regrettably, we do not have a copy of that particular book in stock, but if I might suggest—'

'Could you order it for me?'

The request was accompanied by a smile of such sweetness that the young man actually gulped. 'Well, yes, of course, though I don't know how much luck I will have in finding it. Perhaps Savary's *Letters on Egypt*?'

'Again, entertaining, but I have been told Volney's book is far more detailed.'

'It is,' Laurence said, slowly stepping forwards. 'And while it does not have as many sketches as I would like, his rendering of the

Temple of the Sun at Balbec is quite exceptional.'

The lady turned her head, the quick move-
ment setting the feathers on her bonnet swaying
and treating Laurence to an unobstructed view
of an exceptionally lovely face. Eyes, large and
expressive framed by dark lashes that appeared
even more so against the pale gold of her complexion, stared back at him, but with curiosity
rather than alarm. 'It is?'

'Yes. I would be happy to lend you my copy
as long as you promise to return it to me once
you are done.'

A pair of sable-smooth eyebrows rose above
a small nose lightly dusted with freckles. 'You
would lend such a valuable book to someone
with whom you were not acquainted?'

'No, I would lend it to someone I knew to be
as interested in the subject as I,' Laurence said
with a smile, 'after having taken the liberty of
introducing myself so that we would no longer
be unacquainted.' He touched the brim of his
beaver hat and bowed. 'Laurence Bretton, student of history and reputable lender of slightly
used books. And you are…?'

His enquiry was met by a startled pause and
then by a flash of amusement in eyes the colour of Cleopatra's emeralds. 'Joanna Northrup.
Dedicated researcher and devotee of all things

Egyptian.' She extended her hand. 'It seems we are well met, Mr Bretton.'

The proffered hand was encased in a smooth calfskin glove, but it was not the directness of the reply or the firmness of her grip that took Laurence by surprise. 'Northrup,' he repeated thoughtfully. 'Not, by any chance, related to Mr William Northrup, former Oxford lecturer and archaeologist involved in explorations in the upper Nile Valley in Egypt?'

Her look of startled surprise was followed by one of cautious interest. 'He is my father. Did you have the good fortune to attend one of his lectures?'

'Regrettably no, though, given his fondness for throwing chalk, it may have been to my advantage.'

'He does have exceptionally good aim,' she agreed.

'I know of several gentlemen willing to attest to it. Nevertheless, I would have liked the opportunity. He is a legend to those who have an interest in the study of ancient Egypt.'

'And have you such an interest, Mr Bretton?'

Recalled to the hours he had spent devouring anything he could find about the Rosetta Stone, a centuries-old block of igneous rock discovered in Egypt and said to be the key to translating ancient Egyptian hieroglyphs, Laurence nodded. 'You could say that, yes.'

'Then I wonder if you would be interested in attending a lecture my father is giving at the Apollo Club tomorrow evening? Attendance is by invitation only, but...' Miss Northrup dug into her reticule and pulled out a card '...if you present this at the door, you will be admitted.'

Laurence glanced at the card, upon which the address of the club, and underneath, the initials, JFN, had been written. 'Thank you, I will most certainly attend. I wasn't sure if your father was still involved in Egyptian explorations, given that I haven't heard much about him for quite some time.'

'We have not been much in society of late,' Miss Northrup said, her glance briefly dropping away. 'We suffered a series of...unfortunate deaths in my family and are only recently emerged from mourning.'

'I am sorry to hear that,' Laurence said, aware from the expression on her face that the memories were still painful. 'Such things are never easy.'

'No, they are not, especially when one's life is so drastically altered by the outcome.' Miss Northrup paused, as though reflecting on some private memory. Then, she drew a bracing breath and said, 'However, we bear it as best we can and move on.'

'Yes, we do,' Laurence said, seeing no point in telling her that while the dramatic changes in

his own life had not been inspired by such griev-
ous events, they had kept him fully occupied in
areas that had nothing to do with archaeological exploration. 'At what time does the lecture
commence?'

'Seven o'clock, but I suggest you come early if
you wish to secure a good seat,' Miss Northrup
said. 'Given that it is Papa's first lecture in quite
some time, we are expecting a large turnout.'

'Then I shall make every effort to do so,'
Laurence said, tucking the card into his pocket.
Then, because it was important that he know,
said, 'Will you be in attendance as well?'

'Oh, yes. While my father is one of the most
meticulous archaeologists I know, he tends to be
considerably less so when it comes to the organ-
isation of his lectures,' Miss Northrup admitted with a smile. 'He would no doubt leave half
of his notes at home and end up wandering off
into a lengthy dissertation about the pyramid of
Djoser, which has nothing to do with his more
recent work in the area around Thebes. I am
there to make sure he adheres to the program.'

Observing the fashionable gown, the elegant
bonnet and the cashmere shawl fastened at the
throat by a fine pearl brooch, Laurence was
hard-pressed to imagine the delicate creature
before him taking an interest in what his youngest sister had once called the most boring subject
on earth. 'You don't find the subject a little dry?'

'Not at all. I have worked at my father's side for a number of years, transcribing his notes, organising and labelling his finds, even helping him to map out his future expeditions. And last year, during a visit to the temple complex near Dendera, I was fortunate enough to find the most incredible piece of—'

'*You* found at Dendera?' Laurence repeated in astonishment. 'Are you telling me you actually *went* to Egypt with your father?'

It was a mistake. The lady's eyes narrowed and her lovely smile cooled every so slightly. 'Yes, I did. My second trip, in fact, and, in many ways, even more remarkable than the first. Words cannot describe the size and scope of Tentyra, or the magnificence of the Temple of Hathor. Such things truly must be seen to be appreciated.'

'Of that, there can be no doubt. And I meant no offence,' Laurence said, aware that she *had* misinterpreted his reaction and clearly thought less of him as a result. 'I am simply envious of your good fortune in being able to visit a country I have been reading about for so many years. To travel up the Nile and to see firsthand the wonders being discovered in the desert would be the culmination of a dream.'

She raised an eyebrow, but her voice was scblueeptical when she said, 'It would?'

'Good Lord, yes. Oh, I've read all the books,

studied the drawings, even talked with gentle-men who've been there,' Laurence said, 'but nothing could possibly replicate the experience of actually standing in a crowed street in Cairo, being assaulted by the sounds and smells of the markets or deafened by the babble of a thousand voices. One must *go* there in order to experience such things.'

The lady tilted her head, as though in recon-sideration of her first impression. 'And is it your intention to go there one day, Mr Bretton?'

'I sincerely hope to, yes,' Laurence said, knowing that if the opportunity were presented to him, he would go in a heartbeat. The conse-quences—and there would be consequences—could be dealt with once he got back. Right now it was important that he convince Miss Northrup of his sincerity, since he had obviously damaged his credibility and commitment to the field by having had the audacity to question hers.

Thankfully, the earnestness of his reply must have convinced her of the true extent of his in-terest, for she nodded briefly and said, 'Then I will offer you a few words of advice. If ever you do go, be sure to stay at Shepheard's in Cairo. It is an exceedingly civilised hotel and the view from the terrace is quite splendid. Also, when dealing with the locals, take time to negotiate anything you are offered. You will be hideously overcharged if you do not.'

'Thank you,' Laurence said, relieved he had not done irreparable damage to a relationship he had every intention of pursuing. 'If I am ever fortunate enough to find myself haggling over the price of a fellukah, I will be sure to remember your advice.'

'A fellukah is fine if you are only looking for transportation across the Nile, but if your trip is to be of a longer duration, I would suggest a dahabeeyah,' the lady said. 'They are far more comfortable, some being quite luxurious, though the price will reflect that, of course.'

'Of course.' This time, Laurence knew better than to smile, though he was strongly tempted to do so. He'd never met a woman who knew what a dahabeeyah was, let alone one who was able to tell him it was the preferred method for travel along the ancient river. 'Shall I bring Volney's *Travels* with me to the lecture tomorrow evening?'

'If you wouldn't mind. Unless…' Miss Northrup turned back to the clerk, who was still gazing at her with adoration and said, 'Is there any chance of you being able to procure a copy of the book for me before then?'

The young man's face fell. 'I shall do my best, but I very much doubt it.'

'Ah. Then I would be most grateful for the loan of Volney's *Travels*, Mr Bretton,' Miss Northrup said, turning back to him with a smile.

'And I promise to return it as soon as I am able. As one who has experienced the difficulty in finding reliable source materials, I know how hard it is to let such an exceptional volume out of your hands.'

'In this case, I have no concerns,' Laurence assured her—knowing that as long as *she* had the book, *he* had an excuse for seeing her. 'Volney and I will see you at the Apollo Club tomorrow evening. Good day, Miss Northrup.'

'Good day.' She started to turn away, and then stopped. 'Oh, Mr Bretton, there is…one more thing.'

Laurence turned back. 'Yes?'

She opened her mouth to speak, but then a tiny furrow appeared between her brows and she closed it again. Clearly, she wanted to say something, but for whatever reason was reluctant to do so. In the end, she merely shook her head and smiled. 'Never mind. You will find us upstairs in the Oracle Room tomorrow evening. Please try not to be late. And don't forget to bring the card.'

It was not what she had been going to say. Laurence was certain of that. But, hardly in a position to demand that she disclose what had so briefly tugged at her conscience, he simply assured her that he would not be late, offered her a bow then returned to his earlier browsing, all the while blessing the Fates for having sent him to this particular bookshop on this particular day.

To think he would actually be sitting in on a lecture given by the renowned archaeologist William Northrup! It was almost too good to be true, especially given the time he had devoted of late to activities that, while necessary to his family's well-being, did absolutely nothing to quench his thirst for knowledge. He was first and foremost a student of history and tomorrow evening, he would have an opportunity to talk with like-minded gentlemen about the exciting discoveries taking place in the area of Egypt known as the Valley of the Kings.

It was a long time since he had found himself looking forward to anything as much…except to seeing the intriguing Miss Northrup again, Laurence admitted, casting another glance in her direction. A woman of rare beauty, she obviously shared her father's love of ancient Egypt and, contrary to what society expected, had been allowed to travel with him to share in the excitement of his explorations. There had been no mistaking the enthusiasm in her voice when she had spoken of her impressions of the ruins at Dendera, and if she had worked at her father's side for so many years, there could be no question that her interest in the subject was genuine.

Laurence could think of no other young lady—and he had met a great many over the last eight months—who would welcome such an adventure, which was all the more reason for getting to know the charming and decidedly intriguing Miss Joanna Northrup a great deal better.

Joanna did not speak to Laurence Bretton again. Though she was aware of him browsing through a selection of books on a table close to the window, she could think of no reasonable excuse for approaching him a second time—other than to correct his erroneous assumption that she was *Miss* Joanna Northrup—and so, tucking her purchases under her arm, left the shop and climbed into the waiting carriage.

Why she had allowed the error in address to stand was something she was not so easily able to explain. She'd had eight months to come to terms with the fact that she was now Lady Joanna Northrup. Eight months to accept that as a result of the untimely deaths of her uncle and his heir, her father was no longer a humble academic, but the Fourth Earl of Bonnington. Surely that was time enough to come to terms with such a drastic alteration in one's circumstances.

'Obviously not,' Joanna murmured as the carriage clipped smartly towards her new home on Eaton Place. Otherwise she would not have allowed a handsome but completely unknown gentleman to come up to her in a shop, offer to lend her a book then use the offer as an excuse to introduce himself, all without informing him of her true position in society.

The Practice, as her father's eldest sister was so fond of saying, was to wait for a person acquainted with both the lady and the gentleman to make the introduction, then for the lady to enter into the conversation to the degree to which she felt it appropriate, that degree being determined by the gentleman's position in society and, to a much lesser degree, by the nicety of his manners and comeliness of his person.

From what little Joanna had been able to glean of Mr Bretton's situation in life, the conversation was not one of which her aunt would have approved.

Of course, had he *not* introduced himself, she would not be in the enviable position now of having Mr Volney's book to read over the weekend. She would still be scouring London's many bookshops, quizzing inexperienced clerks in her search for the elusive volume and probably meeting with the same disappointing results as she had in all of her previous attempts. So, in fact, her meeting with Mr Bretton had been most fortuitous in that it had saved her from all those endless hours of tedium!

The fact he had initially been sceptical of her interest in Egypt was a failing Joanna was willing to overlook. She had encountered it countless times before, both from gentlemen who thought she hadn't a brain in her head and from women who couldn't understand her desire to be more than a wife or mother. But given that his interest in the subject was surely as keen as her own, she was willing to forgive him his boldness in approaching her, and to excuse herself for having encouraged the conversation. She was even looking forward to seeing him at her father's lecture tomorrow evening.

It would be a pleasure talking to a London gentleman who really did know more about pharaohs than foxhunting and wasn't ashamed to admit it!

Upon arriving home, Joanna turned her attention to the events of the upcoming days. Now that the family's period of mourning was at an end, invitations had begun arriving again. While she wanted to believe that most were extended out of a genuine desire to welcome the new Lord Bonnington and his daughter to society, she suspected that just as many were prompted by morbid curiosity.

After all, in the blink of an eye, her father had gone from being the ignored younger son and brother of an earl, to being the Earl of Bonnington himself, while she had been elevated from a bluestocking nobody to the highly eligible Lady Joanna Northrup.

Astonishing, really, how far reaching the effects of a single gunshot could be.

'Ah, there you are, Joanna,' Lady Cynthia Klegston said as Joanna walked into the morning room. 'All finished with your shopping?'

'For now.' Joanna bent to kiss her aunt on the cheek—a token of respect rather than affection. She had never been entirely comfortable in the company of her father's eldest sister, a brusque, plain-speaking widow with two married daughters who had paid little or no attention to her youngest brother before his unexpected elevation to the peerage and who only did so now because she realised it was in her best interests to do so. 'I left your necklace with the jeweller to be repaired, checked on the order for your stationery and advised Madame Clermont that you would be in to see her at two o'clock this afternoon. She said that would be convenient.'

'Of course it will be convenient,' Lady Cynthia snapped. 'I bring her a great deal of business. It behoves her to find it convenient. And I think you had best come with me. I've decided you shall have a new gown for the dinner party. As a young lady who is not engaged or married, we cannot afford to have you appear anything less than your best, especially now that you *are* Lady Joanna Northrup and in need of a wealthy husband. Dash it all, where *are* my spectacles? I can never find the wretched things when I need them.'

Having noticed the spectacles on the small table next to the wing chair, Joanna silently went to retrieve them. As a rule, she tried to stay out of her aunt's way. Lady Cynthia was a forceful presence, who, like her late older brother, hadn't bothered to keep in touch with her younger brother's family until death had forced her to do so.

Ironic, really, that her aunt, who had once been so openly disapproving of every aspect of William's life, should now be heard to say that she was doing all she could to help her poor brother and niece cope with the unexpected changes thrust upon them.

'Speaking of convenient,' Lady Cynthia said, 'did you find whatever it was you were looking for?'

'It was a book and, no, I did not,' Joanna said, surprised her aunt would even remember that her niece had gone out for reasons other than to see to her own errands. 'But I happened upon a gentleman who offered to lend me his copy.'

'How thoughtful.' Lady Cynthia gazed up at Joanna over the rim of her spectacles. 'I take it you were acquainted with the gentleman?'

'No, but he knew Papa,' Joanna said, stretching the truth a little. 'He will be coming to the lecture tomorrow evening.'

Her aunt's expression was blank. 'Lecture?'

'Yes. The one Papa is giving at the Apollo Club. I did tell you about it,' Joanna said. 'Just as I told you that I would be in attendance as well, given that many of my drawings will be on display.'

Her aunt's reaction was exactly what Joanna had been expecting. She took off her glasses and said with a sigh of frustration, 'Joanna, I really cannot understand why you and your father persist in this ridiculous occupation. He is the Earl of Bonnington now and with that comes an obligation to his name and his position in society. Both of which are far more important than sitting around with a bunch of stodgy old men talking about Egypt.'

'I understand your concern, Aunt,' Joanna said as patiently as she could. 'But *you* must understand that up until now, archaeology and the study of ancient Egypt have been the focus of my father's life.'

'Of course, because his position in the family made it necessary that he find something to do with his time,' Lady Cynthia said, 'though why he could not have gone into the church or purchased a commission is beyond me. Either of those occupations would have been far more suitable. However, with both Hubert and

Trevor gone, your father is now the earl and he must accept the responsibilities inherent with the title. That includes seeing to your welfare and he *must* know that your chances of making a good match will *not* be improved by his conduct,' Lady Cynthia said, the expression on her face leaving Joanna in no doubt as to her displeasure. 'Circumstances demand that you marry well, and your bluestocking tendencies and your father's willingness to encourage them will not improve your chances.'

'I doubt it will be my conduct or my father's that will have a negative impact on my eligibility, Aunt,' Joanna was stung into replying. 'I suspect much of society knows that Papa is heavily in debt as a result of his brother's and nephew's recklessness and if you would find fault with anyone, it seems to me it should be with those who are truly to *blame* for the predicament in which we now find ourselves!'

It was a sad but true commentary on the state of their affairs. Joanna's late uncle had gambled away a large part of the family's fortune, and his son had squandered the rest on women and horses. Both had met with dramatic ends: her uncle from a fall off a cliff in a drunken stupor, and her cousin from a gunshot wound sustained during a duel with the angry husband of the woman with whom he had been having an affair.

The sad result was that, while Joanna's father

had inherited a lofty title, there was precious little to go along with it. Bonnington Manor, a once-beautiful Elizabethan house, had been left to moulder in the English countryside, its stone walls overgrown with vegetation, its lush gardens choked with weeds. Even the town house in London was in desperate need of refurbishment. While both residences had come with a handful of loyal retainers, the list of unpaid bills that accompanied them was enough to make a king blush.

Little wonder her father had not embraced his elevation to the peerage, Joanna reflected wryly. By necessity, one of his first duties was to find a way of raising enough money to carry out the extensive repairs required—and she was not so naïve as to believe that *she* did not play a role in that solution.

'Well, no matter what the state of your father's affairs, I do not intend to let you sit like a wallflower in a garden of roses,' Lady Cynthia said. 'You are a fine-looking girl. With luck, we will be able to attract a gentleman of means and to secure an offer of marriage, which we both know is your father's *only* hope of salvaging the estate given his own stubborn refusal to marry again. Speaking of which, I hope you have not forgotten that we are going out this evening?'

Joanna had, but given her aunt's decidedly

prickly mood, decided it would be wiser not to let on. 'No, of course not.'

'Good, because while I do not particularly care for Mrs Blough-Upton, it is important that you be seen as often as possible now that you are out of mourning. You will be one and twenty on your next birthday and I do not intend to allow this obsession with Egypt to ruin your chances for making a good marriage.'

Sensing there was nothing to be gained by continuing the conversation, Joanna bid her aunt a polite good morning and then went upstairs to her room. She was well aware that her aunt's only concern was to find her niece a rich husband. And that she could not understand why *anyone* would be so passionate about a country that was dirty, poverty stricken and populated by the most inhospitable people imaginable.

Joanna thought the opinion a trifle unfair given that her aunt had never set foot in the country, but neither could she entirely find fault with the assessment. Egypt *was* dirty and poverty stricken and populated by some very questionable types—but there was so much to see and discover that the one negated the other. Tremendous finds had been made in the last few decades. Travellers were flocking to the banks of the Nile to see the wonders being discovered there, while explorers following in the footsteps of James Bruce and Giovanni Belzoni were setting out to uncover the tombs of long-dead kings, hoping to find in those burial chambers a cache of precious metals and jewels. And, more importantly, clues to deciphering the mysteries of the past.

Joanna sincerely hoped her father would find such a tomb one day and that she would be at his side when he did. Together, they would see sights no English man or woman ever had and perhaps be able to write another chapter in the history of the world.

It was hard to believe *anyone* wouldn't view such a marvellous trip as the opportunity of a lifetime.

Mr Laurence Bretton certainly had. His candid statements and earnest manner had left Joanna in no doubt as to his desire to visit Egypt and, despite the impropriety of his conduct, she was not sorry he had come up to her in the shop. Though he reminded her of one of her father's students with his wire-rimmed spectacles, rumpled jacket and studious air, he was clearly an educated man. Intelligent, well spoken and dedicated to uncovering the mysteries of a bygone age, he was a far cry from the dandies and fops who were more concerned with the cut of their coats than with the secrets of the past. She was looking forward to seeing him again for that reason alone.

The fact he had the most astonishing blue

eyes and one of the most attractive smiles she had ever seen really had nothing at all to do with it.

At half past nine that evening, Laurence stood in his dressing room as his valet ran a brush over the back and shoulders of his perfectly fitted black velvet coat. Though the cut of the *habit à la française* was at least a decade out of date, it was perfectly in keeping with the role he would be playing tonight. That of Valentine Lawe, the wildly successful playwright, whose most recent work, *A Lady's Choice*, was once again playing to packed houses at the elegant Gryphon Theatre.

'Laurence, are you almost ready to go?' his sister enquired from the doorway. 'If we do not leave soon we are going to be late and that would be shockingly bad mannered given that you *are* the guest of honour.'

'I am not the guest of honour, Tory,' Laurence said, surveying the froth of lace at his throat with a critical eye. It was a touch more flamboyant than usual, but, given the nature of the event, he doubted it would go amiss. Lydia and her friends did so love a touch of the dramatic. 'I am but one of the many guests Lydia will have invited and, in such a crowd, I doubt she will even notice what time we arrive.'

'Oh, she'll notice,' Victoria said with a feline

smile. 'The widow is over the moon at being able
to tell her friends that the famous playwright,
Valentine Lawe, will be at her gathering this
evening. She is but another of your many con-
quests, my dear, and I do believe she is hoping
for an opportunity to further the acquaintance,
if you know what I mean.'

Laurence frowned, all too aware of what his
sister meant and none too pleased by the impli-
cation. 'Thank you, but I have absolutely no intention of becoming the latest in a long line of
Lydia's discarded lovers, nor a potential candidate for her third husband. She may be one of
the wealthiest widows in town, but having spent
more time in her company than I like, I understand why people say what they do about her.'
He cast a last look at his appearance and then
nodded his satisfaction. 'Thank you, Edwards.
As usual, you have done an excellent job of turning me out in a manner suitable to the occasion.'

'My pleasure, Mr Bretton.'

As the valet bowed and withdrew, Victoria
picked up the boutonnière resting on the dressing table and drew out the pin. 'Are you sure you
want me to come with you tonight, dearest? You
really don't need me at your side any more. Lord
knows, you've attended enough gatherings in
the guise of Valentine Lawe to be able to carry
it off without any assistance from me.'

'Be that as it may, I *like* having you there,'

Laurence said, watching his sister pin the velvety-red rose close to his collar. 'You are a refreshing breath of reality in the midst of all this madness.'

'Madness *you* invited upon yourself,' Victoria murmured, stepping back to survey her handiwork. '*You* were the one who volunteered to step into the role of Valentine Lawe. Before that, he existed only in my mind, the *nom de plume* behind which I wrote my plays.'

'Exactly. Valentine Lawe *is* your creation so it is only right that you be there to hear the compliments being showered upon his…or rather, your plays,' Laurence said. 'Besides, what else have you to do this evening? I happen to know that your husband is otherwise engaged.'

'Yes, but don't forget that I am helping his cousin Isabelle plan her wedding, as well as picking out furnishings for the orphanage, and all while endeavouring to write a new play. I have more than enough to do and not nearly enough time in which to do it.'

'Nonsense. Your mother-in-law is overseeing most of the arrangements for Isabelle's wedding,' Laurence said, 'and your husband has more than enough servants to attend to the requirements of his new orphanage. As for the play, I have every confidence in you penning yet another masterpiece that will garner the same high level of praise as your last four. Besides, you know you will have a much better time if you come with me.'

'I'm not so sure about that,' Victoria said. 'Lydia Blough-Upton has never been one of my favourite people. She is an outrageous flirt, an insatiable gossip and she continues to make her feelings for you embarrassingly obvious. Still, I suppose I do owe you a few more favours. Your stepping forwards to assume the role of Valentine Lawe has certainly allowed *my* life to return to normal, though given what it's done to yours, I do wonder if it wouldn't have been easier just to admit that I wrote the plays and see how it all turned out.'

'In some ways, I suspect it would,' Laurence said, removing his spectacles and placing them on the dressing table. He only needed them for reading and, given that they did nothing for the image he was trying to convey, he felt no grief at leaving them behind. 'No doubt you and Winifred would have been shunned by good society for a time and our family would have been ignored by those who felt it wasn't the thing for the daughter of a gentleman to write plays that mocked society and the church.'

'I do not mock the church,' Victoria said defensively. 'Only those who draw their livings from it and you cannot deny there is more than enough room for ridicule in that. As to society, I suspect the furore would have eventually died down, replaced by an even more scandalous bit of gossip about someone placed far higher up the social ladder than me. But when I see how much happier Mama and Winifred are with you in the role of Valentine Lawe than me, I have to believe you did the right thing, Laurie. Even if you did fail to give it the consideration it deserved.'

'I gave it no consideration whatsoever.'

'Exactly, and taking that into account, I think it has all turned out very well. Besides, only think how disappointed the young ladies would be if they were to find out that you are *not* the dashing and very eligible playwright they have all come to know and admire.'

'I doubt it would trouble them overly much,' Laurence said, thinking not for the first time of the lovely and erudite Miss Joanna Northrup, a lady he tended to believe would be far more impressed with his intellectual abilities than his literary ones. 'They are infatuated with the image, not with the man.'

'I'm not so sure,' Victoria said. 'Even I have seen the changes in you since you assumed the role of Valentine Lawe. You are far more confident than you were in the past and, while you have always been charming, there is an added refinement to your manner now that is highly engaging. No doubt Lydia Blough-Upton would like to have you all to herself tonight so she can flirt with you unobserved by your staid and newly married sister.'

'My darling girl,' Laurence said, tucking Victoria's arm in his, 'you will never be staid and it is quite impossible for me to do *anything* unobserved now that the world believes me to be Valentine Lawe. Anonymity is a thing of the past. I am now and for ever will be the public face of your creative genius.'

'Then let us go forth and face the world together,' Victoria said, sweeping her fan off the bed. 'All of London awaits your entrance and none more so than the ever-growing and increasingly ardent fans of the illustrious Valentine Lawe!'

Chapter Two

As Lady Cynthia had predicted, Mrs Blough-Upton's soirée was a breath-stealing crush that Joanna was ready to leave well before the clock chimed the midnight hour. She had forgotten how stifling these affairs could be and how pompous was much of English society. Several well-dressed couples cast curious glances in her direction, and though she was paid flattering compliments by many of the gentlemen to whom she was introduced, a few of the young ladies were not as kind.

'I suppose it is only to be expected that you would come back with imperfections of the skin,' Miss Blenkinsop said, peering with disdain at the offending freckles sprinkled across the bridge of Joanna's nose. 'After all, the sun is so very harsh in India.'

'Egypt.'

'I beg your pardon?'

'My father and I were in Egypt,' Joanna said as patiently as she could. 'Not India.'

'Ah. But the two countries are quite close, are they not?'

'Do you not wear a hat when you are out during the day, Lady Joanna?' Miss Farkington enquired.

'Of course, but with the sun being so strong, it is sometimes difficult to—'

'I would *die* if I were ever to discover a blemish on my skin,' Miss Blenkinsop interrupted dramatically. 'It is the reason I spent most of last summer in the drawing room.'

'Indeed, Mama insists on rubbing *my* skin with lemon juice whenever I have been outside,' Miss Farkington informed them. 'She said an ounce of prevention is worth a pound of cure and that if I wish to go about in the sun, I should wait until after I am married to do so. And preferably until after I have presented my husband with his first heir.'

Having no idea how to respond to such a silly remark, Joanna said nothing, convinced it was the wisest course of action. She had long since come to the conclusion that she had absolutely nothing in common with the Misses Blenkinsop and Farkington, who subscribed to the popular belief that young women should do nothing that might detract from their eligibility as wives. They were like hothouse flowers: best viewed from a distance and preferably in the rarefied atmosphere of a drawing room.

Then, a collective sigh echoed around the room as Lydia Blough-Upton walked in on the arm of a gentleman who looked to be considerably younger than her and not in the least concerned about it. He was dressed formally in black-and-white evening attire, though the cut of the jacket and the heavy use of embroidery were clearly reminiscent of a bygone age. His waistcoat, blindingly white and intricately embroidered with silver thread, had been cut by a master's hand. The smoothness of his satin pantaloons and silk stockings outlined muscular calves and thighs that, given the rest of his build, owed nothing to the effects of padding.

That he looked like an aristocrat was evident to every person in the room. His rich brown hair was styled in a classic crop and his eyes, blue as lapis lazuli, gazed out from a face more handsome than any gentleman's in the room. But Joanna had seen those eyes before. Though they had been partially hidden behind wire-rimmed spectacles, the intensity of the colour had struck her forcibly at the time, as had the sincerity of his smile and the earnest nature of his conversation.

A conversation that had given her absolutely

no reason to believe that Mr Laurence Bretton was anything but the humble student of history he had so convincingly purported to be.

'Isn't he divine?' gushed Miss Farkington. 'I wish he would write something for me.'

'Write?' Joanna's head snapped around as an unhappy memory of a youthful infatuation came back to haunt her. 'Never tell me he's a poet?'

'Dear me, no, he's a playwright. Surely you've heard of Valentine Lawe?'

'Actually, no.'

'How strange.' Miss Farkington blinked. 'His latest play is all the rage. But then you have been in mourning for quite some time.'

'Mama and I have been to see it twice,' Miss Blenkinsop said with a condescending air. 'You really should go now that you are moving in society again, Lady Joanna. It is all anyone can talk about, as is Mr Bretton himself. Is he not the most dashing of gentleman?'

Joanna stared at the man who was making such an impact on the ladies in the room and wondered why he had made no mention to her of his literary accomplishments when they had met earlier in the day. All he'd said then was that he was a devoted student of ancient Egypt —which was obviously not true since his appearance on Mrs Blough-Upton's arm now in clothes that would have put a dandy to shame proclaimed him for the Pink of Fashion he so evidently was.

'Ah, there you are, Joanna,' Lady Cynthia said, pushing her way through the crowd to appear at her niece's side. 'Mr Albert Rowe, eldest son of Lord Rowe and heir to a considerable fortune, is interested in making your acquaintance. I told him I would bring you to him at once.'

'Aunt, that gentleman on Mrs Blough-Upton's arm,' Joanna said, ignoring her aunt's petition, 'do you know him?'

Lady Cynthia turned her head in the direction of their hostess and her eyes widened. 'Well, well, so he *did* come. I'd heard that he had been invited, but no one knew whether or not he would attend. Lydia is so very forward and she has made no secret of her affection for him.'

'Then you *do* know him?'

'Of course I know him, Joanna. Everyone knows Laurence Bretton, or rather, Valentine Lawe as he is better known to theatre-going audiences. His latest play opened at the Gryphon Theatre last season and has been brought back for this one. I know you're not all that fond of theatre, but you really should go. Everyone is talking about the play and Mr Bretton is himself garnering a great deal of attention. I understand he has been invited to dine with one of the royal dukes.'

Joanna turned back to watch the gentleman who had somehow managed to disengage himself from Mrs Blough-Upton's talons and now stood chatting to three young ladies who giggled a great deal and seemed to hang on every word he said. So, he was not the erudite student of archaeology he had led her to believe. He was a successful playwright who, judging by the reactions of the Misses Farkington and Blenkinsop, wrote the kind of romantic drivel so popular with society today—weakly plotted stories about star-crossed lovers, most often portrayed by simpering young women who could cry on cue and impossibly handsome men who could not act.

It was a sobering discovery.

Still, at least now she knew the truth about him. Whatever his true purpose in coming up to her in the bookshop this afternoon, it obviously hadn't had anything to do with his professed love of ancient Egypt. No doubt he'd known *exactly* who she was, even though he had pretended not to, and his offer to lend her a book had been nothing more than a calculated attempt to engage her in conversation without going to the trouble of securing a proper introduction; something she would *never* have countenanced had she known beforehand exactly who and what he was.

And then, the unexpected. Mr Bretton, breaking off his conversation with the prettiest of the three ladies, looked up and met Joanna's eyes across the room.

The contact was startling, the intensity of that brilliant blue gaze unnerving.

Joanna felt hot colour bloom in her cheeks and hastily looked away, but not before seeing him make his excuses to the ladies and then start in her direction.

'Oh, good Lord, he's coming this way,' Lady Cynthia said.

Joanna glanced at her aunt, astonished to hear the same kind of fatuous adulation in her voice as she had in Miss Blenkinsop's earlier. Gracious, was she the *only* woman in the room who was not over the moon at the prospect of talking to the man? 'Really, Aunt, he is only a—'

'Miss Northrup,' Mr Bretton said, coming to a halt in front of her. 'We meet again. And sooner than expected.'

His smile was as devastating as it had been earlier in the day, but Joanna no longer found it quite so endearing. 'Indeed, Mr Bretton,' she said, lifting her chin. 'Or should I say, Mr Lawe.'

To her annoyance, he actually smiled. 'I would prefer Mr Bretton since Valentine Lawe really doesn't exist.'

Yet, he did tonight, Joanna reflected cynically. Standing before her in clothes more suited to the stage than a drawing room, he exuded confidence and seemed blissfully unaware of the furore he was causing in the hearts of the young—and not so young—ladies around him.

Taller than she remembered, his features were more finely chiselled, likely due to the fact he had left his spectacles at home. His mouth was generous and his lips, which had no doubt whispered many a charming endearment in Mrs Blough-Upton's ear, were firm and quite disturbingly sensual.

And he wore a single red rose pinned close to the collar of his jacket.

Joanna hardly knew what to make of him.

Neither, it seemed, did her aunt, who was staring at both of them with unconcealed delight. 'My dear Mr Bretton, can it be that you and Lady Joanna are already acquainted?'

At that, finally, he did falter. '*Lady* Joanna?' His dark brows drew together. 'Forgive me. I was not aware of the distinction.'

'Perhaps my niece did not think to mention it.'

'No, I did not,' Joanna said, smiling sweetly. 'But then, it was hardly relevant to the topic of our conversation. Any more than was Mr Bretton being a famous playwright.' She might be new to the role of earl's daughter, but she too could play the part when called upon to do so.

'Well, it is a great honour to meet you in person, Mr Bretton,' Lady Cynthia said, either unaware of the sparks flying back and forth between Joanna and the playwright or choosing to ignore them. 'I have enjoyed each and every one of your plays, though I must say I particularly enjoyed *A Lady's Choice*. When Miss Turcott walked away from Elliot Black in the second to last scene, I was quite overcome with emotion. I feared for an unhappy outcome, but you ended it splendidly.'

'Thank you, Lady Cynthia,' Bretton said, making her a low bow. 'I am glad to hear it met with your approval and that you enjoyed it.'

'I most certainly did. In fact, I was just saying to my niece that she really must see it now that she is out of mourning. I've always thought it a great pity she didn't have a chance to see *Penelope's Swain*, but I believe it opened while Lady Joanna was in—that is, while she and her father were travelling,' Lady Cynthia said with a smile. 'On the Continent.'

On the *Continent*? Joanna was hard pressed not to roll her eyes. Why could her aunt not just say Egypt? Everyone knew what her father did and where he'd spent his time prior to his elevation, so it went without saying that if she was with him, they certainly weren't in the glittering capitals of Europe.

Of course, Lady Cynthia would never *wish* to openly acknowledge Joanna's fondness for Egypt for fear it might result in a gentleman thinking the less of her. In that regard, her aunt was no less concerned with the proprieties than any mother in the room and if presenting her niece in the best light possible meant omitting a

few pertinent details, she was more than happy
to do so. Especially now, when the securing of
a rich husband was of such vital importance.

What a pity, Joanna reflected drily, that her
aunt was not aware that Laurence Bretton, alias
Valentine Lawe, was already well acquainted
with her niece's lamentable fondness for that
country.

'I wonder, Lady Cynthia, since Lady Joanna
has not yet seen the play, if you would be agreeable to seeing it as my guests?' Mr Bretton offered unexpectedly. 'I would be happy to make
available the use of my uncle's box.'

Joanna's eyes widened in dismay. Spend an
entire evening in his company? Oh, no, that
would never do. Whatever good impression he
might have made in the bookshop had been completed negated by his unexpected appearance
here tonight. And she was quite prepared to tell
him so when her aunt, obviously viewing his
offer as some kind of gift from the gods, said,
'How very kind, Mr Bretton. I can only imagine
that seeing the play in the company of the gentleman who wrote it would add immeasurably
to the experience. Do you not think so, Joanna?'

'I really don't see that it would make any
diff—'

'Thank you, Mr Bretton, we would be most
happy to attend,' Lady Cynthia cut in smoothly.
'But you must allow me to return the favour by

inviting you to a soirée my brother is hosting a week from Friday. As you may or may not know, the family is only recently emerged from mourning after the tragic deaths of our eldest brother and his son and we thought a small gathering of friends would be a pleasant way of reintroducing Lady Joanna to society, as well as to celebrating my youngest brother's elevation to the peerage.'

For the second time that night, Mr Bretton looked nonplussed. 'Mr Northrup's elevation?'

'Yes, he is the new Lord Bonnington. He inherited the title on the death of his nephew,' Lady Cynthia said.

Joanna said nothing, happy not to have been the one to break the news to Mr Bretton. He would have found out at the lecture tomorrow evening anyway, and while she had been feeling somewhat guilty for not having acquainted him with the truth of her situation in the bookshop, she no longer did. If he could keep secrets, so could she.

'Please accept my apologies,' Mr Bretton said quietly. 'I was not aware of your brother's elevation, my ignorance no doubt due to having been too caught up in the writing of a new play. During such times I tend not to study the society pages. As to the passing of both your brother and nephew, Lady Cynthia, allow me to offer my most sincere condolences. Lady Joanna did inform me, in very general terms, of the family's bereavement, but not of the specifics.'

'Likely because the brothers were not close,' Lady Cynthia admitted. 'One cannot always claim a close kinship with one's own family, can one, Mr Bretton? As to the soirée, it will be a celebration of good news rather than bad and we would be most pleased if you would attend. I know that many of the young ladies present will be thrilled to hear that such a famous and very handsome playwright will be found in their midst.'

'You are kind to say so and, if I am not otherwise engaged, I would be happy to attend,' Mr Bretton said, his brilliant gaze catching and holding Joanna's. 'It will give me an opportunity to apologise more eloquently to your niece for not having acquainted her with the truth about my other occupation the first time we met.'

'Pray do not give it another thought, Mr Bretton,' Joanna said, refusing to be charmed. 'As you say, our conversation was as far removed from the world of the theatre as it is possible to imagine and I dare say if you *had* bothered to acquaint me with the facts, it would not have lasted as long as it did.'

The expression in Mr Bretton's eyes left Joanna in no doubt that he knew exactly what she intended by the remark and that he was not in the least discouraged by it, neither of which served to endear him to her. Obviously he found her disapproval amusing and her attempts at putting him in his place a waste of time, especially in light of her aunt's all-too-embarrassing display of devotion.

Before he had a chance to reply, however, Mrs Blough-Upton swept down on them like an avenging eagle anxious to reclaim its prey.

'There you are, my dear Mr Bretton. I have been looking for you this past five minutes. Really, Lady Joanna,' Mrs Blough-Upton said, linking her arm through Mr Bretton's in an unmistakably proprietary gesture, 'it is quite naughty of you to keep the most popular playwright in London to yourself all evening. There are any number of other eligible young ladies here anxious to make his acquaintance and I must do my duty as hostess.' She flashed Joanna an insincere smile. 'I'm sure you understand.'

'Of course,' Joanna said, smiling every bit as insincerely. Really, did the woman think her a fool? Lydia Blough-Upton had no more intention of introducing Laurence Bretton to single young women than she did of flying to the moon! It was simply an excuse to pry him away from his present company and to keep him to herself for as long as possible. A ruse that worked to perfection given that Mr Bretton bowed and allowed himself to be led away, much to Joanna's relief and her aunt's obvious disapproval.

'Well, really! The woman is just *too* forward!' Lady Cynthia stated emphatically. 'Has she no shame?'

'It would appear not, Aunt.'

'And poor Mr Bretton, what a gentleman! He could have refused to go with her, but he obviously knew how humiliating it would have been.'

'I doubt altruism had anything to do with it, Aunt,' Joanna said, surprised that her aunt had been so thoroughly taken in by his act. 'He clearly enjoys being the centre of attention. Look at the way he is dressed. What is that if not a blatant attempt at drawing all eyes to himself?'

'Nonsense, Joanna, it isn't at all like that. You were not here, of course, so you cannot be expected to know, but the first time Mr Bretton appeared in public as Valentine Lawe, that was how he was dressed.'

'I cannot think why, unless his first appearance was made at a masquerade ball.'

'As a matter of fact, it was. Lady Drake's masquerade, to be exact,' Lady Cynthia said. 'No one had any idea who Valentine Lawe was before that. Some thought him a half-mad recluse while others believed it was the *nom de plume* of someone highly placed in society. For a time, it was even whispered that his sister, Victoria, now Mrs Devlin, was the famous playwright and that caused quite a stir, I can tell you. But it wasn't long after those rumours began to surface that Mr Bretton stepped forwards and claimed the role as his own.'

'An interesting story, Aunt, but this is not a costume ball and the gentleman's appearance is years out of date.'

'Of course it is, but you cannot deny how dashing he looks in the part,' Lady Cynthia said. 'The ladies all adore it, of course.'

'I still think it speaks to an outrageous sense of vanity,' Joanna muttered, refusing to admit, even to herself, that the elegant clothes and raffish manner did suit him uncommonly well.

'Nonsense, Mr Bretton is the most humble of men! You heard him just now. There was no arrogance to his speech. No condescension to his manner. He is exactly what he seems. A charming man gifted with the ability to write excellent plays. And to think you already knew him,' her aunt said in a tone of exasperation. 'I cannot imagine why you did not bother to tell me.'

'I did not bother to tell you because I did not know he *was* anyone of consequence,' Joanna said. 'He introduced himself as Mr Laurence Bretton, plain and simple.'

'Well, he is neither plain nor simple and I suspect if he was better placed in society, Lydia would have already snapped him up.'

'His lack of a title doesn't seem to be an impediment as far as she is concerned,' Joanna

drawled. 'But I am astonished you invited him
to Papa's gathering. Will that not throw off your
seating arrangements at dinner?'

'Yes, but I shall send a note to Mrs Gavin and
insist that she bring Jane,' Lady Cynthia said,
referring to Joanna's other aunt and her eldest
daughter. 'It will be a pleasant change for the
two of them to mingle in such elevated society
and it will be a feather in my cap to have Valentine Lawe at my table.'

'I think you overestimate his worth. A number of Papa's colleagues will be there, not all of
whom attend the theatre,' Joanna reminded her.
'Mr Bretton may find himself without an audience to impress.'

'I am sure he will manage just fine.'

'What if he is already engaged for the evening?'

'If he is, I suspect he will do whatever is necessary to disengage himself,' her aunt said with
a complacent smile. 'I saw the way he looked at
you. If I don't miss my guess, he is already quite
taken with you.'

'*Taken* with me?' Joanna said, blushing furiously. 'What a ridiculous thing to say! I barely
know the man and, I can assure you, I have no
interest in furthering the acquaintance.'

'Not in any serious way, no,' Lady Cynthia
agreed. 'Mr Bretton would have to be as rich as
Croesus to even hope to justify such a *mésal-*

liance. Nevertheless, it will not hurt your reputation to be seen as someone he admires and it
may draw the attention of other more suitable
gentlemen, like Mr Rowe, your way.'

Joanna, having caught sight of Mr Rowe
through a break in the crowd, said, 'I am not
at all sure I *wish* to draw his attention my way,
Aunt. He is corpulent, balding and well into his
fifties.'

'Nevertheless, he is the sole heir to his father's
fortune and, given the state of your father's fi-
nances, we cannot afford to dismiss him out of
hand,' Lady Cynthia said, smiling in the portly
gentleman's direction. 'When the roof over one's
head is in danger of collapsing, one cannot be
too picky about the manner of the man who
brings hammer and nails to repair it!'

Laurence was not in the best of moods as the
carriage made its way from Cavendish Square
to Green Street in the early hours of the morning. He knew he had no reason to feel that way.
Compliments about the play had rained down
upon his head and he had been sought after and
celebrated from the moment he had walked into
the house. But it was a house in which he had
not expected to see Joanna Northrup—or rather,
Lady Joanna Northrup—and *that*, Laurence admitted, was most certainly the source of his con-
sternation. Had he known beforehand that she

was going to be there, he would have left off the velvet and lace and worn more conservative attire. But because he'd known that Valentine Lawe was expected, he had dressed for the part and the exquisite Lady Joanna Northrup had seen him in the role.

What must she think of him now?

'You're very quiet tonight, dearest,' Victoria observed from the seat opposite. 'Did something happen at the reception to upset you?'

'Hmm? Oh, no, not at all.' Laurence drew his gaze from the window and rallied a smile. 'The evening was a great success. You must have heard all the praise being lavished upon your plays.'

'I did and it was flattering in the extreme, though even after all these months, it still seems strange to hear people talk about my plays as though they were yours,' Victoria said. 'Do you know, one elderly lady called me Miss Lawe the entire evening? I was happy to play along, of course, but it did make me smile, given that she was far more correct than she knew.'

'Of course, because you *are* the famous playwright and the one deserving of all the praise,' Laurence said. 'God knows I've done nothing to warrant the attention.'

'Don't be silly. You stepped forwards and said you were Valentine Lawe at a time when it was most important that you did and I will always think you a hero for that,' Victoria said. 'Goodness knows what would have happened to our family's reputation if you had said nothing. Still, hearing you talk about my plays as though you wrote them does take some getting used to.'

'Sometimes, I almost forget I *didn't* write them,' Laurence mused. 'But if I don't talk about them that way, people won't find me convincing.'

'Exactly, and I am perfectly content to let my plays be thought the work of my brother so that I can still appear to be the very correct wife of Mr Alistair Devlin,' Victoria said with a twinkle in her eye. 'But are you sure there's nothing bothering you, dearest? You seemed in a much better frame of mind upon arrival at Mrs Blough-Upton's house than you do upon leaving it.'

'It's nothing,' Laurence said, shaking his head. 'I'm fine.'

'Good, then you can tell me about the young lady I saw you with not long after we arrived,' Victoria said eagerly. 'The very pretty one with dark hair and rather astonishing green eyes. I noticed you talking to her just before Mrs Blough-Upton swooped down and carried you off again. Who was she?'

Laurence briefly debated the wisdom of pretending he didn't know who Victoria was talking about, but, suspecting that his all-too-observant sister was unlikely to believe it, said, 'Her name is Lady Joanna Northrup. We met in a bookshop earlier in the day.'

'Lady Joanna.' Victoria's eyes widened. 'Good Lord, isn't her father the new earl? The one who assumed the title after his eldest brother fell off a cliff and his nephew was shot in a duel?'

Remembering fragments of the conversation he'd had with Lady Cynthia, Laurence nodded. 'Yes, I believe so.' He paused, frowning. 'I thought duels weren't fought any more?'

'They're not, but gossip has it that the husband of the lady with whom Lord Foster was involved was so incensed that he punched Lord Foster in the face—'

'A crime punishable by death,' Laurence observed.

'Yes, and believing himself the superior marksman, Foster offered him a challenge, only to find out he was not superior in *any* way. But never mind that, tell me about Lady Joanna. Wasn't her father an archaeologist of sorts before he inherited the title?'

'Yes. He lectured at the university and is a recognised authority on Egyptian history.'

'How delightful! You have finally met a woman who shares your fascination with the past.'

'She may share my fascination with the past,

but she was not at all impressed with my being Valentine Lawe,' Laurence said in a rueful tone.

'Ah, I see. And you're afraid,' Victoria said slowly, 'that having first seen you in the guise of an academic, the young lady will doubt your credibility after having seen you tonight in a far more glamorous and, therefore, less admirable role.'

'Something like that,' Laurence murmured. 'My being a famous playwright didn't impress Lady Joanna nearly as much as it did her aunt.'

'And do you wish to impress Lady Joanna?'

Yes, he did, Laurence admitted. He had been looking forward to attending her father's lecture tomorrow night, not only because he was interested in hearing what her father had to say, but because he wanted to see more of her. He wanted to get to know her better, to find out what she thought about matters of interest to both of them and to ask her about the time she had spent in Egypt.

But how seriously was she going to take him after having seen him tonight in the guise of Valentine Lawe? There had been no mistaking the chilliness of her greeting, nor had her manner improved as the evening wore on, Laurence acknowledged grimly. Did she already believe him a fraud? Think the only reason he had come up to her in the bookshop was to initiate a flirtation? A woman that beautiful must have numerous suitors for her hand, not to mention the fact she was the daughter of an earl and well beyond the reach of a man like him.

'Let's just say, I would rather not have her doubting my reasons for attending a lecture her father is giving at the Apollo Club tomorrow evening,' Laurence said, neatly sidestepping the question. 'She may not believe a playwright would have a genuine interest in ancient Egypt.'

'I cannot think why. We are all entitled to more than one interest in our lives,' Victoria said. 'Why should someone who writes plays be any different?'

'I don't know, but Lady Joanna was noticeably more distant when I spoke to her this evening than she was when we met in the bookshop this afternoon,' Laurence said. 'Which is why I intend to do everything I can to convince her that I am an avid student of history and that my appreciation of all things Egyptian is genuine. And you can be sure I plan on doing it sooner rather than later!'

Acting on his convictions, Laurence did not wait until the lecture to settle matters between Lady Joanna and himself. He suspected he wouldn't have much time to talk to her after the lecture, and that even if he did, it would not be with any degree of privacy, so he decided to pay a call on her at home the following afternoon and to use Volney's book as an excuse for stopping by.

As such, he dressed carefully for the interview, choosing a well-cut jacket of dark-green kerseymere over a linen shirt and breeches. With it, he wore a pristine white cravat, a very pale-gold waistcoat and boots that, though polished to a high sheen, bore no fancy tassels or spurs. He was determined that when he saw Lady Joanna again, his appearance would in no way remind her of the man she had seen last night.

Unfortunately, when he was shown into the elegant drawing room of the house on Eaton Place, it was to find her in the company of an older woman; one whose wide-eyed expression upon hearing his name confirmed Laurence's fears that the anonymity he had hoped for would not be forthcoming.

He advanced, somewhat hesitantly, into the room. 'Good afternoon, Lady Joanna.'

'Mr Bretton.' She looked like a vision of spring in a white-muslin gown encircled by a band of pale-green silk, with a darker paisley shawl draped over her shoulders. Her hair, reflecting shades of copper and gold in a bright shaft of sunlight, was arranged in a loose cluster of curls around her face and she looked, in every way, the picture of feminine grace and refinement. But her brow was furrowed and her expression left Laurence in no doubt as to where he stood in her estimation. 'I had not thought to see you until the lecture this evening.'

'That was my intention,' Laurence said, 'but I had errands that brought me in this direction and I decided to take the opportunity to drop off Volney's *Travels* on the way.' He set the book on the table beside her chair. 'I thought you might like to start reading it before the weekend.'

'How thoughtful.' Her eyes fell hungrily to the book, but Laurence knew good manners would prevent her from opening it. Instead, she looked up at him and said, 'Are you acquainted with my aunt, Mrs Gavin?'

'I have not had the pleasure, no.'

'Ah, but I know you, Mr Bretton,' said that lady with a smile. 'Or rather, I know *of* you and I am *very* pleased to make your acquaintance. Unlike my niece, I have seen all of your plays and enjoyed them very much.'

'Thank you, Mrs Gavin,' Laurence said, liking the rosy-cheeked lady and grateful for her recommendation. 'It is always a pleasure to hear that my work is being appreciated.'

'Of that there can be no doubt. I hear there are even rumours that your next play will be produced at Drury Lane.'

'We are only in the opening stages of negotiation,' Laurence said, not entirely surprised that word of his uncle's discussions with the manager of the Theatre Royal should have reached the streets. In London, only the wind travelled faster than gossip. 'The play is not yet finished and there is still much to be discussed.'

'Ah, but I am sure satisfactory terms will be reached by all parties. Not that I see anything wrong with your work continuing to be shown at the Gryphon,' Mrs Gavin said. 'It is a superb theatre and the cast is exceptional. Your uncle is to be commended for his efforts at making the Gryphon the success it is, as are you for contributing so greatly to it.'

Guiltily aware that he had contributed nothing to his uncle's success, that it was his sister's plays that had taken London by storm, Laurence gruffly cleared his throat. 'Thank you. I will be sure to pass your compliments along to my uncle. But now, I must be on my way. I look forward to seeing you at the lecture this evening, Lady Joanna, and hopefully, to speaking with you afterwards.'

'I doubt there will be time.' The lady's words were clipped, her tone discouraging. 'I expect to be fully occupied assisting my father, both before and after the lecture.'

The remark confirmed Laurence's suspicions that the chances of his changing her mind were slim. Clearly, she had not appreciated his being less than honest with her upon the occasion of their first meeting and, having seen him as something of a performer last night, was not interested in furthering the acquaintance. It seemed that while the lady could keep secrets from him, he was not allowed to keep secrets from her.

'I understand. Nevertheless, I look forward to the occasion.' He turned to offer the other lady a smile. 'It was a pleasure meeting you, Mrs Gavin.'

'And you, Mr Bretton. I look forward to seeing many more of your plays and wish you continued success with all of them.'

Grateful for having received at least one positive endorsement in Lady Joanna's hearing, Laurence took his leave, keenly aware of two sets of eyes following him out of the room.

He had hoped to be able to explain to Lady Joanna why he hadn't told her about his other life as Valentine Lawe, but clearly he was not to be given the opportunity. Whatever positive impression he might have made by offering to lend her Volney's book had been overturned by his appearance at Lydia Blough-Upton's soirée as Valentine Lawe. Lady Joanna was clearly not a fan of the theatre and had not been to see any of the plays. She was an academic and historian like her father and, despite Mrs Gavin's glowing words of praise, Laurence knew her opinion of him was already formed.

It was going to take a lot more than an apology, however heartfelt, to change it.

Chapter Three

'Well, it seems you have been keeping secrets from me, Joanna,' Mrs Gavin said, breaking the silence that followed Mr Bretton's departure. 'You neglected to tell me you were such good friends with one of London's most illustrious playwrights.'

'We are *not* good friends, Aunt Florence,' Joanna said, not quite sure how she was feeling in the wake of the gentleman's unexpected appearance. 'I had no idea he even *was* a playwright until I was informed of it at Mrs Blough-Upton's reception last night. Mr Bretton and I simply met in a bookshop where he offered to lend me his copy of a book I happened to be looking for.'

Her aunt leaned over and peered at the title. '*Travels through Syria and Egypt*. Isn't that more along your father's line?'

'It is.'

'But Mr Bretton is a playwright.'

'Yes, who *professes* an interest in ancient Egypt. He is coming to Papa's lecture tonight.'

'Is he indeed?' Her aunt's eyes twinkled. 'Are you sure he isn't using the book and the lecture as an excuse to further an acquaintance with you?'

'I had no reason to think so at the time, but now I'm not so sure.' Joanna nibbled on her bottom lip. 'It does seem a little hard to believe after what I saw of him last night.'

'Well, I have to believe all this attention is a problem of a most pleasurable sort,' Mrs Gavin said, reaching for her cup and saucer. 'I understand Captain Sterne has been paying marked attention to you of late and that Mr Osborne is in the habit of sending you posies.'

'Yes, which I have asked him to stop,' Joanna said. 'I know he is related in some way to Lady Cynthia, but I cannot bring myself to like him. As for Captain Sterne, he had no time for me when I was plain Joanna Northrup, so naturally I am suspect of his affections now.'

'But at least you have something in common with Captain Sterne,' Mrs Gavin pointed out. 'If memory serves, he accompanied your father on one of his early expeditions to Egypt, so his interest in the subject must be genuine.'

'I believe it to be,' Joanna allowed, 'but I have

always found him to be a rather arrogant man. Perhaps that is what comes of inheriting such great wealth at such a young age.'

Mrs Gavin smiled sympathetically. 'I suspect it does change one's circumstances. As does becoming the daughter of an earl. What about Mr Rowe? I hear you made his acquaintance last night.'

'Yes, and I did not care for him in the least,' Joanna said, remembering with distaste the objectionable way the man had leered at her. 'He may be wealthy and heir to a viscountcy, but not even a king's fortune would persuade me to marry him.'

'Unfortunately, your aunt *is* using wealth as the criteria by which she determines your future husband's suitability and, given the deplorable state of your father's affairs, I suppose it must be a valid concern,' Mrs Gavin said regretfully. 'But I would not wish to see it be the only consideration when choosing the man you will marry.'

'Neither would I, Aunt,' Joanna acknowledged with a sigh. 'I was far happier at the thought of marrying Mr Penscott,' she said, referring to the young man who had worked as her father's assistant for the past three years. 'At least he liked me for who I was and we certainly shared an interest in Papa's work. We could have travelled to Egypt together after we were married.'

'I wouldn't be so sure,' her aunt said. 'Mr Penscott hales from Yorkshire and northern men are very old fashioned in their notions. But it matters not since he is no longer a suitable companion for you. And I am sorry. I know you cared for him.'

'Yes, I did. However, I suppose it is better to use one's head than one's heart when it comes to choosing the man with whom one will spend the rest of one's life,' Joanna said in a pragmatic tone. 'The heart is notoriously unreliable.'

'You're thinking about Mr Patterson again, aren't you?'

Joanna blushed, the unwelcome heat giving her away. 'I wasn't aware you knew about him.'

'Of course I knew about him, child,' her aunt said gently. 'You were madly in love with the man, or believed yourself to be. And why would you not feel that way? He was as handsome as a young god and equally blessed when it came to the gift of oratory. I once heard him recite a poem at Lady Saxton's summer fête and by the time he'd finished, I all but fancied *myself* in love with him,' Mrs Gavin said in a wry tone. 'But, I feared he would break your heart. He was very good at flirting with the young ladies, but not so good at following through on his promises to them.'

Joanna glanced down at her hands. 'It all seems so silly now. But it was very painful at the time.'

'First love always is. And you didn't have my sister around to give you the guidance and support you so desperately needed.'

Joanna nodded, remembering how much she had longed for her mother's advice at the time. 'He wrote such romantic poetry. I thought…I truly believed that he had written the words just for me.'

'No doubt he told you he had,' her aunt said with an understanding smile. 'But I am not sorry nothing came of it, Joanna. Mr Patterson would not have made you a good husband. Men like that never do. Most likely he'll end up some rich woman's *cher ami*, or wind up in debtor's prison. Creativity is all very well, but sometimes the more brilliant the mind, the more unstable the person.'

Joanna smoothed her hand over her skirt, wondering why Laurence Bretton's face suddenly came to mind. He hadn't struck her as being in the least unstable, though there was no denying that he was two very different people— and extremely convincing in both roles.

'So Mr Bretton is planning to attend your father's lecture,' her aunt said, unwittingly tapping into Joanna's thoughts. 'Interesting. I suspect you will see him in a very different light this evening.'

'Of course, but in which light does he shine the truest? Writing plays must take a great deal of dedication, especially plays as successful as his,' Joanna said, getting to her feet. 'How can he divide his time between that and the study of ancient Egypt?'

'Obviously, he makes time for both. It is not a bad thing to have such diverse interests.'

Joanna managed a grudging smile. 'You like him.'

'Yes, I do. I sense he is a good man and I like his manners and humility very much,' her aunt said. 'You were not kind to him today yet he did not speak harshly to you.'

Joanna flushed at the criticism. 'He was not honest with me when we first met. He should have told me who he was and what he did, rather than leave me to find out at Mrs Blough-Upton's reception.'

'I suspect he had his reasons for keeping silent. Nor am I saying that you should think of Mr Bretton as someone you might wish to marry because quite clearly he is not. He is far from being your social equal and that is something you must now constantly bear in mind.'

It was a truism Joanna had not yet come to terms with, even though it was one of the principles that guided society. 'I fail to see why. Dukes marry actresses and are not thought any the less of for it.'

'Unfortunately, dukes can do whatever they wish,' Mrs Gavin said, chuckling. 'With rank comes privilege and I know a number of ladies and gentlemen who have made excellent use of both. But I am confident you will make the right choice when the time comes,' she said, getting to her feet. 'Just remember that a promise once given is difficult to retract and a vow once spoken is spoken for life.'

Joanna glanced at the book Mr Bretton had left for her, beginning to wish she had never encouraged the conversation with him in the bookshop. He confused her…and Joanna didn't like being confused. Indeed, life in general seemed to have become a great deal more complicated since her father had become Lord Bonnington. 'Thank you, Aunt Florence,' Joanna said, slipping an arm around her aunt's waist. 'You know how much I value your opinion.'

'Poppycock. You likely think my notions as old fashioned as I am, but are too kind to say so. Well, never mind. All I want is to see you happy. Money is not the only reason to wed, just as having your heart broken once is no reason to shy away from love. But I'm sure you already know that.'

Joanna nodded and kissed her aunt's cheek before bidding her a fond farewell. Only then did she turn her attention to the book Mr Bretton had left for her. She was glad the brusqueness of her words at Mrs Blough-Upton's reception had not affected his decision to lend it to her, but she was sorry his arrival today had coincided with her aunt's—who seemed as enamoured of the man as everyone else.

Was she the only one who thought his not telling her the truth was a problem?

Joanna picked up the book and held it reverently in her hands. It was a lovely copy: leather bound, beautifully engraved and in excellent condition. Mr Bretton certainly took good care of his books, but then, who *would* have more respect for the written word than a man who made his living by them? A playwright would be as respectful of books as her father and Mr Penscott were of the ancient scrolls they found buried in the tombs.

But could the dashing Laurence Bretton, more famously known as Valentine Lawe, really be as interested in *those* artefacts as he was in his wildly successful plays? Did his reasons for wanting to attend the lecture tonight stem from a genuine desire to learn more about the distant past? Or were they, as Joanna was beginning to fear, little more than an excuse for spending time with her, as her aunt was all too inclined to think?

The Apollo Club was a favoured haunt of gentlemen who gathered to share ideas and exchange views on a variety of interesting and diverse topics. It was also where Ben Jonson had written *The Devil is an Asse,* thereby serving to unite Laurence's literary leanings with his more historical ones. No doubt that was why he felt so at home as he strolled into the room known as the Oracle of Apollo a full fifteen minutes before the clock struck seven.

For once, he was in his element, surrounded by fellow students of history all caught up in the excitement of hearing about William Northrup's—correction, Lord Bonnington's— latest expedition to Egypt and of the wondrous things he had seen there. Valentine Lawe didn't belong here any more than an orchid belonged in the desert and Laurence was heartily relieved when no one seemed to recognise him. No doubt the conservative clothes and spectacles helped.

He glanced towards the front of the room where Lady Joanna and her father were busy getting ready for the lecture and allowed himself the pleasure of watching her unobserved for a few minutes. She was dressed in a dark-blue pelisse over a pale-blue gown, the fitted lines of the garment making her look even more slender than she had in the bookshop. She had set her bonnet aside, allowing the candlelight to catch the highlights in her hair, and her cheeks were slightly flushed as a result of her efforts at getting everything ready.

'Joanna, where are my samples of pottery

from the fourth week's dig?' her father asked abruptly. 'Don't tell me I forgot to bring them!'

'You did, Papa, but I did not,' Lady Joanna said, calmly lifting a wooden box on to the table. 'All ten pieces are here, labelled as to their place of origin and date of discovery.'

'And the papyrus scrolls?'

'In the glass cases. I wasn't willing to risk curious onlookers being overly enthusiastic in their handling of them.'

'Excellent,' Lord Bonnington said, regarding the neat arrangement of glass display cases with approval. 'Now, if we can just get these last few pieces of statuary in place—ah, there you are, Mr Penscott,' he said as a lanky young man wearing a dark-brown jacket over fawn-coloured breeches walked up to the table. 'Give me a hand with this stone head, will you?'

'Of course, my lord,' Penscott said, bending to pick it up. His sandy-coloured hair was swept back from a wide forehead bronzed by the sun and he had a pleasant, amiable countenance. 'It's my job to do the heavy lifting. Isn't that right, Lady Joanna?'

The tone was affectionate and the remark, judging from the colour that blossomed in Lady Joanna's cheeks, was not entirely unwelcome, making Laurence wonder as to the nature of the relationship. 'It is indeed, Mr Penscott.' She looked up from her notes and smiled. 'That, and making tea over a campfire, which you do exceptionally well.' Then she saw Laurence and the smile froze on her lips. 'Mr Bretton. You're…early.'

'Am I?' Laurence pulled out his pocket watch and flicked open the lid. 'A few minutes, perhaps, but you did tell me I should come early if I wished to secure a good seat. A sound piece of advice given how crowded the room is already.'

She appeared flustered, as though she hadn't really expected him to come. 'Yes, well, as I said, this is the…first opportunity my father has had to speak about his trip to Dendera since we emerged from mourning. It is only to be expected that there would be…a great deal of curiosity about what he found.'

Laurence closed the watch and slipped it back into his pocket, finding her distress curious. Was she embarrassed that he had witnessed her light-hearted exchange with the other man?

Mr Penscott didn't seem to care. After a cursory glance in Laurence's direction, he went back to unpacking boxes and even her father didn't raise his head. Clearly, the reasons for the lady's discomfort were her own. Deciding not to make an issue of it, Laurence said, 'I would not have expected otherwise. Your father's reputation is well known in London.' He set his satchel on one of the vacant seats. 'For that reason, I hope there will be an opportunity to speak to him after the lecture concludes.'

'That will depend on how many questions he is asked,' Lady Joanna said. 'Upon occasion, he has been known to run very late.'

'Except when you are on hand to keep him to his schedule,' Laurence said, gently reminding her of the comment she had made upon the occasion of their first meeting. 'I'm sure he is grateful for your help in that regard, as well as in the organising of matters beforehand.'

'It is…a necessary part of planning the evening,' Lady Joanna agreed. She glanced back down at her notes, her brow furrowing. 'Now if you will excuse me, I must get back to work. There is still much to be done before the lecture gets underway.'

Laurence inclined his head. 'Of course. I would hate to be the cause of any delay.'

Joanna glanced at him briefly, then turned and walked away. She wasn't sure why she felt so flustered all of a sudden. She had done enough of these presentations that standing in front of a room full of men didn't bother her any more. What, then? Embarrassment that he witnessed her comfortable exchange with Mr Penscott?

Surely not. There was nothing wrong with colleagues enjoying a laugh together. Certainly no one else seemed to think so. After a brief glance at the newcomer, Mr Penscott had gone back to unpacking boxes and her father seemed not to have heard the exchange at all. Even Mr Bretton did not seem unduly concerned. Following his last comment, he had sat down and taken a small leather-bound notebook from his satchel, which he had proceeded to open and lay flat upon his lap. Joanna had seen lines of writing, along with what looked like hieroglyphic symbols covering the page from top to bottom. A moment later, he'd taken out a pencil and began making notes and hadn't looked at her again.

Unreasonably miffed, Joanna had carried on with her preparations. So, the great Valentine Lawe had deigned to make an appearance. How gracious of him. He had even dressed for the part, looking every inch the academic in a dark jacket over breeches and boots, his appearance smart but decidedly understated. He had abandoned his fancy lace jabot for a conservatively striped neckcloth and the signature rose was nowhere in sight. He was even wearing his wire-rimmed spectacles again.

Did he really need them, Joanna wondered, or were they little more than a contrivance?

Not that it mattered, she reminded herself. Laurence Bretton was only one of the many gentlemen who had come to hear her father speak and though she had given him an invitation, it did not entitle him to any special consideration. She had extended the invitation for the same reason he had offered to lend her the book— because they shared a common interest in Egypt.

That was all. Joanna had no intention of getting to know the gentleman better because despite Lady Cynthia's beliefs that Mr Bretton was interested in her, Joanna knew all too well the fickleness of the writer's heart. She had experienced it firsthand. Her infatuation with Aldwyn Patterson had scarred her to a far greater degree than anyone knew because only Joanna knew what he had whispered to her in the folly when they were alone. Only she knew the sweet promises he had made and the lyrical poetry he had written extolling her glorious emerald eyes and the sweetness of her face.

Only she knew how madly and stupidly she had fallen in love—only to discover his true nature when she had found out she was not the only young lady to be on the receiving end of his flattery.

Such was her disappointment in having discovered Laurence Bretton's true calling. Though he was a different kind of writer, Joanna had no reason to suspect he was any different at heart. He lived in a world of fictional characters and implausible scenarios.

Witness his appearance as Valentine Lawe.

What was that if not just another role in his world of make believe?

But her world wasn't like that any more. Joanna was no longer in control of her own destiny. She was the daughter of an impoverished earl, fated to marry a man of means; one who possessed either wealth or a title, or better yet, wealth *and* a title, and who was willing to spend a large part of that wealth on the restoration of Joanna's home.

That was the only hope her family had. Personal feelings didn't enter into it. She was to be married off to the highest bidder—and she was deceiving herself if she thought to call it anything else.

For Laurence, the next two hours flew by. Lord Bonnington offered a highly informative talk concerning his explorations of the ruins at Dendera and of the many unexpected finds he and his team had made along the way. Numerous samples were documented and described, some that were passed around during the course of the discussion, while the more delicate articles were kept at the front of the room for viewing. Mr Penscott, who turned out to be a former student of Bonnington's as well as his assistant, was often called upon to elaborate a point, though his explanations, being more straightforward than the earl's, were better suited to the laymen in the audience.

Then there were the engravings, incredibly lifelike drawings of hieroglyphs and friezes, drawn in greatly reduced scale, but in such exquisite detail that Laurence could almost picture himself sitting on the artist's stool, gazing at the magnificent scenes before him. And *she* had drawn them. Lady Joanna Northrup. To his surprise, the lovely and refined young woman who was destined to become mistress of a grand house in London was also one of the finest illustrators he had ever seen.

His admiration and respect for her only grew.

Unfortunately, as the evening went on so did his awareness of the differences between them. She was the daughter of an earl; a woman who lived in a world vastly removed from his and whose privileged life included servants, magnificent houses and all the conveniences money could buy.

He was the son of a gentleman and a minister's daughter. Though better educated than most and with opportunities greater than some, Laurence knew he would never achieve the lofty heights necessary to be considered someone with whom Lady Joanna might associate.

She was a goddess and he a mere mortal bound to earth. Not surprisingly, the discovery left him with a decidedly hollow feeling.

'Smashing good lecture, eh what?' said the gentleman seated next to him. 'I'd have given my eye-teeth to be on that expedition. But, I'm the first to admit my travelling days are over.'

Laurence regarded the gentleman, who didn't appear to be much over fifty, with amusement. 'You look as though you still have a good few trips left in you.'

'Appreciate you saying so, m'boy, but traipsing through the desert is work for younger men than me.' He turned his head and levelled a surprisingly keen look at Laurence. 'Ever been to Egypt, Mr...?'

'Bretton. And, no, I haven't. Everything I know about the subject has been learned from books and from following the exploits of men like Lord Bonnington.'

'Pity. Reading about the pyramids is nothing like standing at the top of one of those magnificent structures, knowing as you gaze out over the desert that it holds a thousand secrets you're never going to be able to uncover. You can't get any of that from a book.'

Laurence smiled, recognising in the man beside him the spirit of a true adventurer. 'You've been there.'

'Oh, yes,' his companion said, 'and I was younger than you when I made my first trip. Not many young bucks were making the journey back then. Most of them went to Florence and

Rome on their grand tours. But Egypt is becoming popular now and I hear there are even ladies making the trip, though I don't hold with all that nonsense. The desert's no place for a woman.'

'I heard that, Mr Dustin,' Lady Joanna said in a tone of mild amusement as she came up behind them. 'And I take leave to disagree with you.'

'Of course you do, my dear, because you are your father's daughter and every bit as stubborn, though I won't hold that against you,' he said, winking. 'However, if you'll excuse me, I want a word with Bonnington before he leaves. I've a slight difference of opinion when it comes to his theory about Seti the First, though he'll likely tell me I'm talking through my hat.' Abruptly, Mr Dustin turned and extended his hand to Laurence. 'Don't forget what I said, young man. If you ever get the chance to go, take it! You won't regret it.'

'I'll be sure to remember your advice,' Laurence said, shaking Mr Dustin's hand. It was only as he did that he noticed the ebony-topped cane gripped in the gentleman's other hand and realised why Mr Dustin's travelling days were over.

'Well, Mr Bretton, did you enjoy the lecture?' Lady Joanna enquired when they were alone.

Her tone was no warmer than it had been earlier, but aware that she had, at least, come to speak to him, Laurence decided to make the most of it. 'Very much. I am more envious than ever of what you saw and experienced while you were there.'

Her brow furrowed, but in confusion rather than disagreement. 'Why would you say that? You are a famous playwright. A man much admired in society. What reason can you have for being envious of anyone?'

'I am envious because I haven't seen everything I want to see, or travelled to all the places I wish to travel,' Laurence said. 'Just because I write plays doesn't mean I can't have other interests.'

'But the study of ancient Egypt must be one's passion,' Lady Joanna said. 'A person could spend a lifetime engaged in such work and never know all there is to know. I'm sure the same could be said about writing plays.'

'Yet, did Shakespeare not write a play about Caesar and Cleopatra?' Laurence countered. 'One that would have necessitated his having a thorough understanding of the history of the time in order to be able to write about two of its most colourful characters?'

'Of course, but Shakespeare was first and foremost a playwright. Any research he did would have been undertaken to validate the dialogue and the lifestyles of the characters about which he wrote. You claim an interest in a field that is as strongly felt as what you must feel for writing.'

Laurence couldn't argue with that because he couldn't tell her that his first love really *was* history and that he wasn't a famous playwright at all, that the mask he wore as Valentine Lawe was precisely that. But neither could he deny that her persistent doubts were beginning to bother him. 'Lady Joanna. You do not know me well. Indeed, you do not know me at all, but I trust you will believe me when I say that I am capable of having interests in areas beyond those for which I have gained renown. Yes, I am a student of the classics and have read and enjoyed the works of Socrates and Shakespeare,' he said quietly. 'However, I also enjoy music, art, sport and history. Egyptian history, in particular. I have followed the exploits of Mr Burckhardt and Monsieur Champollion, having been fascinated by the latter's *précis du système hiéroglyphique*, and I am here tonight because I admire your father's work and want to learn more.'

'But what I saw of you last night—'

'Has nothing to do with who or what I am now,' Laurence said in frustration. 'Had you *not* seen me at Mrs Blough-Upton's house last night, we would not even be *having* this conversation. But you did and we are and this difference in opinion is the result. But believe me when I say that I am not here under false pretences. I've come to sit at the foot of a man I have long admired and to learn from his experiences. Now, are you going to grant me the promised introduction, or shall I ask Mr Dustin to do it for you?'

Laurence knew his words had made an impression. Lady Joanna obviously hadn't expected him to take exception to her remark, nor to contest it as vigorously as he had. But he wasn't about to stand here and be questioned about a subject he was genuinely interested in, simply because Lady Joanna Northrup believed him more interested in something else!

The seconds ticked by as she stared at him. Then, obviously coming to a decision, she nodded her head. 'That will not be necessary. If you will follow me, I will introduce you to my father.'

It was not an apology and Laurence knew better than to mistake it for one. He might have come away the victor in this small battle of wills, but he was a long way from emerging triumphant in the war. Lady Joanna had more respect for her father's assistant than she did for him. When she looked at Penscott, she saw a man whose interest in Egypt was as keen as her own and whose credibility in the field had been established as a result of the years of work he had done at her father's side.

All she saw when she looked at *him*, Laurence

reminded himself, was a man who made up stories about people who existed in make-believe worlds. One who wore fancy clothes and was admired for the extent of his imagination rather than the sharpness of his intellect.

Well, that was going to change, Laurence decided as he followed her towards the front of the room. He might not succeed in winning her heart, but he was damned if he was going to walk away without at least having gained her respect!

Chapter Four

At the front of the room, Lord Bonnington stood in the company of several other gentlemen, most of whom Laurence knew either by name or reputation. Lord Kingston, a prominent peer whose collection of Egyptian artefacts was said to be one of the most impressive in England, was engaged in conversation with Mr Geoffrey Toberston, a well known historian, while beside them, Sir Guthry Mortimer, the noted cartographer, chatted with Mr Dustin and Lord Amberley, who according to the papers had funded several of Bonnington's expeditions.

Also present were Mr David Sheppard, an ambitious young man who was currently in the throes of planning his first expedition to Egypt, and Captain James Sterne, son and heir of Lord Rinstrom and a man who had accompanied Lord

Bonnington on one of his early expeditions to Egypt.

'Papa, allow me to introduce Mr Laurence Bretton,' Lady Joanna said, drawing Laurence into the centre of the group. 'We met in a book-shop where he kindly offered to lend me his copy of Volney's *Travels*. In return, I invited him to your lecture.'

'Did you indeed?' Bonnington's sharp gaze fell on Laurence. 'I don't believe I've seen you at any of my lectures, Mr Bretton.'

'You haven't, my lord, but I am very familiar with your work. I've been following your ex-ploits for years and have read all of your reports with great enjoyment.'

'Have you now. And what did you think of tonight's presentation?'

'Fascinating. I only wish I could have been at Dendera with you.'

'As do I,' Mr Dustin spoke up. 'Might have been too, if it wasn't for this blasted leg.'

'Which I told you to have reset after you broke it the last time,' Bonnington said drily. 'But would you listen to me? Oh, no! Told me what I could do with my advice, as I recall.'

'Well, what did you expect?' Dustin muttered. 'You're an archaeologist. Not a bloody surgeon.'

Laurence smiled, recognising the friendly bickering for what it was. No doubt Mr Dustin, having either been a rival of Bonnington's or a one-time member of his team, had been rendered incapable of travelling by a series of unfortunate accidents; something he no doubt lamented every day of his life, especially on evenings such as these.

'The desert does get into one's blood,' the older man murmured now.

'Volney's *Travels*, eh?' the earl said, turning back to Laurence. 'Not an easy volume to find.'

'No, but I have an excellent source for such books and have been able to amass a fairly substantial library.'

'Which is more than I can say for some of the shops I visited,' Lady Joanna said. 'The clerk at the last one was quite relieved when Mr Bretton offered to lend me his copy.'

'On the contrary, he would have been more than happy to help,' Laurence said, remembering the look of infatuation on the young man's face and aware of feeling much the same way at the time. 'But given that I had the book at home, I saw no point in making him go to the trouble.'

'Bretton,' Captain Sterne said slowly. 'That name's familiar. Why do I know it?' He tapped one finger against his lip and then smiled, a little too innocently. 'But of course, you're that writer chap. The one all the ladies chatter about. Lang, isn't it?'

'Lawe,' Laurence said, aware of the patronising tone. 'Valentine Lawe.'

'That's right, Valentine Lawe. What a coincidence. I went to see your play last Season,' Sterne said. 'Quite good for what it was.'

Laurence smiled, amused by Sterne's condescension in light of the play's runaway success. 'Thank you. The response has been gratifying.'

'Still, I wonder, sir, what brings you here tonight? I cannot suppose you to have become lost on your way to the theatre, but neither can I think of any reason why a playwright would be attending a lecture such as this.'

Laurence heard a few snickers from the gentlemen standing close by, but ignored them. He'd run into Sterne's type before. 'As Lady Joanna said, we discovered a mutual interest in Egypt whilst browsing in a shop and she extended the invitation at that time.'

'Really. And I suppose a man like you would think a *mutual* interest in a subject like that reason enough for approaching a lady with whom one is not acquainted,' Sterne drawled. 'And whose social consequence is so vastly superior to one's own.'

'Actually, no,' Laurence said, recognising an adversary and wondering if Sterne tried to intimidate anyone who attempted to speak to Lady Joanna in such a way. 'But in hearing Lady Joanna's conversation and recognising an interest as keen as my own, I decided the circumstances warranted the offer being made. It was only after

I did so that I became aware of the lady's identity.'

'Indeed, the first thing he asked after I told him my name was if I was related to you, Papa,' Lady Joanna said quickly.

'Did he indeed? Well, I'm not about to find fault with a gentleman whose intentions are so obviously good. If you've a mind to talk about Egypt, Mr Bretton, feel free to come by the house,' Bonnington said. 'My door is always open to young men who share a passion for the field. Captain Sterne, perhaps you would care to join Lord Amberley and myself for dinner tomorrow evening? I've begun making plans for a trip to Abu Simbel and I remember you saying you would be interested in going.'

'I would indeed,' Sterne said. 'I regretted having to miss Dendera, but it was necessary that I be in America at the time. There were business concerns that needed attending to.' His glance shifted, coming to rest on Lady Joanna. 'I hope we will have the pleasure of your company once again, Lady Joanna? I have yet to meet an expedition artist more talented…or more beautiful.'

Laurence saw two bright spots of colour appear in the lady's cheeks. 'You are too kind, Captain Sterne. Yes, I hope to be included, but it is Papa's decision to make.'

'Actually, I suspect your aunt will have a say in it too,' her father said. 'She doesn't hold with the idea of you travelling abroad. And given that this trip is to be of a longer duration than the last, it may not be appropriate. There are matters here at home that need attending to.'

The remark hung in the air, pregnant with meaning. Laurence saw the expressions on the faces of the men around him and knew what they were thinking. Lady Joanna needed a husband and she wasn't going to find one on an expedition to Egypt. Unless Sterne intended putting himself forwards as a candidate, and judging by the way he was looking at her, that wasn't unlikely.

'Well, I must be off,' Lord Amberley said. 'Excellent presentation on Dendera, Bonnington. I look forward to talking to you and Sterne about Abu Simbel tomorrow evening. Shall we say seven o'clock at my club?'

'Fine by me,' Bonnington said.

'And me,' Sterne replied. 'I've business earlier in the day, but it should be concluded by then. Good evening, Lady Joanna.'

'Captain Sterne,' Joanna said.

Laurence thought her expression looked a little strained as she smiled back at the man, but Sterne seemed not to notice and left the room in the company of several other gentlemen, their laughter and backwards glances in Laurence's direction leaving him in no doubt that he was the source of their amusement.

Finally, only Mr Dustin, Mr Penscott, Lady Joanna and her father remained.

'Well, come along, Mr Penscott, let's get packed up,' the earl said. 'I've no wish to be here until midnight. You may as well go home, Joanna. There's no point in you waiting around.'

'But won't you need the carriage to take everything back to Eaton Place, Papa?'

'Ah.' Bonnington paused, as though the thought hadn't occurred to him. 'Yes, I suppose I will.' He glanced at the boxes, then at the three gentlemen remaining. 'Mr Penscott, how did you arrive here this evening?'

'By hackney, my lord.'

'And you, Dustin?'

'Sir Mortimer was good enough to offer me a ride.'

'Pity. He's already left. What about you, Mr Bretton?'

'I have a carriage waiting outside.'

'Splendid, then perhaps you would be good enough to see my daughter home,' the earl said with relief. 'I don't like the idea of her travelling unescorted at this time of night.'

Lady Joanna's eyes widened. 'You may not like me travelling unescorted, Papa, but neither is it appropriate that I travel alone with Mr Bretton in his carriage.'

'Nor need you,' Laurence said quickly. 'I shall

have my coachman drive you home and make other arrangements for myself.'

'I wouldn't dream of putting you to all that trouble,' she objected. 'I can wait here until Papa is ready to leave.'

'No need,' Mr Dustin said. 'If Mr Bretton is determined to take on the role of Sir Galahad, I am happy to offer my services as chaperon. As a married father of five, I think I've experience enough to play the part. And given that it's come on to rain, I would very much appreciate a dry ride home. What say you, Lady Joanna? Does that meet with your approval?'

Laurence waited for the lady to answer, sincerely hoping that Mr Dustin's presence would provide the reassurance she needed while still giving him a chance to spend time in her company. He was determined to put things right between them and a carriage ride, no matter how short, might be just the place to start.

Fortunately, her father cast the deciding vote. 'Yes, do go with him, Joanna, otherwise poor Mr Bretton here will be forced to listen to Dustin's tall tales the entire way home and I would not wish that on my worst enemy.'

'I will have you know every one of those stories is true,' Mr Dustin said huffily. 'And I have entertained far better men with them than you!'

'Yes, I know. Several of whom expired from boredom on the way!'

'Stop it, you two!' Lady Joanna said, laughing. 'The way you carry on, you'd think you didn't like each other, and I know that you have been great friends these many years.'

'In point of fact, I have put *up* with him for these many years,' her father said. 'There is a difference.'

'Don't I know it!' Mr Dustin said with a snort. 'Well, come along, Lady Joanna. It's time I was at home by the fire. My leg plays me up on damp nights like this.'

'You and Mr Bretton go on ahead,' the lady said. 'I'll just gather up a few things and meet you downstairs.'

'I shall wait for you by the door,' Laurence said, wondering if her reasons for lingering had anything to do with Penscott, who had been gazing at her with admiration throughout the entire lecture. 'Thank you, Lord Bonnington, for a most enlightening evening.'

'My pleasure, Mr Bretton. Well, get a move on, Mr Penscott,' the earl said gruffly. 'I've no desire to be locked up in here for the rest of the night!'

Joanna gathered up her drawings, happy to have a few minutes alone to sort through her feelings before finding herself in a carriage with Mr Bretton for the drive home. She had no idea why she found his company so unsettling, but it definitely *was* his presence that set her on edge. She'd felt as flustered as a Bath Miss the entire evening and she really had no explanation as to why.

Yes, he was as handsome. Even without the dramatic costume, those compelling blue eyes and disturbingly sensual mouth would always capture a lady's attention, as would his broad shoulders and tall, athletic build. But surely she had learned to look beyond the physical aspects of a gentleman's appearance. Surely her regrettable experience with Aldwyn had taught her the folly of allowing herself to put stock in such insubstantial attributes.

'Thank you for your assistance this evening, Lady Joanna,' Mr Penscott said, coming up to her. 'The presentation was favourably received and your sketches were, as always, much admired.'

'Thank you, Mr Penscott. I think it went very well.'

'How could it do otherwise when you were so intimately involved in the arrangements? You have always been a great organiser,' he said with an engaging smile. 'It is a shame your involvement will soon be coming to an end.'

'An end?' Joanna regarded him quizzically. 'Are you aware of something I am not, Mr Penscott?'

'No, of course not. I simply thought…that is,

Lady Cynthia led me to believe that you were… soon to be wed, in which case I thought it was unlikely that you would be able to…or indeed that you would *wish* to, continue travelling with us,' he stammered, cheeks darkening.

'I see no reason why my marriage should have any bearing on that,' Joanna said. 'I am hopeful of my husband sharing my interest in the work and perhaps even of his being willing to do it with me.'

'Yes, of course, that would be the ideal situation,' Mr Penscott said, not quite meeting her eyes. 'I know I would have been…more than happy to do so had our circumstances not altered so…dramatically.'

As if realising he'd said too much, Mr Penscott bowed and hastily walked away, leaving Joanna to stare after him and mull over the significance of his words. She had long been aware of his feelings towards her and of his one-time hopes in her direction. But they both knew those hopes could no longer be entertained. She was the earl's daughter and he the earl's employee. Their worlds were far too distant to permit such an association.

Breathing a sigh of regret, Joanna slipped the rest of her drawings into the case and set it on the table. The evening had started off well, but had deteriorated as the hours passed—and it was not over yet. There was still the carriage ride home and knowing she could not delay it any longer, Joanna bid her father and Mr Penscott a good evening and then made her way downstairs. She was glad Mr Dustin would be riding in the carriage with them—indeed, his presence was the only reason she had agreed to go—but she knew she would be expected to make conversation and, given the way Mr Bretton had spoken to her earlier, that wasn't going to be easy.

He certainly hadn't been backwards in telling her what he thought of her opinions of him.

Still, after tonight she doubted their paths would cross again. Apart from their interest in Egyptian history, it was obvious they had nothing else in common and so had no reason to seek one another out. She neither expected him to follow through on his invitation to the theatre, nor to seek out her father's company. Nor had *she* any intention of using Volney's *Travels* as an excuse for seeing him. She would post the book back to him or deliver it to his house at a time when he was not there.

Mr Bretton had made very clear his feelings about her conduct towards him tonight. She did not need to be told again.

London was never pleasant at night and in a grey, driving rain and with the overpowering smells of the street rising up to meet her, it was even less so. But, true to his word, Mr Bretton was waiting for her at the door and, in the street beyond, Joanna saw an elegant carriage drawn by two perfectly matched greys. Obviously being a successful playwright paid well.

She picked up her skirts and, with the gentleman at her side, made a dash towards the carriage, glad she had only a short distance to go.

'I say, what a dreadful night!' Mr Dustin said as she climbed into the luxuriously appointed interior. 'Wouldn't like to be waiting around for a hackney on a night like this.'

'Indeed not, Mr Dustin.' Joanna sat down beside him and wiped the rain from her cheeks, savouring the warmth rising from the heated bricks. 'We are most grateful for your offer, Mr Bretton.'

'My pleasure,' that gentleman said, having climbed in behind her and closed the door.

'Don't see many young bucks owning fine carriages like this,' Mr Dustin observed.

'Nor do you see one now.' Mr Bretton rapped the head of his cane against the ceiling. 'It belongs to my uncle, Theodore Templeton.'

'Templeton! Not the chap who owns the Gryphon Theatre?' Mr Dustin said. 'Took my wife and eldest daughter to see a play there last year. Can't remember the name of it just now, but it was very good.'

Mr Bretton just smiled and removed his beaver, knocking the rain from the brim.

Joanna, having no desire to hear him brag about his fame, turned her attention towards the window and gazed out into the night. She was quite sure he would provide the name of the play and then go on to talk about his other accomplishments, no doubt pleased at having been recognised this evening even if the nature of Captain Sterne's compliment had been of a decidedly condescending nature. A man who spent his life close to the theatre would surely be inured to such snubs.

To her surprise, however, Mr Bretton did not launch into a recital of his talents, but instead turned the conversation back on her.

'I was very impressed with the work you had on display tonight, Lady Joanna,' he said in a quiet voice. 'The rendering of the pyramid of Giza was particularly well done. Did you employ a camera lucida or draw it freehand?'

Joanna blinked. She hadn't expected him to know what a camera lucida was, let alone to ask if she used one. 'I...prefer to draw freehand, but I have used a camera lucida in the past. It depends on whether or not the lighting is good enough to reflect the image back on to the paper.'

'I have heard that, in dim light, it is easier to draw by hand,' he said, 'but that must make it much more difficult to keep the scale of a temple or an obelisk accurate, as in the column in the Temple of Hathor, for example.'

'I do struggle with that on occasion,' Joanna admitted, 'which is why I tend to draw such things from the bottom up. I count the lines of hieroglyphs, of which there were eleven in the case of that particular column, and then attempt to space them in relation to the height of the column.'

'I don't know how she does it,' Mr Dustin said. 'I can't draw a straight line, never mind replicate the detailed drawings that appear on so many of the temples. But then, she started painting at a very early age, didn't you, Lady Joanna.'

'How early?' Mr Bretton asked as his gaze settled on her again.

'I was probably around six.' Joanna's mouth curved into a smile. 'My mother was a wonderful painter. She would sit for hours in the garden, sketching flowers or birds, or the horses grazing in the field nearby. She had a marvellous eye. She could duplicate every detail of a butterfly's wings and in such perfect scale that I oftimes didn't know whether I was looking at a painting or at the real thing.'

'So she was your teacher as well,' Mr Bretton observed.

'Yes, and I loved spending time with her,' Joanna said, remembering those golden afternoons when the two of them would sit in the shade of a tree with their brushes and easels and paint whatever caught their eye. 'My mother was incredibly patient, always insistent on getting the lines and the spacing right. It was from her I learned composition and scale.'

'She was also very good at portraits,' Mr Dustin said, yawning. 'I remember the one she did of you as a child. Beautiful likeness it was, and as good as any done by the recognised portraitists.'

'Papa used to say that Mama could have exhibited her paintings at Somerset House if she had been so inclined,' Joanna said fondly. 'But her health wasn't very good and she tired quickly.'

'She was a remarkably beautiful woman and as talented an artist as I've ever met,' Mr Dustin said, settling back and closing his eyes. 'And it's long been obvious to me that she passed many of her best traits along to you.'

Joanna was surprised to feel tears spring to her eyes. Funny, she hadn't spoken of her mother to anyone outside the family in years. Not because she was reluctant to do so, but because talking about her brought back so many other memories of the past.

Joanna had adored her mother. It had been her job to look after her when her health had begun to decline and she had done so without complaint, making the vegetable broths her mother was able to eat and bringing her the delicate pastries and sweets she was so fond of. She had sat with her and read to her in the hopes her mother would get better, but despite all the love and care lavished upon her, Frances Northrup had not survived. She had passed quietly in the night with only her husband and her daughter at her bedside to grieve.

Joanna had been fifteen at the time and to be suddenly deprived of the woman who had been at the centre of her life for so many years had seemed unbearably cruel. She had withdrawn into herself, unprepared for the pain of loss and seeking comfort in the thoughts and memories that no one could take away from her.

Her father had fared even worse. He had become a shadow of his former self, burying his grief in work and seldom raising his head from the books that became his solace. He hadn't been able to sleep, had lost all appetite for food and, when at the height of his misery, he had made the suggestion that the two of them travel to Egypt for a time, Joanna hadn't hesitated. Less than three weeks later, they had left England and spent the last four months of their year of mourning in the desert.

The trip had been life altering for Joanna. Not only because she had seen and experienced things she had only read about before, but because being away from London somehow made her mother's absence more bearable, as though they were only separated by distance rather than by the veil of mortality. It was as though for those four months, Joanna was able to block out her sadness, as though the unhappy memories were locked away in the world she'd left behind.

Unfortunately, upon their return to London the loneliness both she and her father had suffered had returned with a vengeance and Joanna understood why her father had immersed himself so deeply in his work. She had thrown herself into it for the same reason, needing something upon which to focus her attention, and in doing so had discovered a fascination with Egypt and its far-distant past.

But her love of painting—a love inspired by her mother—was still what brought back the sweetest memories and Joanna closed her eyes as the tears welled up again.

'I'm sorry,' Mr Bretton said, his voice low so as not to wake Mr Dustin. 'It wasn't my intention to dredge up unhappy memories.'

Joanna opened her eyes and was surprised to see him holding out a large white handkerchief. 'You didn't,' she said, slowly reaching out to take it. 'The memories I have of my mother are not unhappy. But I do miss her, so very much.'

'How old were you when she died?'

'Fifteen.'

'An impressionable age,' he said. 'An age when a girl needs her mother.'

'She was…a remarkable woman,' Joanna said, her voice husky. 'My father adored her. They married without my grandfather's approval. Papa said it didn't matter. As the youngest son, he knew he wasn't of consequence. His older brother would inherit the title, and when my cousin came along, Papa just moved further down the line.'

'How did he become interested in archaeology?' Mr Bretton asked. 'Most younger sons go into the church or take up a commission.'

'Papa wasn't interested in either,' Joanna said. 'But he was fascinated by history—Egyptian history in particular. So he started reading and eventually he began travelling. And the more he learned, the more he wanted to.'

'Did your mother ever go to Egypt with him?'

'Once. She wasn't as taken with it as he was,' Joanna said with a smile, 'but she wanted to be with him and he took very good care of her when they were away. They loved each other so much,' she mused. 'Neither one was happy when the other wasn't around.'

'I'm surprised your father didn't remarry soon after his return to London,' Mr Bretton said. 'Most men see it as a way of easing their loneliness.'

Joanna shook her head. 'Papa has never expressed a desire to marry again. He buries his loneliness in work.' She dried her eyes and then held the handkerchief out to him. 'Thank you.'

He shook his head. 'Keep it. My aunt sends me two dozen every Christmas. I have long since run out of places to store them all.'

In spite of her tears, Joanna felt a smile work its way to her lips. 'My aunt sends me lace caps. I don't know why. I never wear them. But they are beautifully embroidered and I cannot bring myself to say no.'

'Then perhaps we might come to some arrangement,' Mr Bretton suggested. 'My eldest sister is now married and in need of such things, so I will trade you a dozen caps for as many handkerchiefs and we will both think ourselves better off for it.'

Joanna ran her thumb over the softness of the handkerchief and was again tempted to smile. What a strange moment. She had just revealed something of a very private and personal nature to Mr Bretton, but rather than feeling embarrassed for having shared such heartfelt emotions, she actually felt better for having told him. Perhaps because he had encouraged her to believe that his interest in what she said was genuine.

She looked up and saw him watching her, half of his face in shadow, the other half bathed in the light of the coach lamp. He was mystery and magic rolled into one, and in the intimacy of the carriage Joanna was suddenly aware of what a powerful a combination it was…

'I say!' Mr Dustin said, jostled awake as the carriage turned a corner. 'If there are any lace caps or handkerchiefs going spare, I wouldn't mind a few of each. I've five daughters at home and not one of them any good with a needle.'

Abruptly, Joanna laughed, and felt lighter in mood than she had all evening. Somehow, Mr Bretton had taken a melancholy moment and turned it into something positive. What an unusual man he was turning out to be. Contrary to what she expected, he was not arrogant or boastful, nor had he looked at all out of place at the lecture this evening. He had listened intently, asked intelligent questions and fit in very well with the gentlemen who had gathered to hear her father talk about Egypt. All of which made it more and more difficult to figure out the nature of the man seated across from her.

Was he Laurence Bretton…or Valentine Lawe? And why did it matter that she be able to tell the difference?

The following afternoon Laurence was seated in the fifth row of the elegant Gryphon Theatre, watching his uncle coach his two lead actors during a rehearsal of Victoria's play. He had come to the theatre at his uncle's request, but try as he might to concentrate on what the actors were saying, he found his thoughts drifting to Lady Joanna and the events of the past two days.

To say he was fascinated by her was putting it mildly. As a man who had experienced the attentions of any number of women since assuming the role of Valentine Lawe, the arrival on the scene of one who seemed not in the least impressed by his notoriety was a new and refreshing experience. Lady Joanna did not flutter her eyelashes when she spoke to him, or gaze rapturously into his eyes when he spoke to her. Indeed, there were several occasions upon which they'd met when he wished she might have been a great deal *more* receptive to his overtures!

Still, having watched both of his sisters fall victim to the idiocy of love, Laurence had derived comfort from the knowledge that such amorous ups and downs were unlikely to befall him as long as his heart remained unengaged.

It was disconcerting to find out that it only took the arrival of the *right* woman to turn that belief on its head!

'Much better, Victor,' Theo Templeton said at the conclusion of the actor's soliloquy. 'You delivered your lines with far more emotion than you did last night and made the whole scene eminently more compelling. Make sure you give it the same effort tonight.'

'I will, Mr Templeton,' said the handsome leading man with a nod.

'What about me, Mr Templeton?' the actress playing opposite him enquired saucily. 'Is there anything you feel I should work on?'

Despite his preoccupation with Joanna, Laurence allowed himself a small smile. Signy Chermonde was one of London's most beautiful and talented actresses, as well as being one of the cleverest. No doubt she had asked the question expecting to be told that her performance was perfect and that she had no need to improve on anything. But Theo Templeton had not achieved the level of success he had by allowing the members of his troupe to grow complacent. No one was allowed to rest on their laurels—and that included the fiery and tempestuous Signy Chermonde.

'As a matter of fact, I would prefer that your response to Victor not be quite so melodramatic, Signy,' Theo said now. 'Elizabeth Turcott knows what she stands to gain by marrying Lord Greystone, but at the same time, she knows what she stands to lose. I need you to be convincing, not maudlin, and I know you can carry that off. You have more than enough talent to make it believable.'

Aware that he was watching a master at work, Laurence sat back and silently applauded his uncle's skills. Signy was famous for her emotional outbursts, but rather than being offended by Theo's criticisms, she actually agreed that she could do the scene better. After casting a last lingering glance in Laurence's direction, she regally exited the stage. Theo came down a short time later, shaking his head as he settled into the chair next to Laurence's.

'Little minx. I saw the way she was flirting with you. At times she seems to forget that she still finds her way into Lord Collins's bed every night.'

'It's just a game she likes to play,' Laurence said, unconcerned. 'She thinks now that I'm Valentine Lawe, I'll take her to Drury Lane with me, but you and I both know she's better off here. No one can hold a candle to you when it comes to wringing the most out of an actor's performance.'

'It helps when you've been on the other side of the fence,' his uncle said, shrugging off the compliment. 'I received several harsh reviews from bad directors when I started acting and it didn't help my performance one little bit. But a good director can make all the difference in the world. Still, it's outrageous the way she flirts with you.'

'As I say, it's just for show,' Laurence said. 'Signy has no more intention of leaving Lord Collins's bed than I have of putting her in mine.'

'You did once.'

'Yes, until I found out she was the one responsible for the rumour that nearly destroyed

Victoria's reputation,' Laurence said. 'I could never share my bed with a woman I didn't trust or respect. I feel foolish now for even having *thought* she was what I wanted.'

'Don't be too hard on yourself, lad. You're not the first man to succumb to Signy's wiles and you certainly won't be the last,' Theo said. 'She's a damn good actress, both on and off stage, and I expect she'll get what she wants one way or another. But never mind that, I didn't call you down here to talk about Signy,' he said, pulling a letter from his pocket. 'This came from Loftus this morning. He wants to know how you're coming along with your new play.'

Laurence frowned as he read the flowing lines of script from Sir Michael Loftus, noted theatre critic and the man whose unexpected appearance in the Brettons' drawing room one day had been the turning point in Laurence's life. 'I thought he was going to talk to me directly about the play.'

'I did too, but for whatever reason, he seems to want me involved. Maybe because he fears that bad blood between us may not be to his advantage. He wants your next play—'

'Victoria's next play,' Laurence said automatically.

'Right, Victoria's next play to be staged at Drury Lane. But since all of her previous plays have been produced here, he's afraid I'll be put out over the amount of money I stand to lose. Frankly, I don't give a damn about the money, but there is your future to consider—'

'Victoria's future.'

Theo sighed. 'Pardon me, Victoria's future, and I have to agree it would be better served at Drury Lane, especially if she wants to do a work of serious drama. The Gryphon isn't licensed for that kind of performance.'

Laurence folded up the letter. 'I'll speak to Victoria and see where things stand. Between all the preparations for Isabelle's wedding and my own hectic schedule I haven't had much time to talk to her these last few weeks.'

'Fine. Then I'll tell Loftus it's up to you… or rather, Valentine Lawe, to decide when and where his next play will be produced. That should keep relations between Loftus and myself on an even keel, and believing you'll choose the Theatre Royal over the Gryphon will keep Loftus happy with you. We don't want to make an enemy of the man.'

'Duly noted,' Laurence said, getting to his feet.

'By the by, how did you enjoy Lord Bonnington's lecture last night?' Theo enquired.

Laurence stared at his uncle in surprise. 'You *heard* about that?'

'Dear boy, there's not much I *don't* hear about when it comes to my family. I have eyes and ears at every door.'

'I shall be sure to bear that in mind. But the presentation was excellent. Bonnington is an authority in his field.'

'He also has a very pretty daughter.'

Laurence supposed he shouldn't have been surprised. For all of his uncle's considerable business savvy, he was still an unapologetic romantic at heart. 'Yes, he does. But the lady is not particularly impressed with Valentine Lawe right now,' he said, before going on to inform his uncle of the circumstances surrounding his initial meeting with Lady Joanna at the bookshop and of his less-than-stellar follow up with her at Lydia Blough-Upton's soirée.

'Well, never mind, lad. I dare say you'll do well enough elsewhere,' Theo said. 'Lady Joanna is a lovely young woman, but there are plenty of others who'll be happy to be seen at your side, Lady Mary Bidwell being one of them.'

'Thank you, uncle, but Lady Mary is the daughter of a duke,' Laurence said, not about to mention that she was also a far cry from Lady Joanna in every way imaginable. 'Even Valentine Lawe's name won't carry me that high up the social ladder!'

Chapter Five

~~~~~~~~~~~~~~~~

After dinner, Laurence spent a few hours with his parents and younger sister in the drawing room before bidding them all goodnight and heading up to his room. While he loved his family dearly, he was getting a little tired of listening to his mother and youngest sister go on about Henry Fulton. Everyone knew that Winifred was in love with the man and that she was hopeful of receiving his proposal of marriage very soon. But the courtship had been going on since well before Laurence had assumed the role of Valentine Lawe and, frankly, he was getting tired of listening to her extol the man's virtues as though he were some kind of newly anointed saint.

For everyone's sake he hoped Fulton would just make up his mind and get on with it.

Then there was his father, who'd sat in the

other corner happily immersed in his book and his cognac, chuckling to himself every now and then over some cleverly written phrase or amusing witticism. Ever since his eldest daughter's highly successful marriage to Lord Kempton's heir, Mr Bretton had taken to indulging in a glass of brandy before bed, saying that it helped him fall asleep and that it kept the nightmares at bay.

Laurence suspected it was just his father's way of celebrating the good things that were happening to the family. Given how close they had come to complete ruination, he really couldn't blame him.

'So, how's your new play coming along then, Mr Bretton?' his valet asked as he helped Laurence out of his evening clothes and into a heavy silk robe. 'The girls are all curious about it below stairs.'

Laurence smiled as he tightened the belt around his waist. 'It's coming along fine, Edwards, thank you. In fact, I plan to be up for a good few hours yet, so I'll likely need fresh candles in the morning.'

'I'll make sure to tell Betsy, sir,' the valet said. 'Goodnight.'

Laurence waited until the door closed again before crossing to his desk and taking out a slim stack of papers. He'd started the play last year, just before the news that he was Valentine Lawe went public and not surprisingly, in the months following that stunning disclosure, he'd had precious little time to work on it. His days had been filled with literary readings and luncheons while his evenings had been taken up with attending the many glittering society events to which he was routinely invited.

But now that the initial frenzy was over, Laurence found himself with more free time and was able to get back to working on the play.

The problem, nothing about the play *was* working. Not the plot or the characters, not even the dialogue. Sometimes, in a brief moment of clarity, the words he wanted to say would magically appear on the page in exactly the way he wanted to say them, but more often than not, all he saw was a blank sheet. Too many times the conflicts he'd thought strong ended up being weak and far too easily resolved. Either that or his characters' motivations were not compelling enough, or worse, made no sense at all.

Those were the moments through which Laurence struggled. He felt like he was waging an ongoing battle with characters over whom he had no control and who kept taking the play in a direction he didn't want it to go and he honestly didn't think it was supposed to be that way.

He remembered how happy Victoria had been during the writing of her second and third plays. Her head had been filled with ideas and her hands had flown across the pages in an effort to get the words and the story down.

Of course there had been moments of frustration, but for the most part, it had been an uplifting and fulfilling experience.

There was nothing even remotely uplifting about what Laurence was doing. If he was being honest with himself, he wasn't even sure he *liked* the story any more. He certainly didn't like his characters. What did *that* say about his skills as a playwright?

'It says,' Laurence murmured in disgust, 'that you are not cut out to *be* one.'

Unfortunately, he didn't have a choice. If, as he suspected, Victoria was not working on a new play, it meant someone else had to—and that someone was him. When he had assumed the role of Valentine Lawe, he had also assumed the obligations. By confirming the man's existence, he had established a belief that there would be more plays because society—and Sir Michael Loftus—expected that of him. If he didn't produce, both would turn on him like a vengeful lover.

Theo had said it himself. Sir Michael could be very helpful to those he liked, but if you crossed him, you risked arousing the devil.

Laurence had no desire to arouse the devil. Too many people had played that game and lost, which meant that this book, or rather, this pathetic collection of words and thoughts with virtually no plot, seriously flawed pacing and a cast of characters even the best troupe of actors would be hard pressed to make interesting, would have to do.

The devil was close by and no one knew better than Laurence how wretchedly unprepared he was to do battle.

It was nearly two weeks before Joanna finished Volney's *Travels*. The book contained a far more detailed account of life in that time than any of the other books she had read, but the fact she had made notes as she went along contributed much to the time it had taken. The author offered such fascinating insights into life in the Ottoman Empire that she had found herself reading many of the sections several times over. She could see why Mr Bretton had recommended it.

Equally aware, however, that she had kept it longer than intended, Joanna set out for Green Street the very next day. She had some shopping to do and so would not be taken much out of her way to return the book on her way there. With any luck, Mr Bretton would not be at home.

Joanna knew it was silly she should feel that way, but the truth was, she still wasn't comfortable in his company. While she had moved past the issue of his not having told her the truth about his being a successful playwright the first time they'd met, she could not so easily dismiss the events that had taken place on the night of her father's lecture. First the scene in the hall when Mr Bretton had taken her to task over what she had said about his not being able to be both a historian and a playwright—even though it was *his* omission of the facts that had caused the conflict in the first place—and then that disturbing interlude in the carriage on the drive home when he had displayed such kindness.

Joanna had not expected compassion or understanding from the man when she had talked about her mother, and his demonstration of both had left her feeling decidedly confused. So she had chosen avoidance as the way of dealing with him and had drawn out the time for as long as she could. But one could only hold on to another's possessions for so long and, knowing she had gone past that point, Joanna set out, hoping simply to drop the book and leave.

Unfortunately, as so often happens when one has wishes to the contrary, Mr Bretton *was* at home and when Joanna was shown into an elegant drawing room, it was to see him seated at the pianoforte playing an extremely complicated study. She heard only a few bars of the piece before he looked up and saw her, but it was enough to give her yet another tantalising glimpse into the complexity of his character.

'Lady Joanna,' he said, getting to his feet.

'Mr Bretton.'

At the same time, his sister, whom Joanna's aunt had pointed out to her at Mrs Blough-Upton's reception, rose to greet her. 'Lady Joanna, how nice of you to call. I am Mrs Devlin.'

'Good afternoon,' Joanna said. 'I hope I am not intruding.'

'Not at all. I just came to pay a call on my brother and said how pleasant it would be if someone else were to arrive as well, and now here you are.'

It was impossible not to like Victoria Devlin. Her natural vivacity and bright, sparkling eyes were guaranteed to make a guest feel at ease and Joanna found herself smiling back at the lady as though they were friends of long standing. 'I was en route to do some shopping and thought I would return Mr Volney's book on the way. Your brother was kind enough to lend it to me and I have enjoyed it immensely.' Joanna turned to look at the gentleman who was still standing by the pianoforte and said, 'Forgive me for keeping it so long, Mr Bretton, but there was a great deal of material to be covered.'

'No apologies are necessary, Lady Joanna, I was not anxious for its return,' he assured her. 'I have been reading *Viagio che o fato l'anno 1589 dal Caiero in Ebrin navigando su per el Nilo.*'

Joanna's eyes opened wide. 'By the gentleman who called himself Anonimo Veneziano?'

'The same.'

'How interesting. I wasn't aware it had been translated from the original Italian.'

'It hasn't.'

She blinked. 'Oh.'

'May I ring for refreshments, Lady Joanna?' Mrs Devlin enquired with a smile.

Stifling a sigh, Joanna shook her head. It seemed that once again she had severely underestimated Mr Bretton's abilities. 'Thank you, no. My maid is waiting outside and I have several more errands to attend to.'

'It was good of you to take the time to bring the book back,' Mr Bretton said, finally moving away from the piano.

'As I recall, it was condition of it being lent,' Joanna said, though her cheeks grew warm under the intensity of that crystalline-blue gaze. 'You play very well, Mr Bretton. I have not known many gentlemen who are as musically gifted.'

'I find it a relaxing pastime,' he replied. 'It takes my mind off other things.'

'Unlike writing, which demands that one's mind be present and engaged at all times,' Mrs Devlin said. 'Isn't that right, Laurence?'

Joanna saw the affectionate glance that passed between brother and sister and envied them their closeness. It was at times like these that she wished she had siblings of her own. While she was fond of her cousins, it wasn't the same as having a brother or sister with whom she could share confidences.

'Speaking of which, Lady Joanna, I recently came into possession of another book you might be interested in reading,' Mr Bretton said. 'It is by the French archaeologist, Denon, entitled *Travels in Upper and Lower Egypt*—'

'—*during the campaigns of General Bonaparte in that Country,*' Joanna said, excitement lending a slightly breathless quality to her voice. 'Yes, I am familiar with it, but however did you manage to find a copy?'

'The owner of a small bookshop on Oxford Street knows of my interest in such things and keeps his eyes and ears open for the rare and unusual. He contacts me whenever something new comes his way. Being an artist yourself, I think you will find it very entertaining.'

'Yes, I'm sure I would. Thank you, Mr Bretton,' Joanna said, blushing. 'It was…very kind of you to think of me.'

'Speaking of which, I understand we are to make up a party for the theatre,' Mrs Devlin said.

Joanna sent her a blank look. 'We are?'

'Yes. My brother received a very nice letter from Lady Cynthia, asking if his offer to escort the two of you to a performance of *A Lady's Choice* was still open.'

'And I wrote back to say that it was,' Mr Bretton said. 'I have also invited Victoria and her husband to join us, so we will be five.'

'Unless there is someone else you would like to include?' Mrs Devlin added quickly.

'Someone else?' Joanna said, glancing from one to the other.

'Your aunt indicated that Mr Osborne or Mr Rowe might be interested in accompanying you,' Mr Bretton said in a carefully expressionless voice.

Joanna felt her face burn. How *could* her aunt have suggested such a thing? Mr Osborne was of no more interest to her than Mr Rowe, but now Mr Bretton and his sister had reason to believe otherwise. 'I regret that my aunt thought to take advantage of your offer, Mr Bretton, by including people with whom you may or may not be acquainted. But I can assure you I am happy with the company as it stands. And I am looking forward to the evening.'

It was a comment made more out of obligation than because she genuinely felt it. Joanna had never been an avid theatre goer given that so many of the plays she *had* seen were not in the least memorable. The writing was poor, the acting worse and once the audience began hurling orange peelings and fruit at the stage, the evening degenerated even further. But as she sat in the carriage heading for Bond Street a short time later, she realised she was looking forward to giving the theatre another try, if for no other reason than to see what manner of playwright Laurence Bretton really was.

She had seen him shine in a world that was not his own. She was curious to see how he conducted himself in one that was.

That evening saw Joanna and her father, along with Lady Cynthia and Mrs Gavin and her husband, engaged for cards and dancing at the home of Lord and Lady Breckinridge. Not surprisingly, her cousin Jane did not attend.

'She's at home, poor darling,' Mrs Gavin murmured in response to Joanna's question. 'Her stomach wasn't quite the thing so I sent her off to bed with a posset.'

Joanna offered a suitable response, but in truth she hadn't expected anything else. Jane often came down with an illness right before a social engagement. Her mother tended to put it down to a delicate stomach, while Lady Cynthia was of the opinion the girl suffered from a weak constitution. Only Joanna knew the poor girl was paralytically shy and that she would do almost anything to avoid having to appear in public.

How she was ever to find a husband was a

question no one seemed willing to address, but as Joanna walked into the magnificent Park Lane mansion, she thought it just as well Jane hadn't come tonight. The fashionably dressed crowd, most of whom occupied the upper echelons of society, would certainly have made Jane's knees tremble. Joanna was thankful *she* had chosen to wear the newest and most elegant of her gowns, knowing that anything less would have been deemed inappropriate. Fashioned in exceedingly flattering lines, with a bodice cut low enough to expose the rounded tops of her breasts and in a shade of pink not deep enough to be called rose, it was as stylish as any in the room.

'Why look, Joanna, there is Mr Bretton,' Mrs Gavin said as they moved into the largest and most ornate of the reception rooms. 'And keeping very good company, I might add. Lord Trucklesworth is to his right, Lord and Lady Kempton are to his left and he is speaking to Mr Devlin, who is, of course, married to his eldest sister. And is that not Lady Mary Bidwell standing with them?'

'I do believe it is,' Lady Cynthia said, 'and looking quite fetching in that gown, though the colour does make her look somewhat pale. I wonder if her parents are here.'

'I suspect the duke and duchess are at cards,' Mrs Gavin said. 'They are both mad for whist.

So much so that I generally try not to end up at their table. I love my husband dearly, but he is quite hopeless at the game.'

'Why don't you go over and say hello, Joanna?' Lady Cynthia suggested. 'I believe I saw Mr Bretton glance over this way just now.'

'I suspect he was looking at someone else,' Joanna said, self-consciously redirecting her gaze. 'Besides, I have no wish to intrude on their conversation. I do not know Lord Trucklesworth or Lord and Lady Kempton.'

'Pish-tosh, these are the circles in which you now move and you must start feeling comfortable in them,' Lady Cynthia said. 'Mrs Devlin will surely introduce you to Lord and Lady Kempton, given that they are her in-laws. Besides, it will be good for you to be seen standing next to Lady Mary, given how much prettier you are than her.'

The cutting remark, so typical of her aunt, did nothing to make Joanna feel better as she reluctantly made her way across the floor. She was well aware that she was expected to move in a different circle now and that being the daughter of an earl entitled her to be treated as an equal. But she had lived too many years as plain Miss Joanna Northrup to feel at home in the company of lords and ladies. Unlike Mr Bretton, whose relaxed posture and enviable poise seemed to suggest he found nothing in the least awkward about mingling with his betters.

'Why, good evening, Lady Joanna,' Mrs Devlin said, again greeting her with that warm and engaging smile. 'How lovely to see you. I don't believe you are acquainted with my husband?'

Joanna replied that she was not and the necessary introductions were made. Mr Devlin, in turn, introduced her to his parents and then to Lord Trucklesworth, all of whom were familiar with her father and his expeditions.

'I suspect you were surprised to learn that Bretton here, famous for his plays, was also an avid student of Egyptian history,' Lord Kempton said.

'I was indeed,' Joanna said, aware of Mr Bretton's eyes on her. 'He is a man of many talents.'

'And accomplished in them all, from what Lord Parker tells me,' Lady Mary said, casting flirtatious glances in Mr Bretton's direction. 'I am informed that Lord Parker challenged him to an archery contest last week and that Mr Bretton's arrow landed in the very centre of the target from a distance of one hundred paces. Is that true, Mr Bretton?'

'I do not believe it was a hundred paces—'

'Don't be so modest, Bretton, I know for a fact it was more,' Mr Devlin spoke up. '*And* I watched him place a second arrow no more than an inch below the first one a few minutes later.'

Despite her ambivalence, Joanna had to admit to being impressed by Mr Bretton's accomplishments. Who would have thought a man who wrote plays, spoke Italian like a native and played difficult études for relaxation, would also turn out to be such a skilled archer?

'A lucky shot, Mr Bretton?' she ventured.

'Luck always plays a part in such endeavours, Lady Joanna,' he replied with a smile. 'My father taught me to shoot when I was a boy and it seems some skills carry over into adulthood.'

'Are you as adept with a pistol are you are with a bow and arrow, Mr Bretton?' the duke's daughter enquired breathlessly.

'I really cannot say, Lady Mary, never having fired one. But given the nature of my occupation, I suspect the chances of my ever having to do so are extremely limited.'

'You never know, Bretton,' Trucklesworth said with a wink. 'You might be called upon to defend yourself from a jealous husband whose wife is so enthralled by your prose that she believes herself in love with you.'

'Really, Trucks, you do say the most ridiculous things,' Mr Devlin drawled.

'Only to amuse the ladies.'

'But what *would* you do, Mr Bretton,' Joanna said, 'if such a thing were to happen?'

Lady Mary's softly indrawn breath was indicative of Joanna's having strayed beyond the bounds of polite conversation, but Mr Bretton didn't bat an eye. 'Never having experienced such a situation, I really cannot say, Lady Joanna. But I would never choose to be the cause of marital discord and would do my utmost to assure the fellow that his lady was in love with the words, rather than with the man. I might even suggest he try writing a love letter to her himself.'

'Like your hero did in *Penelope's Swain*,' Lady Kempton said.

'Did he?' Mr Bretton looked momentarily bemused. 'I'd almost forgotten.'

'It is no wonder, given that you have written four such excellent plays,' Lady Mary said in a voice that left no one in any doubt as to her affection for him. 'I think your stories are *wonderful*. And so terribly romantic.'

But not nearly so romantic as the playwright.

The thought sprang unbidden to Joanna's mind, where it remained, unexpected and unwelcome. It became even more so when Mr Bretton suddenly looked at her and said, 'You do not care for romantic fiction, Lady Joanna?'

'I...did not say that, Mr Bretton.'

'No, but you smiled when Lady Mary said my plays were romantic. I thought perhaps you did not care for such things.'

'I am not a fan of mawkish love stories, no,' Joanna said, uncomfortable at being centred out for attention but exceedingly glad that he *had* misinterpreted her reaction. 'Though I'm sure yours are not in any way of that nature.'

His mouth twitched. 'How diplomatic. Tell me, what *do* you like to see in the way of theatre?'

'I suppose I would have to say classical works by Shakespeare and Marlowe. The operas of Rossini and Mozart, and more dramatic works by the contemporary playwrights of our day.'

'Dear me, it seems we have a dissenter in our ranks,' Mr Devlin said, clearly amused by the exchange. He glanced with affection at his wife. 'Will you not go to the defence of your brother's works, my love?'

'Certainly not,' Mrs Devlin said. 'Laurence is perfectly capable of defending himself. Besides, I believe you and I are engaged for this dance.'

'So we are. If you will excuse us, ladies and gentlemen.' Mr Devlin took his wife's hand and winked at his brother-in-law. 'You're on your own, Bretton. Don't let the side down.'

They left, as his parents did, to take their places on the dance floor. Shortly thereafter, Lady Mary excused herself to find her mother and Lord Trucklesworth slipped away, muttering something about never being able to find a servant when you needed one.

The exodus left Joanna alone with Mr Bretton, who was still smiling at her in that all-too-familiar way.

'It would seem something amuses you, Mr Bretton,' she said, careful to keep her focus on the people moving around them.

'Indeed, Lady Joanna. You.'

'Me?' Her eyes flew back to his. 'What have I done to arouse your mirth?'

'Nothing, other than be yourself.'

'I hardly think that noteworthy.'

'I beg to differ. You are unique. As different from any other woman in this room as a sovereign is from a penny.'

Joanna felt an unfamiliar quickening of her pulse. 'You hardly know me well enough to say.'

'Ah, but I do, and a great deal better than you think.'

His piercing blue gaze remained fixed upon her face. He neither blinked nor looked away. Joanna found it distinctly unnerving. 'I do not think it appropriate that you look at me in that way, Mr Bretton.'

'What way?'

'You are staring at me.'

'Am I?'

'Yes. And it is entirely possible someone might notice and misconstrue your intent.'

His smile broadened. 'But I have no intent, other than to serve my own pleasure.'

'I can assure you, your pleasure would be better served by staring at someone else,' Joanna told him in a wry voice. 'Lady Mary Bidwell, for example.'

'Come now, Lady Joanna, you know as well as I do that staring at Lady Mary would be a poor use of my time. A duke's daughter is hardly like to marry a poor playwright.'

'I think you cry poor when you are nothing of the sort,' Joanna said. 'You live in a fine house and conduct yourself with the manners of a gentleman. You are embraced by society and mingle with the likes of viscounts and earls.'

'Nevertheless, I am not titled myself and know better than to set my sights so high.'

'So you admit to wishing to marry well.'

'I admit to wishing to be happily married,' he corrected her. 'If I achieve wealth into the bargain, so be it. But there are many rich men whose wives do not love them yet are happy to say they do. I would rather be without wealth and know my wife loves me for who I am, than be rich and constantly wondering. Why, Lady Joanna, you're blushing. Surely the topic doesn't embarrass you?'

'Not at all,' Joanna replied, wishing not for the first time that her cheeks were not such a visible barometer of her emotions. 'I simply do not think it is an appropriate topic of discussion for a single lady and an unmarried gentleman to be having.'

'Perhaps, but as someone who studies human nature in order to weave emotion into the heart of a story, it behoves me to talk about such things,' Mr Bretton said. 'Love, hate, jealousy, betrayal—the strongest emotions make the best foundations for a story. The man you claim to admire wrote one of the most compelling love stories of all time, using words as romantic as any ever written. "One fairer than my love, the all-seeing sun,"' he quoted softly. '"Ne'er saw her match since first the world begun."'

Joanna blushed even as her brow furrowed. The words, undeniably romantic, were familiar, but she couldn't place them…

'"O, she doth teach the torches to burn bright,"' he continued. '"It seems she hangs upon the cheek of night. Like a rich jewel in an Ethiope's ear; beauty too rich for use, for earth too dear."' He broke off, smiling. 'I think you recognise it now. Your cheeks have gone quite pink again.'

'It is only that the room is so warm,' Joanna said. 'And that a gentleman I barely know is quoting lines from *Romeo and Juliet* to me.'

'Ah, so you know the Bard's words,' he said, even more softly.

'My governess adored Shakespeare. I spent nearly a year studying his writings. I found the language…difficult.'

'But you cannot deny the elegance of it.' He

stopped and looked at her, his eyes leaving her nowhere to hide. 'Shakespeare had a way of telling a woman how beautiful she was without falling back on trite, conventional phrases. I thought the repeating of them to you now seemed... appropriate.'

The feelings came unbidden—an unexpected rush of excitement, followed by an even stronger one of guilt. 'Mr Bretton, I really must insist—'

'That I continue?'

'That you keep such words to yourself!'

He watched her in silence for a moment, then nodded. 'Yes, perhaps you're right. After all, there can be no harm if I reflect, in my own mind, that in that gown you remind me of the first rose of spring. Or that the delightful sprinkling of freckles across your nose, no doubt the bane of your existence and despaired of by your aunt, is one of your most charming features. Far better to keep thoughts like that to myself.'

Joanna closed her eyes and waited for her erratic pulse to slow. 'It is no wonder you have achieved such fame with your plays, sir. Were those lines drawn from one of them?'

There was a very brief silence before he said, 'I would never say something to you that had been written for someone else. Pardon me if the lines sounded...clichéd.'

Joanna slowly opened her eyes. His smile was as she remembered, but the expression in his eyes had changed. She had offended him and that was the last thing she wanted to do. 'They did not,' she said hastily. 'I simply wasn't... expecting them.'

He watched her for a long time, as though trying to draw out everything there was to know about her. Had she ever been observed so closely? Had a gentleman's eyes ever probed so gently, yet so intently?

Joanna thought not. Until now, she had never had any reason to engage in such an intimate discussion with any one, let alone a man who had no business dwelling so stubbornly in her thoughts.

'No, of course not,' he said finally. 'Because we both know I had no right to speak to you in such a manner and for that I apologise.' His anger, quickly aroused, seemed to die an equally swift death. 'It was not my intention to embarrass you or to make you feel uncomfortable.'

The apology, far more earnest than Joanna had expected, left her feeling even worse. 'You did not embarrass me.'

'Then why did you blush?'

'Because I wasn't—' She broke off, unsure of herself and of the situation. It was not the first time he had spoken to her seriously. He had done so at her father's lecture and then again in the carriage on the drive home. But now, as then, she had no idea how to respond. 'Mr Bretton, I really don't know what to say—'

'Then say nothing. It is enough that you know my apology was sincerely intended and that I will not trespass on your feelings again.' He glanced down at the floor, then briefly at a lady passing by. 'I am promised to Lady Mary for the next dance. Will you honour me with the one following?'

The invitation, surprising as it was unexpected, brought a rush of colour to Joanna's cheeks. 'I'm sorry, but it is already reserved.'

'Of course. The next one?'

She shook her head, regretfully. 'That one too.'

'And the one after that?'

For the space of a second, their eyes met— and Joanna felt the rhythm of her heart change. 'I'm sorry.'

It was not a lie. She *was* engaged for the next three dances…but not for the fourth. Unfortunately, Mr Bretton did not ask for the fourth. She waited, because it must always be the gentleman who asked, but he did not ask again.

Instead, with a regretful smile, he bowed and walked away, leaving her to stare after him, confused without knowing why. Hurting when there was no reason to hurt. Surely she did not *wish* to dance with Mr Bretton. He was a playwright.

Someone she did not wish to know better. Some-one she would not be *allowed* to know better.

But she did wish to know him better…and three times he had asked her to dance. Why did it suddenly matter so much that he had not asked her a fourth?

Upon returning home from the soirée, Lau-rence did not go immediately to bed. He was too unsettled, the memory of his conversation with Lady Joanna playing over and over in his mind.

Something had happened tonight. Something that had changed the tenor of their relationship. He knew it as surely as he knew his own name. Before tonight, Lady Joanna had struck him as being a supremely confident young woman—one who knew what she wanted and how to go about getting it. Only once in the carriage when she had talked about her mother had she dem-onstrated any signs of vulnerability.

Yet tonight, during the latter moments of their conversation, he had seen that vulnerabil-ity again. Her confidence had faltered and she had been unsure of herself, her words saying one thing while her eyes said another. And though she held fast to the belief that it was he who had spoken out of turn, Laurence knew, on a deeper and more instinctive level, that he had not.

There was a difference between a woman who blushed upon hearing something she did not

like and one who blushed upon hearing something she did.

Still, what did it matter if she coloured at his
compliments? Rumour had it she was being
courted by gentlemen far more worthy of her
affections than him. The Honourable Albert
Rowe, heir to a viscount and a substantial fortune. Mr John Osborne, a barrister distantly related to the earl. And Captain James Sterne, son
of Lord Rinstrom and already possessed of a
considerable fortune.

What had he to offer when compared to men
like that?

Or perhaps she was the type of woman who
enjoyed the attentions of one man while flirting with another. If so, he was better off without
her. It was only a matter of time before a woman
like that broke a man's heart.

Hoping to distract himself with work, Laurence pulled out the manuscript and sat down
at his desk. He had made some small gains in
the story, amending the plot to reflect a darker
and more difficult goal for his protagonist, and
combining two of his less important characters
into one. It had added a sense of urgency to the
story and had briefly inspired what Laurence
had hoped might be a burst of creative brilliance.

But three hours later, with two empty wine
bottles on the floor and all of the candles burned
low, he shoved the papers back into the drawer

and called it a night. He had written only ten lines—and crossed them all out again.

Clearly, this was not a good time for creative endeavours. His mind was too wrapped up in Joanna and with all of the reasons he shouldn't care about her.

The problem was, he did care about her and, more than ever, Laurence realised that his infatuation with Signy Chermonde had been just that: a silly infatuation based entirely on the actress's winsome beauty and seductive manner. What he felt for Joanna was already so much deeper because she was different from any woman he'd ever met. There were depths to her that would take a lifetime to plumb. She would challenge him and he her. They would meet as intellectual equals, their discussions about subjects of interest to each of them being both well researched and highly stimulating.

And there would be passion. Oh, yes, there would most definitely be passion. Joanna was the type of woman who felt things deeply. Laurence remembered the excitement in her voice when she had spoken to him about her time in Egypt. Remembered how her eyes had glowed with pleasure when she had stood at her father's side during his lecture and explained what each of her drawings was about. If that enthusiasm for work was equated to passion for a man... for him...

But, no, it was foolish even to entertain the thought. Laurence knew he was not the one destined to introduce such intimacies into her life. Another more suitable man would have that pleasure. He was doomed to remain for ever on the periphery of her life; a fellow she might encounter a few times a year, perhaps in a shop or at the theatre or whilst riding in the Park. They would greet each other as friends and enquire after one another's health. Then they would move on, perhaps feeling better for having had the conversation.

But he wouldn't feel better. In fact, Laurence couldn't imagine anything worse. He had no desire to engage in polite conversations with Joanna. He wanted more. A lot more. And the realisation he wasn't going to have that opportunity brought home the futility of his hopes.

He was beginning to care deeply for Lady Joanna Northrup. And he had no need of anyone telling him that down that road lay the path to destruction.

Chapter Six

The days leading up to Lady Cynthia's dinner party were not restful ones for Joanna. Aside from being assiduously courted by Mr Rowe and Mr Osborne—who had taken to appearing almost daily in her drawing room—she was subject to the ever-changing whims of her aunt, who became more of a tyrant the closer the party came. Nothing was done to her satisfaction and the servants were kept busy from morning until night polishing silver, sweeping floors and dusting furniture.

For her own part, Joanna sought solace at the British Museum. The building on Great Russell Street had become a refuge of sorts and she had spent many hours gazing at Mr Towneley's classical sculptures or admiring the marble statuary Lord Elgin had acquired from the Parthenon and Erechtheum.

Today, however, it was not the stone busts or intricate friezes that drew her attention, but the fragment of black granite taken in the looting of Alexandria after Napoleon Bonaparte's defeat. The famous Rosetta Stone.

As she approached it now, breathless in the face of such a monumental piece of history, Joanna wondered about the people who had carved it. It was a substantial block of granite, standing almost four feet high, two feet wide and about twelve inches thick. Tiny lines of script covered the entire surface of the stone, each distinct and different from the other. Each, clearly, its own unique language.

But what did it say? Joanna wondered as she ran her finger over the lines. What secrets did it really hold—?

'The bottom portion is Greek,' a voice said quietly to her left. 'The middle contains a cursive script known as Demotic, and the top portion is hieroglyphic. Scholars have been able to translate the Greek portion because the knowledge of the language is still with us, but it is only recently that the meaning of the hieroglyphic portion has become known.'

Joanna inhaled sharply. She had not expected to see Laurence Bretton today and the degree of pleasure she felt upon hearing his voice was undeniable. She strove to keep any sign of it from her voice. 'Does anyone know how old it is?'

'The Greek inscription indicates that the stone is a decree originating in 196 BC,' Mr Bretton said, his expression as solemn as hers as he gazed at the stone. 'Which would place it in the reign of Ptolemy V. But what matters is that the identical inscription is written in each of the three languages, thereby allowing scholars to isolate similar letters and words in each. Once they knew what the letters were, it was possible to form an alphabet and then go on to decipher other hieroglyphic writing.'

Joanna knew that what he was telling her was not imparted with a view to impressing her with his knowledge, but rather in the hopes of educating her and to share his enjoyment of this incredible piece of history. 'I really don't know very much about it,' she admitted.

'No one does. Jean-Francois Champollion was the first to decipher the hieroglyphs. He was well schooled in the ancient languages and said the symbols were basically phonetic in nature.' Mr Bretton reached out and reverently touched the stone. 'I have a feeling we will learn a great deal more about it in the centuries to come.'

Joanna slid a sideways glance in his direction, aware that it was becoming more and more difficult to equate the educated scholar with the flamboyant playwright she had glimpsed so briefly on that one occasion. There were so many levels to this man, so many facets to his personality. And as each new facet was revealed, Joanna felt herself being more and more hopelessly drawn in.

'I think about that every time I travel to Egypt,' she said now. 'I find myself wondering about the discoveries yet to be made and if I will be fortunate enough to be there when they are.'

'You are lucky just to have *been* to Egypt,' Mr Bretton said. 'Most men and women will learn no more than what is to be found in their books and see no more than what is on display in this room.'

'But I should like to feel I have *participated* in some way.'

'You have. Your sketches will serve as an invaluable record of all you have seen.'

'I know, but wouldn't it be marvellous to be the one who stumbles upon the tomb of some great king and who shares his history with the world?' Joanna said, feeling the thrill of it even as she spoke. 'At the very least, I would like to be like Mr Champollion, able to decipher and read the words of the ancients.'

Mr Bretton's mouth lifted in a smile. 'Champollion is a brilliant man. He has dedicated his life to the study of languages and many years to deciphering the writing on the stone. Knowledge like that isn't gleaned overnight.'

'I know,' Joanna said. 'It's just that…I would so like to be able to look back on my life and feel I had made some kind of worthwhile contribution to historical exploration.'

'Do you really place such little value on your art?'

'No. I know my work is good,' Joanna said. 'But I am not in any way unique. There are many artists far more talented than I.'

'There may be artists *as* talented, Lady Joanna, but I doubt there are many as unique,' he said. 'You have far gone beyond what is expected of a woman in our society. You are fearless, and for that must always be thought unique. But I'm sure I am not the first man to tell you that.'

'In fact, you are,' Joanna said, blushing. 'Other than my father, of course, but one cannot put too much stock in what a father says.'

Mr Bretton laughed, the sound drawing appreciative glances from a group of young ladies clustered around a display case on the other side of the room. 'Of course you can. Not all fathers believe their children are unique. If your father compliments your work, it is because he truly believes you are deserving of it.'

'But surely yours must think the same of you,' Joanna said. 'Not many sons can be as gifted in so many ways.'

She was surprised to see him look momentarily uncomfortable. 'Gifted goes far beyond what I am able to do, Lady Joanna. Gifted is a doctor who is able to heal the sick. Gifted is a composer like Mozart, whose music seems to come from the heavens. All I do is write stories that amuse people.'

'Oh, now I really must take exception to that,' Joanna stated. 'I am told you are quite brilliant. If you would be so critical of your own abilities, do not think to elevate mine.'

'You have not yet seen my play.'

'I don't need to. Enough people of my acquaintance have and they would not say you were brilliant if you were not,' Joanna said. 'You know how fickle society can be.'

'Oh, yes, I know,' Mr Bretton acknowledged. 'But what brings pleasure to one brings pain to another. I do not care for the sound of the bagpipes, yet its music has stirred countless generations of Scots for centuries.'

Joanna wrinkled her nose. 'If it is of any consolation, I do not care for the music of the pipes either. I am surprised they even consider it music. But then, the Scots view many things differently from us.'

'Aye, they do that.'

Aye? Joanna glanced at him, an unwelcome suspicion dawning. 'Please don't tell me *you* have Scottish ancestry?'

'No, but my Aunt Templeton does,' he said, grinning. 'Fiona Anthea McTavish she was before she married my uncle, with flaming red hair and eyes as green as shamrocks.'

'Marvellous,' Joanna said, laughing so that he might know she was teasing. 'And here I was, hoping to make a good impression.'

'Who says you haven't?'

Her laughter died as his eyes caught and held hers. Suddenly, she felt like a breathless girl who had just received her first compliment. One that meant more than any other ever would—because it had come from him.

Needing time to gather her thoughts, Joanna moved away to examine some of the other display cases. 'Tell me about…your sisters, Mr Bretton,' she said.

'My sisters?'

'Yes. What it is like to have them.'

He watched her for a moment and then smiled, as if recognising her need to change the subject. 'I have two sisters and they could not be more different. The eldest, Victoria, whom you've met, is accomplished, beautiful and uncommonly wise for her age. The youngest, Winifred, is more beautiful, less accomplished and far more inclined towards silliness.'

'Are the three of you close?' Joanna asked.

'Victoria and I are. We share a number of common interests and see things in much the same way. Winifred and I have become closer over these last few months, but she is still very silly. All she thinks about is marrying Mr Henry Fulton.'

'That is not uncommon for young ladies in our society,' Joanna said. 'It is what we are expected to do. Some of us more than others,' she added, her voice dropping away.

'But surely that will not be a problem for you. You must have numerous suitors for your hand.'

'I do, but which ones are courting me *because* I am Lady Joanna Northrup?' Joanna said. 'Why do you think I didn't tell you who I was the first time we met?'

'I assumed it was because you didn't *want* me to know,' Mr Bretton said.

'You're right, I didn't. I wanted to talk to you as though we were just two people who shared a common interest in Egypt,' Joanna said. 'One not affected by who I was or my position in society.'

'I wouldn't have spoken to you any differently had I known you were titled,' he told her. 'You are still who you are. And we still share that common interest.'

'Yes, but it would have put a distance between us, as it does now,' Joanna said sadly. 'I wanted, for those first few minutes, to be able to talk to you as though we were equals.'

'Even though you knew we were not.'

Joanna nodded. 'Even though. I had very few obligations in my old life, Mr Bretton. I was

happy to work at my father's side and content
to arrange his meetings and catalogue his finds.
Mr Penscott and I developed a very good system for doing so.'

'You are fond, I think, of Mr Penscott.'

'He and I share an interest in my father's work,'
Joanna said. 'Our friendship developed as a result of that.'

'Is that all it is? A friendship?'

'It is all it can ever be.' She stopped and drew
a long, deep breath. 'The daughter of an earl
does not associate with one of her father's employees, Mr Bretton.'

Joanna heard the brittleness of her voice and
knew he had too. 'No, she does not,' he said.
'Nor, if she is wise, does she associate with a
playwright, which I should think would be even
more damaging to her reputation.' He smiled,
and glanced over at her. 'However, if it is of any
consolation, we all bear obligations of one kind
or another, my lady. Some are simply more onerous than others.'

'I cannot imagine you having such onerous
obligations,' Joanna said, wishing for a moment
that they could change places so that he might
understand the restrictions of her life. 'You can
come and go as you please. You have achieved
success doing what you love and are free to
marry anyone you wish, and given how famous

you are, I imagine you have quite a variety of young ladies from which to choose.'

His mouth pulled into a cynical smile. 'You might be surprised. I have only recently become famous, as you call it. Before that I led a quiet life and was content to do so.'

'So you do not care to be the object of all eyes.'

'Not of all eyes, no.' He paused and then said, 'Only of one lady's.'

Joanna looked up—and found his clear blue gaze steady on hers. Unwavering. Surely he didn't mean—

'Mr Lawe?'

An unexpected voice intruded—and the moment was lost. Joanna turned to see that one of the ladies who had been admiring Mr Bretton from the other side of the room had come over in the hopes of talking to him.

It was the excuse she needed…and strangely, did not want. 'Well, I must be on my way. Lady Cynthia will be wondering where I am.'

'I hope I have not unduly delayed your departure,' he said, ignoring the lady at his side.

'Not at all. I found our talk most…informative,' Joanna said. And then, prompted by some flight of madness, added, 'I look forward to seeing you this evening.'

'As I do you, Lady Joanna. And I hope,' he said with a wry smile, 'that by the time the evening is over, you will feel I have been considerably more than just…informative.'

Not surprisingly, Joanna was on tenterhooks for the rest of the day. When it came time to dress for the evening, she changed her gown twice, had her maid arrange her hair with a band of small silk roses, only to change to ribbon at the last moment, and looked through an assortment of fans before she found just the right one. She tried to assure herself it was because of her aunt's insistence that she look well for Mr Rowe and Captain Sterne, but Joanna knew that wasn't the case.

Her wish to look as lovely as possible had nothing to do with either of those gentlemen.

In an effort to calm her nerves, Joanna went in search of her father. She knew he would avoid showing his face for as long as possible and suspected he had taken refuge in his study—a bolt hole where the two of them had spent many a pleasurable hour talking about subjects of interest to them both. It was here her father had first mentioned the possibility of her going to Egypt with him in the months following her mother's death and here they still met to discuss his ongoing expeditions to that most fascinating country.

Tonight, he was in a particularly good mood as a result of a letter he had received just that afternoon from Lord Amberley, confirming his intention to fund the trip to Abu Simbel. Now, preparations could begin and her father was never happier than when planning an expedition.

'Yes, it is very good news,' he said, 'given that there is absolutely no way I could have covered the costs of the trip myself. There isn't enough money left in the estate. This way, I suffer no guilt but still have the funding I need, which means I can start mapping out our next trip.'

'A trip you *are* planning to take me on, I hope, Papa?'

'Eh?' Her father looked up and his bushy brows drew together. 'Oh, well, I don't know about that, Joanna. Your aunt is not at all keen on the idea. This is going to be a much longer expedition than those I've undertaken in the past and she is concerned that your first priority be to find a husband. Unless you have already made up your mind in that regard?'

Joanna glanced at him in surprise. 'Why would you think I had?'

'Because Captain Sterne asked me if he might speak to you, which in turn led me to believe that *you* may have offered him some… encouragement.'

'I can assure you, Papa, I have offered him no encouragement whatsoever,' Joanna informed him. 'We have spoken together a few times, but that is all.'

'But is he a man to whom you could give

your heart? He is not a bad fellow by all accounts. Indeed, I don't mind spending time with him, though he can be somewhat overbearing at times.'

'A great deal overbearing,' Joanna murmured. 'And not a little arrogant.'

'No, I cannot disagree with you there,' her father admitted. 'Still, he is exceedingly wealthy and stands to become even more so after his father dies, which is certainly why your aunt keeps encouraging the association. He also shares your interest in Egypt, which is more than can be said for Mr Osborne, who I am quite sure doesn't even know where Egypt is!' her father said in disgust. 'Mr Rowe, at least, has some understanding of the country and its politics, though I doubt he has any interest in going.'

'I cannot think the heat or the exercise would be good for his health,' Joanna agreed, thinking of the man's size.

'I suspect not. However, all that aside, it is important that you be married, my dear. And while I cannot deny the need for you to marry a wealthy man, I would hope it would be someone for whom you could feel a genuine affection.'

'Is that why you have no wish to marry again, Papa?' Joanna asked. 'Because you are still in love with Mama?'

For a moment, the joy left her father's face, making him look like an old man. 'I loved your mother with all my heart, Joanna. The day she became my wife was the happiest of my life. But when she died, it was as though…a light went out in my world,' he said quietly. 'I didn't know how to go on. Indeed, for a time I had no desire to. Even now, not a day goes by that I do not think about her. How fair would it be to marry someone else, knowing how little of my heart I had to give her?'

It was a question for which Joanna had no answer. The infatuation she had felt for Aldwyn Patterson was insignificant when compared to the way her father had felt about her mother, but even so, she remembered how much it had hurt when Aldwyn had left.

What must it be like to know the person you loved more than any other was never coming back?

'You have your whole life ahead of you, Joanna,' her father said, cupping her chin in his hand. 'You need to be with a man who loves you and who you love madly in return. Whoever that man is, he will have my blessing. But I will not deny that if he were rich, it would go a long way towards solving a great many of our difficulties.'

'What will happen if our debts are not paid?'

'I suspect this house, and everything in it, will have to be sold,' her father said, regretfully. 'And quite likely Bonnington Manor too. Our debts are high and we have nothing else to fall

back on. My brother and his son were quite…
extravagant in their lifestyles.'

'You mean irresponsible.'

'Yes, I suppose I do.' Her father stared down
at his desk, then gamely rallied a smile. 'However, the wolves are not yet at the door. We still
have time and I do still hold out hopes of you
making a good marriage.'

'But if I do not,' Joanna asked, hearing what
he said…and what he did not, 'our entire way of
life is going to change, isn't it, Papa? How then
will we survive?'

He looked at her and, for the first time, Joanna saw the weight of the burden he was carrying—and trying so hard to conceal. 'We will do
what we did before, my dear. We will live simply
and within our means. We could become explorers in search of adventure and set off for places
unknown. Who knows? Perhaps we might join
a Bedouin tribe and ride across the desert on a
camel!'

It was wishful thinking…and they both knew
it. Her father was Lord Bonnington and the responsibilities owed to the name could not so
easily be put aside. He had to do all he could to
preserve the good name of the family, so while
he might not wish her to marry a rich man whom
she did not love, neither could he afford to see
her marry a poor man she did.

And it was becoming clearer by the day who the two men were who occupied those roles.

Truly, salvation came at a steep price.

Not surprisingly, Joanna's aunt and uncle were the first of the dinner guests to arrive.

'I did try to hold him back,' Mrs Gavin said, looking exceedingly elegant in a deep plum-coloured gown and matching turban, 'but you know how he hates to be late.'

'Bad manners to be late,' Mr Gavin stated flatly. 'Evening, Joanna.'

'Good evening, Uncle Carl, Aunt Florence. And Cousin Jane,' Joanna said, bending down to kiss her cousin on both cheeks, 'how delightful to see you again.'

Jane Gavin was a pretty girl—pale, with fine features and clear, bright eyes. She looked lovely in an off-white gown edged with deep flounces of lace and pink ribbon, though the look of fear in her eyes suggested she would far rather have stayed home. Unfortunately, Lady Cynthia's insistence that she be here to even out the numbers made such a choice impossible.

Either that, Joanna reflected, or her mother had insisted that she attend because she knew there would be a number of eligible bachelors present. After all, Joanna wasn't the only young lady in need of a husband.

'So, how many are we tonight?' Mrs Gavin

asked after they retired to the drawing room and the butler handed around glasses of ratafia for the ladies and stronger libations for the gentlemen.

'Thirty-two,' Lady Cynthia said. 'Lord Amberley and his wife will be here, of course, as well as the Stanton-Howards, Lord and Lady Barker-White, Mrs Taylor, Mr Rowe and the Chesapeakes. I do not believe you are acquainted with the other guests.'

'Mrs Taylor is back in society?' Mrs Gavin frowned. 'I thought she was still mourning her husband.'

'She put off her blacks two months ago,' Lady Cynthia said. 'I met her in Gunter's last month and stopped for a chat. Delightful woman. I've always thought she would do very well for Bonnington.'

Not surprisingly, the comment earned her a dark look from her brother.

'And what have we in the way of single gentlemen?' Mrs Gavin enquired, sparing a glance for her daughter.

'Sadly, my nephew, Mr Osborne, was taken ill at the last minute and is unable to attend, but Captain Sterne, Mr Rowe and Mr Filbert will be here,' Lady Cynthia said. 'And, of course, Mr Bretton.'

'The inimitable Valentine Lawe,' Mrs Gavin exclaimed with pleasure. 'How exciting!'

'Yes, I was most pleased that he was able to join us. I thought since he was kind enough to invite Joanna and myself to share his uncle's box at the theatre, the least I could do was invite him to be a guest at my dinner party,' Lady Cynthia said. 'Such a charming young man, though unfortunately lacking in any particular social status. You really should introduce him to Jane.'

'Oh, no, you mustn't, Mama!' Jane cried, her pale-blue eyes filling with panic. 'He is far too famous. I wouldn't know what to say to him.'

'There is nothing to be afraid of, Cousin Jane,' Joanna assured her. 'Mr Bretton is not at all intimidating. I have always found him very easy to talk to.'

'But you find everyone easy to talk to, whereas I do not,' Jane said in an anxious voice. 'What would I talk to him about? I don't know the first thing about writing plays.'

'No, but you sing like an angel and I happen to know that Mr Bretton also enjoys music and that he plays the pianoforte very well.'

'And how do you know that, miss?' Mrs Gavin asked.

'I happened to hear him play when I called at his house to return a book,' Joanna said.

'Oh, well, I suppose that would be all right,' Jane said, sounding relieved and cautiously optimistic. 'If he likes music, we would have at least one interest in common. I don't think I could speak to him otherwise. He is so very handsome, he quite takes my breath away.'

'Don't worry, my dear.' Mrs Gavin knowingly patted her daughter's hand. 'You are not the only one.'

The rest of the guests arrived within the next ten minutes and the room was soon filled with the light-hearted sound of conversation and laughter. Mr Rowe had come in with Sir Anthony and Lady Clifford, and while his attire was perfectly correct, there was no chance of his ever being mistaken for a Pink of fashion. The claret-coloured jacket looked to be cut one size too small and his ivory pantaloons clung to his short fat legs like a second skin, making them look more like sausages than legs. His bald head was already damp with perspiration and when he walked, Joanna fancied it was to the accompaniment of a wheezing sound.

Captain Sterne arrived a few minutes later with Lord and Lady Amberley, but, unlike Mr Rowe, there was nothing one could find fault with in his appearance. His dark-blue jacket was impeccably cut, his white cravat beautifully tied and on his finger a magnificent ruby sparkled in the candlelight. While one might not go so far as to call him handsome, he did possess a certain rugged appeal that was not unattractive. Given his interest in Egypt, he was far more welcome company than Mr Rowe.

'Lady Joanna, may I say how exquisite you look this evening,' he said, bowing over her hand.

'Thank you, Captain Sterne; it is kind of you to say so.'

'I did not have an opportunity to tell you at your father's lecture how very pleased I was to see you out in society again. You have been missed and by none more than myself.'

It was patter she had heard before and, knowing it was expected, Joanna replied in kind. 'I'm sure you were far too busy entertaining the other ladies, Captain Sterne, to even notice my absence.'

'On the contrary, I could never be so preoccupied as not to notice the absence of one of society's brightest lights,' he murmured.

'Captain Sterne, how very nice to see you again,' Lady Cynthia said, coming to stand beside them. 'Your mother and father are well, I hope?'

'They are, Lady Cynthia. They would have come tonight, but had already accepted an invitation from the Duke and Duchess of Valemore.'

'I am surprised you did not join them, Captain,' Joanna said, knowing of his fondness for elevated society.

'I would rather be here, Lady Joanna,' he said smoothly, 'given that you would be here as well.'

'An excellent reason for coming,' Lady Cynthia commented with approval. 'Now that Lady Joanna is out of mourning, a number of gentlemen have been making their interest in her known and I do not think I am speaking out of turn when I say it would benefit a gentleman to keep that in mind.'

Wishing she could disappear into the floor, Joanna glanced away, just in time to see Laurence Bretton make his entrance. And suddenly, the room seemed brighter and the evening more interesting. Once again, he had left off his dramatic attire for a fashionable black jacket over light-coloured pantaloons and a spotless white shirt. His cravat, tied in the stylish Oriental, was tucked into the neck of an elegant white waistcoat, and while there was nothing flamboyant about his appearance, with the exception of the red rose pinned to his lapel, he was still, in her eyes, the most attractive man in the room.

'My dear Mr Bretton,' Lady Cynthia said, going to the door to greet him. 'How very pleased we are that you are able to join us.'

'It was good of you to invite me, Lady Cynthia,' he said in a voice as rich and as smooth as melted chocolate.

'Come, I am anxious for you to meet our

guests,' she said, drawing him forwards and introducing him to the people he had not met.

Mr Rowe, who had come across the room to stand beside Joanna, Mrs Gavin, and Captain Sterne, watched the introductions with a jaundiced eye. 'Fellow's a little out of his league here, isn't he?'

'Out of his league?' Joanna repeated.

'Of course. Not the thing for a playwright to be mixing with lords and ladies.'

'Ah, but he is not just any playwright, Mr Rowe,' Mrs Gavin said. 'He is Valentine Lawe.'

'That doesn't make him better than any man here, or as good as for that matter,' Mr Rowe said, the fabric of his coat stretched tight across his stomach. 'I was surprised when Sterne here told me that he'd encountered Bretton at your father's lecture.'

'He went to hear Papa talk about his latest trip to Egypt,' Joanna said. 'Mr Bretton has a keen interest in the subject.'

'A playwright interested in archaeology?' Mr Rowe let out a guffaw. 'He was bamming you, Lady Joanna. Can you imagine a man like that labouring for hours under the punishing heat of the desert sun?'

'I take it you cannot, Mr Rowe?' Mrs Gavin said.

'Indeed, ma'am. I suspect he'd wilt like a

pansy in a drought and I'll wager he doesn't know the first thing about Egypt.'

'I'm surprised you would venture an opinion,' Joanna said stiffly, 'given that you know almost nothing about him.'

'I hear what's going around.'

'Do you?' Joanna watched a bead of sweat form on Mr Rowe's forehead. 'If that is the case, you will also know that Mr Bretton is exceptionally well read on the subject.'

'Being well read hardly makes him an authority, Lady Joanna,' Sterne pointed out.

'No, but neither does he claim to be one,' Joanna said, hearing in the Captain's voice the same patronising tone he had adopted during his conversation with Mr Bretton at her father's lecture…and liking it no better. 'But I have, on several occasions, had conversations with him that have convinced me he knows a great deal more than one might think.'

'Well, it will be interesting to see, should the occasion arise, just how much Bretton does know about the subject,' Mr Rowe said, exchanging a look with Sterne.

Joanna watched the bead of sweat on Mr Rowe's head begin to move. It picked up speed, rolling over the smoothness of his bald patch, slowing a little as it hit of the first of the six hairs plastered to his forehead, and then dropped into his left eye, causing him to blink uncontrollably.

Joanna couldn't help herself. She laughed.

Captain Sterne, sporting a smirk, bowed and went to join Joanna's father and Lord Amberley on the other side of the room.

Mr Rowe, his face bright red, bowed, turned and walked away, waiting until he was at the other side of the room before surreptitiously wiping his eye and then his forehead.

'That was not kind, Joanna,' Mrs Gavin said, though her own lips trembled with barely suppressed mirth.

'Neither was what he said about Mr Bretton.'

'What's this? Coming to the defence of the playwright?' her aunt murmured. 'I thought you did not like him.'

'Whether I like him or not has nothing to do with it,' Joanna said. 'I simply do not wish to hear him denigrated by a man like Mr Rowe. After all, what has *he* to recommend himself?'

'Ten thousand a year and the promise of a viscountcy,' her aunt said drily. 'And do not for a moment think that in Lady Cynthia's eyes that does not count for a great deal.'

Joanna's gaze lingered a moment longer on Mr Bretton—who was chatting comfortably with Sir Anthony and Lady Clifford—before moving on to Mr Rowe in one corner and Captain Sterne in the other. Both looked a little too smug for her liking and she sincerely hoped it was not their intention to do or say anything that might embarrass Mr Bretton during the course of the evening.

She would find it very hard to forgive any man such an act of unkindness…even those who circumstances forced her to consider marrying.

Chapter Seven

As expected, conversation around the dinner table was lively and entertaining. It moved, as good conversations do, from topic to topic, the gentlemen discussing politics and life in the country while the ladies discussed fashion and entertainments in town.

Joanna, who was seated across from Mrs Chesapeake and to the left of Mr Blair, glanced at Jane, who was sitting next to Mr Rowe, and thought what a pity it was that she hadn't thought to check with Lady Cynthia about the seating arrangement. She suspected Mr Rowe had few of the conversational skills necessary to put a timid girl like Jane at ease; a suspicion confirmed by her cousin's heightened colour and frequently downcast eyes.

Mr Bretton, on the other hand, was seated a

little further down the table, with Mrs Gavin on his right and Lady Barker-White across from him. Joanna, who was trying to listen to a number of the conversations going on around her, realised that he was perfectly at ease in the countess's company and that he was adroitly fielding questions about having to submit his work to the Examiner of Plays.

'Naturally, I don't agree with such harsh censorship of creative works,' he said. 'Any content deemed to be subversive or inflammatory is removed, but in removing that content, you often risk weakening the story and perhaps losing some of the play's strongest elements.'

'But you have not been so heavily censored,' Sir Anthony Clifford observed. 'I recall a number of passages in *A Winter's Escapade* that must have raised a few clerical eyebrows.'

Mr Bretton laughed with the ease of one long accustomed to such questions. 'Yes, I suspect they did. In truth, the Examiner has not been as critical of my works as he has been of some. But I expect the tide will turn and I will be forced into writing works that do not ruffle the diocesan feathers quite so much.'

Joanna returned her attention to her soup, impressed by Mr Bretton's clever handling of the questions put to him. He might not have been born with a title, but there was nothing in his manner that led her to believe he was not at ease in the company of those who had been.

The same applied when the conversation came around to the subject of her father's work in Egypt. A lively discussion ensued over what he had discovered on his latest trip and what his plans were for the next even longer one in the spring.

'So, Bonnington, are you really thinking of travelling all the way down to Abu Simbel next year?' Sir Clifford enquired.

'In actual fact, we will be travelling *up* to Abu Simbel,' the earl said, 'given that the Nile runs from the mountains in the south to the Mediterranean in the north. So the site is actually in Upper Egypt.'

'Yes, yes, but what matters is that you're planning to go a damn sight further than you've gone before, am I right?'

'Yes, you are, and, yes, I am.'

'How long do you expect to be away?'

'Well, taking the logistics of the trip into account, I'd say the better part of eight months. Nearly two will be spent travelling and, given the location of Abu Simbel and what we expect to find along the way, I don't see how we can do it in less.'

'Really, my lord, I cannot imagine why you would wish to spend so much time in such a barbaric country,' Mrs Chesapeake commented in her usual forthright manner. 'From what I understand, a person takes their life in their hands when they step outside their door, especially civilised people like us. I cannot stop thinking about that poor girl who was shot dead in the streets.'

'I take it you're referring to the daughter of the Swedish consul,' Lord Amberley said.

'I am. That poor child did absolutely nothing to provoke the attack. She was simply on her way to the public baths when an Arab jumped out and shot her.' Mrs Chesapeake turned a censorious eye on Joanna's aunt. 'I don't know how you can let your niece go on these expeditions, Lady Cynthia. I would fear for her safety every hour she was away. A young woman has no place on an expedition like that.'

'So I have tried to tell her, but I fear she has a mind of her own,' Lady Cynthia said. 'And her father sees nothing wrong with it.'

'No he does not,' Joanna said, smiling so that her aunt would not take offence, but irritated none the less. 'Papa is aware that I am as capable as any man who sets out and that I know better than most what to expect.'

'Only because you have accompanied him in the past,' Mrs Chesapeake said. 'But you could have had no knowledge of what to expect the first time you went.'

'On the contrary, I read extensively about the

conditions and had Papa's knowledge of previous expeditions to guide me,' Joanna said. 'When I went, I was very well prepared.'

'What do you think, Bretton?' Lord Amberley said. 'I'm sure you're a more liberal thinker than most, being so intimately connected with the theatrical world. What are your sentiments on women being allowed to go on such expeditions?'

Joanna flushed, her attention immediately shifting from Lord Amberley to Mr Bretton. 'I hardly think it fair to ask Mr Bretton a question like that, my lord.'

'It's quite all right, Lady Joanna,' Mr Bretton replied, looking remarkably at ease, even though the eyes of the entire room were on him. 'Like you, I believe it is up to the individual to decide whether or not he or she wishes to go on such an expedition. I have read accounts of women who travelled to Egypt, either with or without a husband, and for the most part they enjoyed the experience immensely. It gave them a chance to step outside the confines of their normal lives and to see wonders they would never have seen otherwise.'

'You sound as though going to Egypt is something you would like to do, Mr Bretton,' Mrs Taylor observed with a smile. 'Yet you have established your fame as a playwright.'

'A man may have many interests in his life, Mrs Taylor. Writing is but one of mine.'

'Well, personally, I cannot imagine anything pleasurable in the finding of a dried-out old mummy in the depths of some stuffy old tomb,' Mrs Blair said with a shudder. 'God knows what manner of blight or disease it might be harbouring. Plague is quite common in Egypt, is it not, Lord Bonnington?'

'It is, though I suspect any form of life that might once have existed in the tombs died out thousands of years ago.'

'Speaking of such things,' Captain Sterne said, casting an amused glance in Mr Bretton's direction. 'Lady Joanna has given us to believe that you are quite knowledgeable on the subject of ancient Egypt, Bretton. Is that right?'

Mr Bretton's eyes narrowed. 'I enjoy reading about it, yes.'

'Then what is your opinion of Henniker's famous disappearing mummy? I'm sure you're familiar with Antonio Lebolo and his work in Thebes.'

Joanna only just managed to stifle a gasp of outrage. Antonio Lebolo was an antiquities dealer who had discovered the Archon Sotor's tomb in the winter of 1819. Inside the tomb were fourteen coffins, each with a well-preserved mummy inside. Mr Frederick Henniker, a tourist, purchased one of the coffins from Lebolo, but upon reaching Cairo reported that the coffin, which he assured everyone had not been opened, was empty—hence the mystery of the disappearing mummy.

The story had made the rounds of the archaeological community, but it was highly unlikely anyone outside that would be familiar with it. 'Again, I hardly think it fair to put Mr Bretton on the spot—'

'And again, I do not mind answering.' Mr Bretton's blue eyes glowed with quiet enjoyment. 'I am familiar with Antonio Lebolo's discovery of Sotor's tomb, though I suspect the mystery of the disappearing mummy has more to do with greed than it does with any supernatural influences. As I recall, Mr Henniker was present when the tomb was opened and he bought one of the coffins that supposedly contained the body of Sotor Cornelious, governor of Thebes. Knowing of the fabulous wealth that was often deposited in mummies, especially those of noble birth or position, I suspect he unwrapped the mummy during his trip back to Cairo in the hopes of finding gold coins or jewels hidden within. When no such bounty was found, he disposed of the mummy and claimed when he arrived in Cairo that it had mysteriously vanished.'

'But that's disgraceful,' Mrs Taylor said.

'Yes, it is, but not all that surprising when

you consider that the main interest of men like Lebolo and Henniker is the *value* of what is to be found in the tombs rather than the historical relevance of the find itself.'

'So, do you share the layman's view that such things should be left where they are?' Mr Chesapeake asked. 'Or do you side with the archaeologists who feel they owe it to the world to bring such treasures home?'

Again, Mr Bretton smiled, tracing with his index finger a pattern of embroidery on the tablecloth. 'I understand the value in bringing such treasures to light and thereby giving historians a chance to find out about the civilisations that existed long before ours, but I do take issue with the tombs being plundered without thought.'

'By the natives, certainly,' Mr Rowe said. 'But surely you do not disagree with British explorers removing whatever antiquities we happen to find?'

'Would it matter to you if the person breaking into your family crypt and carting off bits of your ancestor's belongings was an Englishman or an Arab, Mr Rowe?'

The remark elicited the expected round of laughter and Joanna smiled too—until she saw the thunderous expression on Mr Rowe's face. Clearly, he was not amused by Mr Bretton's remark, though whether his annoyance stemmed

from the comment itself or from the fact Mr
Bretton had been instrumental in turning the
question back on him, it was difficult to know.

'But it is different now, isn't it,' she said
quickly. 'We don't bury our dead with the same
pomp and ceremony that was employed in ancient times.'

'We certainly don't have our entrails plucked
out, sealed in a jar and placed in the grave with
us,' Mr Chesapeake said.

Several of the ladies went pale, a fact that did
not go unnoticed by Joanna's father. 'I think,
Chesapeake, that the ladies might prefer a little
less detail. As for Mr Bretton's comment, I understand what he is saying, though I'm not sure
how we go about achieving it.'

'Well, I don't agree with him at all,' Captain
Sterne said with a tight, cool smile. 'The world
deserves to know about the treasures being
found in that part of the world. The Arabs have
no interest in such things. They open up the
tombs, hoping to find treasure, and when they
don't, they grind up the mummies and sell the
dust, claiming it has magical medicinal pow-
ers. I say we get out as much as we can as fast
as we can.'

'How? By blowing up the entrances to the
tombs?' Mr Bretton said, his expression darkening. 'Far too much wanton destruction is being
caused by such heavy-handed methods. Time

needs to be taken to excavate the sites properly and precautions must be put in place to prevent random looting.'

'A nice idea, Mr Bretton, but how do you propose to enforce it?'

'I doubt anyone at this table has the answer to that, Captain Sterne,' Joanna said, painfully aware of the tension between the two men. 'And certainly not Mr Bretton. He hasn't had the advantage of visiting the sites the way you have.'

'Yet *he* was the one who made the suggestion,' Sterne tossed back. 'If he has an opinion, let him state it. I would be interested in hearing what he has to say.'

'My opinion is simply that extreme care must be taken in the exploration of these ancient sites,' Mr Bretton said. '*And* that accurate records must be kept. Lady Joanna and those with similar skills render an invaluable service to the archaeological community. They have the ability to sketch, in almost perfect detail, the temples and structures that are being found. A number of years ago, a French archaeologist did a sketch of the chapel of Amenhotep III. His decision to do so was providential given that the chapel was torn down a few years later. That would have been a piece of history lost had it not been for the fact that someone had taken the time to capture it on paper.'

'Is that what you do, Lady Joanna?' Mrs Taylor asked. 'Draw pictures of what you see?'

Joanna nodded. 'Yes, it is.'

'So you're saying, Mr Bretton,' Mrs Blair said, 'that you approve of women being allowed to go on these expeditions?'

'Not all women, no. Some have a romanticised idea of what they're going to find and are totally unprepared for the conditions they meet,' Mr Bretton said, smiling at Joanna across the table. 'Lady Joanna knows what to expect and enjoys being able to put her skills to good use.'

'But to be away for such a long time,' Mrs Chesapeake said, 'and to work under such horrendous conditions. Surely a lady should not be exposed to such hardships.'

'With all due respect, I think if a person has a talent that serves such a useful purpose, he *or* she should be allowed to make their own choice.'

'Well, from what I read in the paper,' Mr Blair said, 'there are plenty of tombs being discovered and no doubt the potential for many more. What does it matter if the contents of a few are lost along the way?'

'It matters a great deal!' Joanna said fervently. 'These are relics from an ancient civilisation. Who can say that a piece of sculpture tossed indifferently to one side might not hold a vital clue to the deciphering of an as yet undiscovered language, as happened with the Rosetta Stone?'

'Well, there can be no question that my daughter is as passionate about the subject as anyone at the table,' Lord Bonnington said indulgently. 'But I think the rest of the ladies are finding it somewhat less interesting.'

'Indeed, I would far rather ask Mr Bretton about his next play,' Lady Barker-White said, stifling a yawn.

'And I fear the gentlemen would find that equally tedious,' Mr Bretton countered with a smile. 'Surely there is something about which both genders can talk with equal interest.'

'Good God, the man's a diplomat as well as a playwright,' Lord Amberley said. 'You would do well to take him with you next year, Bonnington. Aside from knowing his history as well as anyone at this table, you might just be able to make use of his negotiating skills when you run into a hostile tribe.'

'Don't be ridiculous, Lord Amberley,' Mrs Stanton-Howard said. 'If Mr Bretton went to Egypt, we would have no new Valentine Lawe plays and that would be most disconcerting. I can't imagine that sitting in a tent in the middle of the desert could be conducive to writing fiction.'

'On the contrary, I expect a wealth of new ideas would arise,' Mr Bretton said. 'But Lord Bonnington has assistants far more capable than myself. I have no experience in the field.'

'And you won't get any if you don't put your-self forward,' Lord Amberley said.

'Very true,' Bonnington agreed. 'And perhaps Mr Bretton and I will have some discussions in that regard, but for now, I would like to propose a toast to Lord Amberley. I believe we are on the verge of tremendous discoveries and it is men like Lord Amberley, whose ongoing generosity has made these expeditions possible, to whom we owe our gratitude. Raise your glasses please. To Lord Amberley!'

'To Lord Amberley!' came the refrain, and then a moment of silence as the earl's good health was drunk.

Shortly thereafter, Lady Cynthia stood up, a signal to the ladies that it was time to leave the gentlemen to their pleasures.

Glad to be excused from the company of cer-tain gentlemen and their opinions, Joanna got up and marched out of the room. She did not look at Mr Rowe or Captain Sterne as she passed, too angry with the pair of them over their offensive treatment of Mr Bretton.

How dare they try to belittle him like that! They should have known better than to draw attention to a guest at her father's table, and as gentlemen they should *never* have tried to hu-miliate him in such a manner. Thank goodness Mr Bretton had done such a splendid job of standing his ground. He had shown himself in possession of far more knowledge than anyone had given him credit for and, as far as Joanna was concerned, he had emerged far and away the better man.

More than that, his position on the removal of antiquities was exactly the same as hers and thinking on that brought to mind a book her father had found in a market in Cairo years ago. It was an old volume, one she suspected even the diligent Mr Bretton would not have found, and thinking to give it to him as an apology of sorts for the shoddy treatment he had received during dinner, Joanna slipped downstairs to her father's study, intent on finding it prior to joining the other ladies in the drawing room.

'Ah, good evening, Lady Joanna,' Quenton greeted her as she opened the door. 'I was just stoking the fire in case his lordship came down later.'

'I suspect he will,' Joanna said, knowing how much her father liked to end his days with a quiet glass of brandy. 'He'll likely have Lord Amberley with him, so you might like to top up both of the decanters.'

'Very good, my lady.' The butler collected the two crystal decanters from the credenza and then left, pulling the door closed behind him.

Joanna turned her attention to the bookshelves along the back wall, eventually finding the slim red volume tucked between her father's trip journals. She was engrossed in reading a description of the Sphinx when the door opened again a few minutes later.

Expecting to see Quenton with the refilled decanters, Joanna looked up, only to catch her breath when she realised the gentleman standing in the doorway was not definitely a servant.

'Mr Bretton! What are you doing here?'

He stood quietly in the doorway, making no move to enter or to retreat.

'Forgive the impertinence, my lady, but I was hoping to have a word with you in private. I suspected there wouldn't be an opportunity for that once we were all gathered in the drawing room again.'

Joanna smiled, but her heart was racing. If they were to be discovered here…if someone were to find them alone together… 'How did you know where I was?'

'I came looking for you. I noticed you weren't in the drawing room and when I passed your butler on the stairs, I asked him if he had seen you. He told me you were here. And you needn't worry,' he said, walking into the room, but leaving the door open. 'Having had two sisters at home, I am well aware of what is and what is not appropriate behaviour. But I don't intend to keep you long. Only long enough to apologise for my behaviour at dinner tonight.'

'*Your* behaviour?' Joanna said, frowning. 'What on earth have you to apologise for?'

'It wasn't my intention to provoke a heated discussion at your father's table,' Mr Bretton informed her. 'Though I have been known for expressing unpopular opinions in the past, I generally refrain from inciting arguments over dinner and in company where I am not well known.'

The remark was so unexpected that Joanna actually laughed. 'Mr Bretton, I can assure you, you owe no one any apologies. Indeed, if I am to apportion blame, it is Mr Rowe and Captain Sterne to whom the lion's share must go. They were beastly in their behaviour towards you. Indeed, I thought your responses were remarkably restrained.'

Amusement twinkled in the depths of those hypnotic blue eyes. 'You are kind to say so, but I think we both know I did more to incite their anger than to defuse it, especially in Sterne's case. He didn't like me taking the stand I did.'

'What he didn't like,' Joanna said, 'was your knowing as much about Egypt as you did. He wasn't expecting that. Nor was anyone else.'

His voice dropped as he walked towards her. 'Does that include you?'

Joanna blushed, as though she had been a child caught stealing sweets. 'Yes, if I am being completely honest, though I'm not even sure why I say that any more. Every time I'm with you, you prove me wrong.'

'Because you still believe me first and foremost a playwright.'

'Probably.' She raised her head and looked at him, trying to see past a wall of preconceived notions augmented by her memories of Aldwyn Patterson. 'Is that so wrong?'

He shrugged. 'The playwright is all many people see. Only those who know me well are privy to my secrets.'

'And have you…many secrets, Mr Bretton?' Joanna asked softly.

'Everyone does. Some are good. Some are bad. And some…' he said, reaching for her hand and raising it to his lips, 'are life altering.'

Joanna stared at his mouth, watching it move across her fingers, feeling the warmth of his lips and his breath soft against her skin. 'Am I forgiven?' he murmured.

She was drowning in the intimacy of what he was doing. His head was bent over her hand, the dark fringe of lashes concealing his eyes. 'Forgiven for what?' she whispered.

'For provoking Mr Rowe and Captain Sterne. I would hate to think my behaviour tonight had changed your opinion of me.'

Aware of the slow thumping of her heart, Joanna shook her head. 'It has.'

'For the better or the worse?'

The air crackled between them. 'I'm afraid that's my secret now, Mr Bretton.'

Something flared in his eyes. An awareness. An acknowledgement. An acceptance of the inevitable. And when he smiled, Joanna knew herself lost. All of her life she had been waiting for this, without even having been aware of what she was waiting for. But the closeness she felt to this man, the desire to be with him in every way possible, was undeniable—and he knew it. As the seconds passed, Joanna watched his smile fade and the expression in his eyes turn serious.

But he didn't say a word. He reluctantly released her hand and sketched an elegant bow. Then he took a step backwards, slowly turned and walked out of the room.

Joanna didn't move. Though her heart was pounding, she did not budge from the spot where he had left her.

She glanced down at the book, which she had forgotten to give him, and at the fingers of her left hand, which he had just kissed. Then she closed her eyes and groaned. Laurence Bretton, the playwright, had become Laurence Bretton, the man.

She was fooling herself if she thought things were ever going to be the same between them again.

* * *

By the time the gentlemen rejoined the ladies, Laurence had had more than enough of high society. While he thoroughly enjoyed his conversations with Lord Bonnington and Lord Amberley, Sterne's presence had been a thorn in his side all evening. Every time he'd looked up, the Captain had been glaring back at him, as though daring him to pick up where they'd left off at the dinner table.

And Albert Rowe was no better. He walked around the room with his chest puffed out, clearly more impressed with his consequence than anyone else, and took pains to avoid Laurence's gaze at every turn.

Thank God for Joanna, Laurence mused. She was the evening's true saving grace; the one person who made him grateful he had come. He was glad he'd had a chance to talk to her in private before the guests had reassembled in the drawing room. Though he had taken a certain amount of pleasure in putting Rowe and Sterne in their places, Laurence hadn't intended to make things awkward at dinner and it was important to him that Joanna know that his apology was sincerely and genuinely intended. So he had sought her out and talked to her.

Kissing her had definitely not been part of the plan.

But now having done so, Laurence wasn't in

the least sorry. If he had his way he'd be doing a lot more than kissing her, though he knew thinking like that was only going to make it that much harder to get over her—

'Mr Bretton,' Mrs Gavin said, breaking into his thoughts. 'We did not have an opportunity to chat before dinner, but my daughter has been most anxious to talk to you about your music. I understand you play the pianoforte exceedingly well.'

'I am no more than average, I assure you,' Laurence replied, surprised that Joanna, who was the only person in the room to have heard him play, would have made mention of it.

'Nevertheless, I wonder if you might consider performing a duet with my daughter,' Mrs Gavin said. 'Jane has a very pretty singing voice.'

'Of course, if your daughter is agreeable.'

'Oh, yes, I would be delighted,' Miss Gavin said, colouring prettily.

'Ladies and gentlemen,' her mother announced, 'we are to be treated to a rare musical performance. Mr Bretton has kindly agreed to accompany my daughter, Jane, on the pianoforte.'

Joanna was standing by the glass cabinet with her aunt and Lady Amberley when the startling announcement was made.

'How unusual,' Lady Cynthia murmured. 'Jane is always so reserved in company. She never volunteers to stand up and perform, let alone to sing with a gentleman.'

'I think Mr Bretton must have put her at her ease,' Lady Amberley said, turning to watch the pair make their way to the pianoforte. 'Such a charming man, is he not? So modest and unassuming.'

Joanna said nothing as the couple took their places, though the countess's words struck a jarring note. Laurence—she could no longer think of him as Mr Bretton—sat down at the pianoforte and began to thumb through the selection of sheet music while Jane stood quietly to one side. He offered a remark to which she smiled and nodded, after which he withdrew two sheets of music that he set on top of the others. Then, placing his fingers upon the keys, he began to play.

Conversation died as the opening strains of an old English love song filled the air. It was a well-known piece and Joanna had heard it played many times before, but not with the level of skill and emotion Laurence brought to it now. It was as though he knew what the composer had in mind when he'd written the melody so many years ago.

Nor could there be any question that he had chosen the piece with Jane in mind. Sweetly sentimental, it suited her golden voice to perfection and the room was soon filled with the sound. She was even able to smile as she looked out over her audience.

Joanna could scarcely believe this was the same girl who had once burst into tears at being asked to recite a piece of poetry in front of her family.

'Gracious, is there nothing the man cannot do?' Lady Amberley whispered. 'I had no idea Miss Gavin could sing so beautifully.'

'Perhaps she has never been given the opportunity,' Joanna whispered, knowing it was Laurence who had allowed Jane to blossom in front of a room full of strangers.

At that point, a beaming Mrs Gavin came over to join them. 'Well, is this not a most auspicious occasion? I have never seen Jane look happier, nor do I remember the last time she appeared so at ease in the company of a gentleman. I fear she is in danger of losing her heart to Mr Bretton and I think he is not unaware of her.'

As though to confirm her words, Joanna saw the two performers smile at one another, and when the piece came to an end to much enthusiastic applause, Laurence stood up and escorted Jane back to her chair. He stood and chatted with her for a moment before moving away to talk to Mr Stanton-Howard, but the smile did not fade from Jane's face. Clearly she had fallen under his spell, the same as had most of the other women in the room, Joanna reflected.

The same way she had—

'Lady Joanna,' Mr Rowe said. 'Forgive the intrusion, but might I have a word with you in private?'

His voice was jarring, a discordant note in the music of her thoughts. 'I hardly think this is the time or the place, Mr Rowe.'

'It will only take a moment.'

Joanna sighed. She didn't want to talk to him and certainly had no wish to be alone with him. But fearing he might say something to her in public that would lead to an even more embarrassing scene in private, Joanne reluctantly rose and led the way on to the landing. Once there, she turned without ceremony to face him. 'Yes, Mr Rowe?'

'Lady Joanna, I can hear in your voice that you are annoyed with me, but I hope you will not continue to feel that way once I have said what I need to,' Mr Rowe said pompously. 'You must know that I care deeply for you and that what I am about to say springs from a sincere concern for your welfare.'

'I appreciate that, Mr Rowe,' Joanna said, all but spitting with impatience. 'But please do get on with it.'

'Yes, of course. This is a little awkward, but I feel I really must make my feelings known—'

'Mr Rowe!'

'I am aware that Mr Bretton is well thought of

by certain members of society,' Mr Rowe said in a rush, 'but I strongly feel I must caution you to be on your guard around him. I think it was obvious to everyone in the room that he harbours inappropriate feelings for you.'

'Inappropriate feelings?' Joanna stared at the man in astonishment. 'Mr Bretton hardly knows me.'

'On the contrary, you must have seen the way he was looking at you. The way he was watching you throughout dinner. The lascivious intent in his eyes. Theatre people are like that, you know.'

'Are they?' Joanna said drily.

'Indeed, and you must be on guard against them! You have your reputation to consider and that is a most sacred and precious thing.'

The reason for Mr Rowe's prolonged bachelorhood was no longer a surprise to Joanna. The fact she had somehow managed to refrain from slapping him was. 'Mr Rowe, while I appreciate your concern for my reputation, it really is not necessary. Nor is this conversation, which is now at an end.'

'But, Lady Joanna—'

'And before you make any more disparaging remarks about Mr Bretton, let me just say that I did not like what I saw of *your* behaviour this evening and I think it decidedly unbecoming in the conduct of a gentleman. You were rude and

condescending and I have no interest in furthering the acquaintance. Good evening, Mr Rowe!'

Joanna turned on her heel and walked back
into the drawing room, leaving Mr Rowe red
faced and spluttering on the landing. What an
obnoxious little man! She didn't care if he had
eighty thousand a year, nothing would have
compelled her to marry him. Laurence Bretton
might be a mere playwright in his eyes, but he
was a prince as far as she was concerned!

And so she would tell anyone else who
thought to ask.

It was almost midnight before Laurence finally bid his host and hostess a good evening.

'A most enjoyable gathering, my lord, Lady
Cynthia,' he said, aware of Joanna standing quietly off to one side.

'We were delighted you were able to come,
Mr Bretton,' Lady Cynthia said. 'Who would
have thought that London's most talented playwright would turn out to be such an informed
historian and liberal thinker, to say nothing of
such an accomplished musician?'

'It was Miss Gavin's singing that elevated
the performance,' Laurence said, knowing that
while it was expected that he would offer the
lady a compliment, what he said was true.

'You are kind to say so, but I think we all

know you have won yet another lady's affection and admiration this evening.'

Laurence acknowledged the compliment, knowing full well there was only one lady whose affection and admiration he wished to win. 'It was a privilege talking to you this evening, Lord Bonnington,' he said, addressing the earl. 'I wonder if I might stop by later this week and ask you a few questions about the Rosetta Stone?'

'The Rosetta Stone. Yes, by all means,' Bonnington said, 'though I must admit to not knowing a great deal about it beyond what has been written by the French. I can give you the name, however, of a fellow who has been studying it rather assiduously.'

Laurence inclined his head. 'I would like that.'

The timely arrival of another couple to bid their goodnights allowed Laurence to move on, but in doing so, he caught Joanna's gaze.

'I'll walk out with you,' she said, and without waiting for his agreement started for the door.

Laurence followed her out to the street, where a young lad was dispatched to find his carriage. He felt the chill in the night air and noticing Joanna's bare arms, said, 'You really should go back inside. The temperature has dropped considerably.'

'I know, but I find it rather refreshing after the

heat of the house.' She crossed her arms in front of her chest, hugging her arms as she stared into the night sky. 'I know it is customary, and of course, polite, to say that one enjoyed the evening as one is bidding goodnight to one's host and hostess, but did you really enjoy it, Mr Bretton?'

Laurence raised an eyebrow in surprise. 'Did I appear as though I did not?'

'No. You were the perfect guest,' she said. 'You were paraded about before dinner, cross examined during it and made to perform when it was over. Yet never once did you look ill at ease or as though you wished you were somewhere else. I simply find myself wondering how enjoyable it really was.' She brought her gaze back to his and her eyes were troubled. 'I know I should have hated it.'

He managed a small smile, touched by her concern. 'I admit it was akin to trial by fire, but it is not the first time it has happened. People seem to think that what a man does is all that he is. I refuse to accept that.'

Her eyes fell before his and she nibbled on her bottom lip. 'I am not without guilt in that regard and I do regret it,' she said in a low voice. 'Just as I deeply regret the way you were treated by... some of the other guests this evening.'

Laurence knew to whom she was referring, but was surprised she would make mention of it, given that she was probably going to marry one of them. 'I was not offended by what Mr Rowe or Captain Sterne said, Lady Joanna. They are as entitled to their opinions as I am to mine.'

'But they were wrong to put you on the spot like that,' Joanna said. 'Their behaviour was uncalled for and I deeply regret that you were treated so disrespectfully.'

'And I appreciate you saying as much, but to be honest, I really don't care what Rowe or Sterne think of me. Only what you do.'

Her eyes flew up to his. 'That matters to you?'

'Of course. How could you think otherwise?'

She shook her head, her expression troubled. 'I don't know. I don't seem to know anything any more. Life has suddenly become…so confusing.'

'I know,' Laurence agreed, thinking of how upside down his own life had become in the last year. 'And in that regard, there is something I *would* have settled between us once and for all.'

A tiny furrow appeared between her brows. 'Yes?'

'When we first met at the Temple of the Muses, I made no mention of my being Valentine Lawe because I was not there in the guise of the playwright,' Laurence said, wanting what few things that could be open and honest between them to be so. 'I was there looking for books about Egypt and when I heard you express the same interest, I saw no reason to discuss the nature of my other occupation. The omission was not calculated in any way, nor would I would want you to think I had approached you with any other purpose in mind.'

Joanna nodded, but the line between her brows deepened. 'I know that your offer was prompted by the most generous of motives, even if I did not know it at the time. You have long proven what kind of man you are and cleared up any misconceptions I may have had,' she said quietly. 'I have seen you with your family, and with friends. I even watched you bring out a side of a young lady I have *never* seen in all the years I've known her.'

He looked amused. 'Miss Gavin?'

'Indeed. Jane has never sung in public before, but she sang with you tonight and even appeared to be enjoying it.'

'She has a lovely voice.'

'Yes, but that's not the point,' Joanna said as another couple walked by. '*You* gave her the confidence she needed to stand up and sing in front of all those people. No one else ever has, which only proves what a very special man you are.'

He swallowed hard and glanced away. 'I am no more or less than I was before, Lady Joanna. It is only that you have come to know me better. But I am not without secrets.'

'Who amongst us is?' Joanna said, her smile

tinged with sadness. 'Who in that room tonight did not have a least one secret they would never wish anyone to know, lest they be thought the less of for its discovery?'

Laurence smiled. 'What secrets have you, my lady, that could possibly make anyone think less of you? I know I could not—'

'Getting a little personal, aren't you, Bretton?'

The words were like a dash of cold water and Joanna jumped. 'Captain Sterne!'

'Lady Joanna. Sorry to interrupt your little tête-à-tête,' Sterne drawled, 'but I wanted to make sure I had a chance to tell you how much I enjoyed your company this evening. I admire a woman who has the courage to stand up for her convictions. You spoke passionately of your beliefs and are to be commended for it. As I told your father over dinner the other evening.'

'Thank you,' Joanna said, though Laurence heard the note of reserve in her voice. 'I wasn't aware the two of you had dined together.'

'Actually, I have enjoyed several meals with your father.' Sterne smiled down at her, completely ignoring Laurence. 'There were matters I wished to discuss with him, one being of particular importance, though this is neither the time nor the place to go into it. The matter can wait until we find ourselves in a more…private setting.' He finally flicked a brief, dismissive glance in Laurence's direction before turning to smile at Joanna again. 'I look forward to the pleasure of calling on you very soon, Lady Joanna. And to furthering what has become, for me, a thoroughly delightful acquaintance.'

Even through the darkness, Laurence saw the blush that rose in Joanna's cheeks and the reason for it struck him forcibly. Rowe wasn't the danger now, Sterne was. Apart from having a demonstrated interest in Egypt, he was the wealthy son of a peer and he was actively pursuing Joanna.

Was that what he had discussed with her father over their several dinners together? Bonnington's plans for Abu Simbel—and Sterne's plans for her?

'Well, I won't keep you any longer, Lady Joanna,' Laurence said, the note of forced joviality grating even to his own ears. 'You should go back inside. The air grows chill.'

'Mr Bretton, wait—'

But Laurence didn't wait. What was the point? After Sterne's little speech, there clearly wasn't anything else that needed saying. Whether she knew it or not, Joanna's life was mapped out—and Laurence wasn't so stupid as to believe that he had any part in it. The gulf between them was too wide, the consequences of such a liaison too far reaching.

Joanna was the daughter of an earl and, by her own admission, earl's daughters did not indulge in romantic liaisons with their father's employees—or with playwrights! Another man—one far more suitable in every way—was going to ask her to marry him and she was probably going to say yes.

If ever he'd needed proof that his hopes in Joanna's direction were wasted, he had surely just been given it.

Chapter Eight

‿‿‿‿‿◈‿‿‿‿‿

In the silence of her bedroom, Joanna sat as still as a statue as her maid went through the nightly ritual of taking down her hair and brushing it out. The bedtime custom was usually a soothing prelude to sleep, but tonight her mind was far too troubled to be calmed in such a way.

Captain Sterne was going to propose. He hadn't come right out and said as much, but Joanna knew that's what he intended. His not-so-subtle reference to the *particular topic* he and her father had discussed had not gone unnoticed because Sterne hadn't intended that it should. He'd *wanted* Laurence to know that he had spoken to her father about marrying her, just as he'd wanted both of them to know that her father had not discouraged his suit.

Laurence certainly knew it. It was the reason,

Joanna felt sure, that after a decidedly brusque goodnight, he had climbed into his carriage and driven away without waiting to hear what she had to say and without so much as a backwards glance. And all the while, Sterne had stood beside her with a smug look on his face and the air of a man well satisfied with what he had done.

And to think *this* was the man her father wanted her to marry!

But was it, Joanna wondered, because he genuinely *liked* Captain Sterne or because Sterne was the *only* man to have come along with the kind of fortune necessary to pay off her father's debts and save the estate—?

'You're frowning, miss,' Sarah said as she drew the brush slowly through Joanna's hair. 'Makes me think you've something on your mind.'

Joanna raised her head and met her maid's eyes in the glass. 'I do, Sarah, but I don't know what to do about it.'

'Has it something to do with Mr Bretton?'

Surprised, Joanna said, 'Why would you say that?'

'Because he likes you, my lady. And a handsome man he surely is.'

Joanna let her gaze drift back down to the table. 'Yes, he is.' Trust the servants to be gossiping about Laurence already. But Sarah was right. Laurence did like her and, worse, she was coming to like him and a great deal more than she should.

But, like Romeo and Juliet, their relationship was destined to fail. She had no idea what Laurence's financial circumstances were, though she doubted they were anywhere near Captain Sterne's. And even setting the matter of wealth aside, Laurence didn't have the standing in society that would allow him to take their relationship any further.

Sterne did. As Lord Rinstrom's heir, he had excellent connections and a fortune to go with it. At one time, that wouldn't have mattered to Joanna. At one time, she had been free to choose who she would marry.

Now she was not. And the knowledge that she was falling in love with a man she could not have only made it all that much worse.

'Thank you, Sarah,' Joanna said, abruptly getting up from the table. 'Goodnight.'

The maid put the brush down on the dressing table and bobbed a curtsy. 'Goodnight, miss.'

As soon as the door closed, Joanna climbed into bed and blew out the candle, though sleep was the last thing on her mind. Instead, she stared a long time into the darkness, hoping to find answers, her mind tracing back over the time she had spent with Laurence this evening, then to every conversation they'd ever had.

Secrets. He'd admitted to having secrets. But were his true feelings for her one of them?

He had tenderly kissed her hand. Quoted lines to her from *Romeo and Juliet*. And he had told her there was only one lady whose eyes he wished to be the object of.

Joanna refused to believe that was nothing more than irrelevant chatter at a society function. This was *not* a case of her callow poet all over again. Laurence wasn't at all like Aldwyn. He was a deeply caring man who was worthy of being admired and loved by everyone who knew him—

But not by you.

The words echoed in the darkness, leaden and bleak. Words that would not be silenced, no matter how hard she tried. Laurence could *not* be the man for her. As respected as he was for the plays that he wrote, he had nothing to offer her by way of a position in society or by the fortune necessary to save her and her father from financial ruin.

She had fallen in love with the wrong man. And as she closed her eyes and prayed for sleep, she couldn't stop thinking about how unfair life was—or how she could have been so utterly foolish…again.

The memory of his departure from Joanna— and of Sterne's parting words—stuck like thorns in Laurence's side, refusing to be dislodged and growing more painful by the day. How many letters did he start to write, only to tear into pieces when he realised there was nothing to be gained.

A woman waiting for a proposal from another man was not going to be swayed by the words and sentiments of a man for whom she could afford to feel nothing. He wasn't rich or titled and he had nothing to offer in comparison to a man like Sterne.

Was it any wonder that as his irritation increased, his family took to avoiding him? Nor was his mood improved by the unexpected arrival two mornings later of Sir Michael Loftus, intent on finding out the progress of Valentine Lawe's newest play.

'Of course, I don't mean to rush you,' the gentleman said. 'But I am curious to know when you might have something ready for me to read.'

'I will keep you apprised of my progress, Sir Michael,' Laurence said, 'but given that *A Lady's Choice* is still playing to full houses, I don't see any urgency to finish a new play.'

'Ah, but we cannot rest on our laurels, Mr Bretton,' Loftus said. 'There is a tremendous amount of work to be done before a new play is presented to the public. The work must be read and most likely revised. A cast must be selected and rehearsals begun. A full-blown production is not mounted overnight. I'm sure you are aware of that.'

'I am, but neither can I just command the words to appear,' Laurence said, and certainly not now when his mind was so conflicted over Joanna. 'These things take time.'

'Yet your first four plays were produced over a relatively short period. Why not this one?'

'Because every play is different. Sometimes the words come easily and sometimes they do not. And given that this new play is going in a slightly different direction—'

'Different direction? The Theatre Royal is not the Gryphon, Mr Bretton,' Loftus said, his brows snapping together. 'The type of plays you wrote for your uncle were of a different stamp altogether from what I expect to see from you now. You have never been able to do a work like this before and I expect you to rise to the occasion.'

'Your confidence in me is flattering and I will produce a new play, but in my own time rather than in one dictated to me.'

Laurence went to turn away, but Sir Michael's arm shot out, stopping him. 'Have a care, lad. I know how talented you are and I respect and admire you for it, but this is a business and I've no time for airs and graces. The last time we spoke you gave me to understand that a new play was underway and that you were eager for the opportunity to see it presented at Drury Lane. Are you telling me now that you've changed your mind?'

Laurence bit back a heated reply. As much as he wanted to tell Sir Michael Loftus to go to hell, he knew he couldn't because it was not *his* career that stood to suffer. Victoria might still want to do both a work of serious drama *and* a children's book, and belligerence towards Loftus now certainly wouldn't help her cause. While Laurence had no desire to kowtow to the man, neither could he afford to make an enemy of him.

'I have not, Sir Michael. It is an opportunity for which I am very grateful. Forgive me if I gave you the wrong impression.'

He watched the other man's eyes narrow into slits, then, thankfully, saw his expression ease into more relaxed lines. 'Not at all, Mr Bretton. It was a misunderstanding, nothing more. Of course, you may take more time. Take all the time you need…though it would be advantageous if you could have something finished before the end of the Season. That would give us time to have the production ready for the New Year, and what a glorious way to start out! With a brilliant new play on the stage of the Theatre Royal, Drury Lane. Quite a feather in your cap, m'boy. Quite a feather indeed.'

Sir Michael clapped Laurence on the back and then took his leave, obviously feeling their business satisfactorily concluded. As soon as he was gone, however, Laurence's forced geniality gave way to a frown.

So, he was expected to finish a new play before the end of the Season. Under normal circumstances, that wouldn't have been a problem, but taking into account Victoria's uncertainty about what she wanted to write and his own inability to produce something worthy of being published, it was far from a sure thing now.

Victoria was the creative genius behind Valentine Lawe and she must be the one to decide whether or not the plays kept on coming. If she decided not to write, Loftus would have to go elsewhere and Laurence would no longer be society's darling…which was fine by him.

'At least Lady Joanna would think better of me,' he muttered under his breath.

It did not make him feel better to know that any improvement in her opinion was no small point in the argument's favour.

Joanna's moment of decision arrived sooner than expected. Two days later, Captain Sterne appeared in the doorway of the drawing room. 'Good afternoon, Lady Joanna.'

'Captain Sterne.' Joanna was hard pressed to conceal her dismay, given that her aunt had just gone upstairs to lie down. 'To what do I owe the pleasure?'

'I actually came to speak to your father about the expedition to Abu Simbel, but I was informed that he has stepped out.'

'Yes, though I expect him back soon.'

'Then…do you mind if I have a moment of your time?'

Joanna inclined her head. 'Not at all. Won't you sit down?'

'Thank you.' He settled his long frame into the chair opposite, looking relaxed and entirely at ease. 'I expect you know what it is I wish to say to you.'

'Actually, no,' Joanna said, stalling for time. 'We are not so well acquainted that I am able to predict the nature of our conversations, Captain Sterne.'

He looked vaguely amused. 'I would have thought you might, given the unfortunate situation in which you and your father find yourselves. And your rather pressing need to find a solution.'

Joanna reached for her tambour—and impaled her finger on the needle.

'Shall I call for a servant?' Sterne enquired solicitously as they both watched a drop of blood appear on the end of her finger.

'Thank you, no.' Joanna reached into her pocket of her apron and pulled out a handkerchief, which she proceeded to wrap around the injury.

Unfortunately, Sterne's sharp gaze narrowed in on it. 'Are those *your* initials, Lady Joanna?'

Joanna's eyes dropped to the embroidered letters in the corner of Laurence's handkerchief and she blanched. 'No. A friend lent it to me when I was in need of it.' She put her free hand over top the makeshift bandage. 'What is this unfortunate situation you wished to speak to me about, Captain Sterne?'

Sterne's gaze lingered a moment longer on the handkerchief before slowly rising to meet hers. 'The situation in which you and your father find yourselves as a result of your late uncle's reckless spending habits. In particular, the part *you* play in providing a solution to the problem.'

'I'm not sure I understand—'

'Let us not beat around the bush, Lady Joanna,' he interrupted. 'I am well aware that vast amounts of money are required to pay off the estate's debts and to restore both Bonnington Manor and this house to their former glory. As your father knows, I have that kind of money. And I am prepared to make it available to him *if* I am promised something in return.'

Joanna kept her gaze on her needlework. 'And that something you wish to be promised?'

'Simple. Your hand in marriage.'

'I see.' Joanna nodded, the roaring in her ears all but drowning out the thundering of her heart. 'But you do not love me.'

He smiled. 'Nor do you love me, but I am confident you will learn to. There would, after all, be much to recommend the marriage. You would never want for anything again. You would have more gowns than you could possibly wear, own finer jewels than anyone in London and have a string of carriages and servants at your disposal at all times. At the same time, your father would find himself free of debt and able to indulge in the kinds of activities a gentleman of his position and stature should. I suspect that should adequately compensate for the absence of feeling between us.'

'So you do not care that I do not love you.'

'In all honesty, no,' Sterne said. 'I am in need of a wife and you are in need of a wealthy husband. Any way you look at it, we both stand to gain by marrying. So, what is your answer to be?'

'I cannot give you an answer to a question that has not been asked,' Joanna said, twisting Laurence's handkerchief more tightly around her finger. She needed time. Time to find out if there was any point in holding out hopes that Laurence might say something to her. What that might be, she had no idea, but she desperately wanted to hear—

'He can't help you, you know,' Sterne said in a silken voice.

Joanna glanced up. 'Who?'

'Bretton. That *is* his handkerchief you're clutching. But he can't help you. Not the way I can.'

'I don't know what you're talking about,' Joanna said, getting to her feet in agitation. 'Mr Bretton is an acquaintance, nothing more.'

'Yet I've seen the way you look at him,' Sterne said. 'And the way he looks at you. And I heard what he said to you outside the house the other night. But believe me, as sweetly compelling as his words no doubt are, he is not the man for you. A man like that could never be an acceptable husband for you. And since you wish me to ask the question, I will. Lady Joanna, will you—?'

'Stop!' she cried, whirling. 'Do not ask! Not today.'

'Why not?'

'Because if you force me to give you an answer today, it will not be the one you are hoping for.'

His eyebrows rose. 'Indeed. And if I were to ask again in a week's time? Would you give me a different answer?'

'I don't know. I only know what I would answer if you were to ask me today.'

Sterne watched her for a long time, his eyes narrowed thoughtfully as he stared at her face. 'Very well. I shall respect your wishes and not ask today. But I *will* come again,' he said, abruptly standing up. 'And when I do, I *will* ask the question and I suggest for your father's sake that you give me the answer I want. I will make you a good husband and him a very wealthy son-in-law.' Sterne glanced at the monogrammed handkerchief and sneered. 'A claim others will never be able to make.'

The night for the outing to the theatre with Joanna and her aunt arrived, but as Laurence stood in the vestibule waiting for them to appear, he knew it would have been better to call it off. Spending an entire evening in Joanna's company was going to be destructive to his physical and his mental well-being because no matter how much he wished otherwise, he was never going to have her.

It didn't matter that he *wanted* to be with Joanna, or that she was the kind of woman with whom he could easily imagine spending the rest of his life. One with whom he could open up and share his deepest secrets. She was destined to be with another man. A man who could give her all the things he could not. And every time Laurence saw her, he would be reminded of that.

It would not do to lose his heart to a woman who could not give it a home. The smartest thing he could do was accept that and move on.

Then she walked in—and all sense of reason and logic flew out the door.

She looked like a goddess in a gown of pure

white silk, her dark, shimmering hair swept up in a glorious crown on top of her head. The skilful cut of the gown caressed every curve upon which it touched and exposed the voluptuous swell of breasts while leaving her arms and shoulders bare.

Was she aware of the magnificent picture she made? Did she see how men turned to admire her, or notice how the ladies stared at her with envy? Did she know what she was doing to his heart as she walked up to him and said, 'Good evening, Mr Bretton. I hope we are not late.'

Laurence shook his head and extended his hand for hers. 'You are not. And even if you were, I could not chastise you for it. You take my breath away.'

He spoke the words quietly but he knew Joanna heard them. He saw the look of longing in her eyes and wondered what she might have said had her aunt not chosen that very moment to appear.

'Ah, Mr Bretton, how delightful to see you again. Forgive my having kept you waiting. I wanted to stop and have a word with my dear friend, Lady Burroughs.'

'Not at all, Lady Cynthia,' Laurence said, dragging his gaze from Joanna's face. 'We still have a few minutes before the curtain rises. My sister and Mr Devlin have already gone up. Shall we join them?'

At the lady's nod, Laurence turned and led the way up to his uncle's box. He was aware of Joanna walking a few steps behind him and several times was tempted to turn around and talk to her, but at the last moment caught himself. It was best for all concerned that he treat this as a convivial evening with friends. It was the only chance he had of getting through it with his heart intact.

'It seems you have drawn another full house, Mr Bretton,' Lady Cynthia said, after the box had been reached and greetings between families exchanged. 'I do not see an empty seat in the place. Oh, look, Joanna, there is Lady Standish. If I'm not mistaken, she is staring this way. How nice.' Lady Cynthia waved in the countess's direction and then sat down in her chair. 'It will be all over London tomorrow that we were here with you tonight, Mr Bretton,' she said, obviously pleased by the knowledge.

'If there is anything going around London tomorrow, I hope it will be Lady Joanna's satisfaction with the play,' Laurence replied. 'I am well aware she is not fond of romantic satire.'

Joanna blushed. 'You are mistaken, Mr Bretton. I said no such thing.'

'On the contrary, I remember very clearly what you said,' Laurence said, not about to tell her that he remembered every conversation they had *ever* had.

He had to believe that, for the sake of a man's pride, it was best that some things remain unsaid.

I should never have come! The thought reverberated through Joanna's head like a crack of thunder. Every time she saw Laurence now, the awareness of her feelings for him made it more and more difficult to remain uninvolved or to pretend uninterest.

She longed for a repeat of their closeness in the library, to feel once again the special affection in which she knew he held her. But Captain Sterne's words had changed all that. His thinly veiled references to her father's approval of his courtship had left Laurence in little doubt as to what his ultimate intentions were. When she had walked into the theatre this evening, she had felt his detachment.

For the first time since she'd met Laurence, Joanna wished her playwright had the heart of a pirate.

'I understand this is your first time seeing *A Lady's Choice*, Lady Joanna,' Mrs Devlin leaned over to say.

'Hmm? Oh, yes, it is.' Joanna made a concerted effort to meet the woman's smile. *Dear Lord, a pirate*? 'My aunt came to see it when my father and I were travelling.'

'In Egypt.'

'Yes.'

'How terribly exciting for you,' Mrs Devlin said, her tone not in the least disapproving or condescending. 'You have made my brother quite jealous with all your escapades. He would dearly love to experience what you have.'

Joanna risked a quick glance in Laurence's direction and saw that he was enjoying a lively conversation with his brother-in-law. Tonight, he wore a beautifully tailored black jacket over another snowy-white waistcoat, the simple elegance of the outfit leaving one's eye free to admire the handsomeness of the face above.

Had she ever noticed that charming cleft in his chin before, or how affecting was the sound of his laughter? Both seemed so obvious to her tonight, yet she could not remember having been so aware of them before…

'Do you consider yourself an archaeologist, Lady Joanna?'

Joanna forced herself to pay attention. 'No, my skills are strictly those of an artist, though I am fascinated by the history of the country.' She paused for a moment, stopping to glance down at her fan. 'I find it strange that your brother professes such a fondness for the subject while still being able to write such popular plays. It seems an unusual combination.'

'Yes, I suppose it does,' Mrs Devlin allowed. 'But then Laurence is an unusual man. He possesses an astonishing intellect while at the same time being able to produce such excellent fiction. I think that is to his advantage, don't you? Single-minded men can become so very tiresome.'

Unwittingly reminded of Mr Rowe, Joanna said, 'Yes, though I suppose that depends on whether or not the interest is shared by the lady he is with.'

'Perhaps, though I admit, my knowledge of men is limited to my father and brother, and now Mr Devlin.'

'Whom I sure you do not find in the least tiresome.'

Victoria's eyes widened in surprise and then, to Joanna's relief, she burst out laughing.

'No, Lady Joanna, I most assuredly do not. Nor is my brother, whom I have always admired for the wide variety of his interests. He is what my husband terms an all-rounder. Apart from being fluent in six languages, Laurence knows more about the planets and the stars than any man I've ever met. He is also a neck-or-nothing rider, quite brilliant in the hunting field and you have already been treated to his brilliance on the pianoforte. But you will never hear him boast about it, nor about any of the other things he does so well. Humility and an unassuming nature will always prevent him from putting himself forwards.'

Mrs Devlin bestowed an affectionate glance on her brother and then, obviously feeling she had said enough, turned to address a remark to Joanna's aunt.

Wishing she had kept on talking about her brother, Joanna sat back and waited for the play to begin. The list of Laurence's accomplishments was growing by the day. Who would have thought that a man so supremely accomplished in so many ways could be as genuinely humble as Laurence was?

Her ruminations were brought to an end by the appearance of the theatre manager on stage and by a noticeable quietening of the audience as he began his introduction. Then, a few minutes later, the curtain rose and *A Lady's Choice* began.

Half an hour into the performance, Joanna knew she was watching magic. Her scepticism had long since given way to surprise, and her surprise just as quickly to pleasure. She was completely caught up in the story of Elizabeth Turcott and Elliot Black. Their seemingly tragic relationship was played out over three acts, but contrary to what Joanna had expected, the play was neither sentimental nor melodramatic. It was clever…insightful…and, above all, intelligent.

An added delight came in the form of the

cast. Everyone, from the stunning Signy Chermonde in the role of Elizabeth Turcott, to the young boy who played a lowly street urchin, was exceptional. Not a line was forgotten, not an entrance missed and the actors' soliloquies were delivered clearly and with exactly the right amount of emotion. Even the most dramatic of scenes were played with absolute sincerity, and when at the end of a highly satisfactory conclusion the audience rose to its feet to pay tribute to the cast, Joanna stood up too, not in the least embarrassed about showing her approval.

Then the chant began. 'Valentine…Valentine…Valentine…'

They were calling for him, demanding that the playwright stand up so they might pay homage to him. The name Valentine echoed throughout the theatre and everywhere Joanna looked, faces were turned in their direction, all eyes directed towards the man sitting beside her.

'Stand up, Laurence,' Mrs Devlin whispered. 'It is time to take your bows.'

Laurence did, but it was clear to Joanna that he did so reluctantly. He stepped to the front of the box and as the chants changed to applause he raised his arm in acknowledgement of their cheers. Then he turned towards the stage and saluted his uncle and the cast.

Joanna laughed when Miss Chermonde blew Laurence a kiss, prompting both whistles and a few off-colour remarks from the dandies in the pit. Clearly, the gentleman's admirers came in many forms.

'Oh, that *was* good,' Lady Cynthia said with an audible sniff when at last the cheering and the applause died down. 'Mr Bretton, you are, quite simply, brilliant. I did not think it possible, but I enjoyed the play even more tonight than I did the first time I saw it. Left me feeling quite emotional, I must admit.'

'Thank you, Lady Cynthia,' Laurence said, though his gaze and his smile briefly rested on his sister. 'I am very glad to hear it.'

'What did you think, Joanna?' her aunt asked.

Joanna was aware of Laurence's eyes on her and suddenly found herself blushing. 'What can I say other than that it was one of the most enjoyable performances I have ever seen? You are to be congratulated, Mr Bretton. You are truly a gifted storyteller.'

The gentleman inclined his head, but again refused to meet Joanna's eyes. Instead, he shared another smile with his sister and then stepped aside to let the ladies precede him out of the box.

Not surprisingly, a veritable sea of people awaited them in the vestibule. Some were chatting with friends; others were going in to see the operetta while others were coming out, making for a constant ebb and flow of people moving past them.

Laurence's sister and husband were soon hailed by another couple and drifted away to speak to them, while Joanna's aunt crossed the floor to chat to Lady Standish, leaving Joanna alone with Laurence—and the hoard of well-wishers eager to congratulate him on the excellence of his play.

Finally, in a quiet moment, he turned to her and said, 'I am sorry about this, Lady Joanna. I doubt you expected to find yourself in the midst of a crush tonight.'

'I did not, but neither do I mind. No, really,' Joanna said, laughing when she saw the doubt on his face. 'It's all rather exciting actually, though I have no idea how *you* manage to stay so calm.'

'Practice,' he said, leaning in closer so that he could be heard. 'The attention was overwhelming at first, but I have done it so many times now, it seems quite natural. I suspect it is like being an actor. You get over your nerves and rise to the occasion.'

'I suppose, though I cannot imagine what it must be like to stand in front of all those people and recite something from memory. I would be terrified.'

'I don't think so. You would likely become caught up in your performance and forget all about the audience,' Laurence said. 'Have you ever stood on a stage?'

'Certainly not!' Joanna said, only to blush

when she realised how conceited her answer must have sounded.

'It's quite all right,' Laurence said, laughing. 'Well brought-up young ladies do not appear on stage or even express a desire to do so. But it can be liberating to pretend to be someone else for a while.'

His voice had assumed a pensive quality and Joanna said in surprise, 'Do you wish to be someone else, Mr Bretton?'

She was astonished to see his cheeks darken. 'No. The role of Valentine Lawe is quite enough for me.'

'But that isn't really pretending to be someone else, is it. You *are* Valentine Lawe,' Joanna said. 'Pretending to be a thief or a king—now *that* would be playing a role, and, yes, I suppose it would be liberating in a sense. We all play at such things when we are children, but when we are grown, we put away those pastimes and become serious and proper adults.'

'I wonder.' He turned to her and Joanna saw the light of mischief dancing in his eyes. 'What character would you play, Lady Joanna, if you were to be given the chance? Cleopatra, the great queen, or Juliet, that most tragic of heroines. Or perhaps Rosalind, a far more gentle and compassionate woman, considered by many to be one of Shakespeare's most-endearing heroines.'

Joanna pressed a hand to her stomach, as

though to still the nerves fluttering there. Was he really asking her to think of herself in one of those roles? What an outrageous notion! A well brought-up lady would never consider such a thing!

And yet, the idea *was* intriguing. Deliciously so. To think that she could step outside herself, just for a short time, and assume the characteristics of another person, to speak in their language and to express their thoughts. To imagine herself as an actress. It really was quite wicked.

'I honestly do not know,' she said at length. 'I haven't your knowledge of the plays and so am not as familiar with the characters, but to even think about entering into such an occupation is beyond anything I have ever contemplated.'

'I sometimes think we should all play another part, even if just for a little while,' Laurence mused. 'Most of us live within such narrow confines. Imagine shedding your skin and pulling on someone else's for a few hours. You must own it has a certain appeal.'

'Yes, but as much as I might be tempted to try it, the thought of the look on my aunt's face would always prevent me. She would be horrified!'

'Never mind that. Is it something *you* think you might like to do?' Laurence asked.

Joanna thought about that for a moment, allowing her mind to dwell on the possibility. The answer surprised her. 'Yes, I think I would. Just as I would love to venture into the deepest recesses of a pharaoh's tomb. But neither of those things is going to happen. I daren't consider the former and my father won't allow the latter,' Joanna said. 'He draws the line at my undertaking anything of a dangerous nature.'

'He is right to do so,' Laurence said staunchly. 'It would cause me great pain to hear that you had been injured during one of your expeditions.'

The teasing tone was gone; the expression in his eyes very serious indeed. Joanna glanced away and fiddled with her fan. For a moment, they stood in silence as she tried to think of something inconsequential to say. People were looking at them and whispering, smiling and nodding as though they knew something she did not. The ladies were frankly envious and Joanna was astonished to see that a number of gentlemen were dressed similarly to Laurence in black and white. Several even sported flowers, though no one was brave enough to wear a red rose. Clearly, only Valentine Lawe was entitled to do that.

'Mr Bretton, it is obvious to me that I owe you yet another apology,' Joanna said at length. 'I had no idea you were such a talented writer. *A Lady's Choice* was wonderful!'

Laurence looked at her for what seemed like a

very long time, though Joanna was sure it could only have been moments. Then, he slowly began to smile. 'You owe me no apologies, Lady Joanna. Most men do one thing well and others moderately so. I, on the other hand, do several things moderately well, yet cannot claim excellence at any one.'

'But that's not true! The play was outstanding,' Joanna said in all sincerity. 'I would never have believed that a man would be capable of writing such a deeply compelling story. You captured the nuances of emotion perfectly. You clearly understood what Miss Turcott was feeling, from the time she was a young woman newly in love until she stood as an old woman looking back on what had gone right and wrong in her life.'

Again, Laurence failed to meet her eyes, focusing instead on the steady stream of people pouring down from the boxes. 'You flatter me.'

'No, I do not. I am simply offering praise where it is so clearly deserved.'

'And yet, what would I not give to be as talented as both you and your father.'

'Nonsense! I am not a trained archaeologist.'

'But you are a gifted artist and you have combined that skill with your love of Egypt. That, truly, is a blending of two passions.'

'Then you must do the same,' Joanna said. 'You must become like Shakespeare, setting your plays against the backdrop of ancient Luxor. Your heroes must be gladiators and emperors, and your heroines, queens and goddesses. Then you would truly be combining your talent and your passion.'

He looked thunderstruck. His eyes focused on her face with such intensity that Joanna had to look away.

Had any man ever looked at her with such focused passion before?

Her infatuated poet certainly had not. Aldwyn had been too busy indulging his muse. Nor had Mr Penscott or Mr Rowe or Captain Sterne. No one had ever looked at her the way Laurence was looking at her now.

What was he thinking? What thoughts were running through his head? For a man to write so convincingly, so passionately of love, he must surely have felt it—

'Good evening, Lady Joanna,' said a brusque voice behind her. 'Surprised to see you out here amongst the hoi polloi.'

Joanna turned around and was surprised to see one of her father's friends standing there. 'Lord Kingston, forgive me, I didn't notice you there. Did you enjoy the play?'

'Didn't get here in time to see it,' Kingston replied, looking decidedly put out. 'Horse threw a shoe on the way over and I had to send for a replacement. But I expect I would have enjoyed it. I like what I've seen of Lawe's plays. Came for my daughter's sake, more than mine.'

'Good evening, Lord Kingston,' Laurence said.

The marquess's brows rose. 'Sir!'

'You remember Mr Bretton, Lord Kingston,' Joanna said, surprised that the older man hadn't recognised Laurence. 'You were both at Papa's lecture at the Apollo Club.'

'We were?' The marquess peered more closely at Laurence's face, then let out a snort. 'Well, I'll be damned, so we were. Sorry, Bretton. Didn't recognise you without your spectacles.'

'Quite all right, my lord. They do tend to change one's appearance.'

'Taking in the play, are you?'

'Actually, Mr Bretton *wrote* the play, Lord Kingston,' Joanna said. 'He *is* Valentine Lawe.'

'Is he, by Jove? And here I thought he was just another of Bonnington's disciples. Why didn't you say you were Valentine Lawe at the time, man?'

'Because I wasn't there in that role,' Laurence said. 'I went to hear Lord Bonnington talk about Dendera.'

'Of course you did, but that's no reason to hide your light under a bushel.'

'Actually, Captain Sterne did draw attention to the fact that Mr Bretton was Valentine Lawe,' Joanna said, remembering how uncomfortable the moment had been. 'But I believe you were talking to Sir Mortimer at the time and may not have heard.'

'Can't say that I did,' Lord Kingston said. 'I'm sure I would have remembered something like that. Well, I must say this is an unexpected pleasure. My wife adores your plays, Bretton. She will be heartily disappointed when she learns that you were here tonight and I had a chance to speak to you and she did not.'

'Lady Kingston is not with you?' Joanna said, knowing the marchioness's fondness for the theatre.

The marquess shook his head. 'Left her at home with a raging toothache and a bottle of laudanum. But…I say, Bretton, we're hosting a small gathering at Briarwood Monday next. Why don't you join us?'

Joanna's eyes widened. Lord and Lady Kingston's *small gatherings* were, in fact, select receptions for some of society's most illustrious members. Invitations were highly coveted and not frequently made available to those outside their gilded circle. The fact Lord Kingston had extended an invitation to a playwright was an honour of the highest degree—and it seemed Laurence was not oblivious to the fact. 'Thank you, Lord Kingston. I would be honoured to attend.'

'Splendid. Never hear the end of it if I were

to tell my wife I'd met you this evening and not extended an invitation,' Lord Kingston announced. 'And you must come too, Lady Joanna, and bring your father and Lady Cynthia. I know Bonnington doesn't care much for these stodgy affairs, but you can tell him there will be one or two other crusty old gentlemen whose company I dare say he won't mind sharing.'

'I will be sure to tell him,' Joanna said, not at all surprised that her father's reputation for avoiding society events was so well known.

The marquess moved away, but before Joanna had an opportunity to talk to Laurence about his unexpected good fortune, her aunt came back to join them, all but rubbing her hands together in glee.

'Well, that was most satisfactory,' Lady Cynthia said. 'Lady Standish was very surprised to see us sitting with you, Mr Bretton, but I made sure to tell her that you had invited us to join you. It does so elevate one's consequence to be seen in the company of those with whom others *wish* to be seen. Well, come along, Joanna, it is time we were leaving.'

'Aunt, we have just been invited to Lord and Lady Kingston's gathering on Monday next.'

Lady Cynthia stared. 'We have?'

'Yes. When I told Lord Kingston that Mr Bretton was Valentine Lawe, he said his wife would never forgive him if he did not invite him to the gathering, and then he kindly invited us as well.'

'Gracious! An invitation to Briarwood?' Lady Cynthia said. 'What an honour.'

'He seemed to think Lord Bonnington might not wish to attend,' Laurence said.

'Not attend one of the most select gatherings in London? He won't have any choice!' Lady Cynthia stated flatly. 'Thank you, Mr Bretton, for a thoroughly delightful evening. I cannot remember when I have enjoyed one more.'

'You're welcome, Lady Cynthia,' Laurence said, his eyes catching and holding Joanna's. 'In all honesty neither can I.'

Chapter Nine

It was hardly surprising that sleep was the furthest thing from Laurence's mind when he got home that night. Not only because Joanna had looked at him with far more warmth than she had on any of their previous engagements, or because she had blushed so prettily when he'd told her how much he had enjoyed the evening.

He couldn't sleep because the germ of an idea had taken root in his brain. An idea sparked by Joanna herself when she'd said, *'...you must become like Shakespeare. Setting plays against the backdrop of ancient Luxor. Your heroes must be gladiators and emperors, and your heroines, queens and goddesses. Then you would truly be combining your talent and your passion...'*

Why hadn't he thought of it before? The material was all there. And, as Joanna had said, it would be combining the two things about which he felt the most passionate—writing and the distant past. His setting would be ancient Egypt, and his characters, the pharaohs and gods who populated that world. He knew enough about both to make the story compelling, but where Shakespeare had used ancient Greece and Rome as his backdrops, Laurence would make them integral to the story. He would introduce the gods and goddesses and make them forces for change in his characters' lives.

It was as though a floodgate had suddenly been opened. Upon reaching his room, Laurence lit the candles on his desk and pulled out a fresh page of parchment. He couldn't remember the last time he had felt so inspired…and it was all because of Joanna. His muse…and his inspiration.

He sat quietly for a moment, thinking pleasurable thoughts of her, while allowing other ideas to eddy and swirl like currents in a stream. Then, as they began to coalesce and take form, he dipped his quill into the bottle of ink, drew the parchment towards him and steadfastly began to write.

Joanna was alone in the drawing room when Mrs Devlin arrived to pay a call a few days later.

'I hope you don't mind my stopping in unannounced,' she said with a smile, 'but my husband was to have taken me for a drive and at the last minute had to cancel and so suggested that I take a friend instead. I wondered if perhaps you might like to accompany me, Lady Joanna. It is such a delightful afternoon and I did so enjoy our conversation the other evening.'

A little taken aback by the lady's singling her out for attention, Joanna nevertheless said, 'Yes, of course, I would be delighted. If you will give me but a moment to change…'

It did take little more than a moment. Joanna exchanged her shawl for a spencer, her slippers for a pair of leather shoes, and her lace cap for the newest and most fashionable of her bonnets. Given Mrs Devlin's stylish appearance, it would not do to go out looking anything but her best.

Less than ten minutes later, they were seated opposite one another in Mr Devlin's comfortable carriage, with Mrs Devlin chatting about this and that as they made their way through the streets.

'Oh, and if it is not too much of a bother, I did say I would stop at the theatre and pick Laurence up on our way back,' the lady said. 'He went down for a meeting with our uncle and was originally to have come back with Mr Devlin and myself. Is that all right?'

'Yes, certainly,' Joanna said quickly, hoping her pleasure at the thought of seeing Laurence again was sufficiently disguised. She hadn't been able to stop thinking about him since their night together at the theatre.

You take my breath away. That was what he had said to her upon her arrival at the theatre, but it was not only the words he had used, but the manner in which he had said them that gave such special meaning to the phrase.

And then, at the conclusion of the play had come that moment when the audience had begun to call his name and Laurence had stood up in the box. Joanna knew she would never forget how handsome he had looked as he'd risen to acknowledge their cheers. How confident he had appeared, yet how unassuming. There hadn't been a trace of arrogance or pride in his manner, yet he must have known he held everyone there in the palm of his hand.

Just as he held her.

The two ladies chatted about inconsequential matters for the next little while: the price of gloves, the scarcity of good lace, where to go for the finest linens. As such, the time passed unnoticed, and before Joanna knew it, they were pulling to a halt in front of the Gryphon Theatre. 'Oh, we're here!'

'Yes, though I did think Laurence would have been outside waiting for us,' Mrs Devlin said, looking around. 'Oh, well, I suppose we shall have to go inside and find him. You don't mind coming in, do you?'

Joanna glanced at the imposing façade of the theatre and briefly wondered if they might not be better sending the coachman in, until she remembered that Mrs Devlin's uncle owned the theatre and that it was very respectable as far as theatres went.

'I suspect he's with my uncle,' Mrs Devlin said as they made their way into the auditorium. 'You can wait for us here if you like. I'll just be a moment.'

Joanna had never been to a theatre when the actors weren't on stage and all the seats were empty. As such, it seemed strange to walk in and not hear the cheers and the laughter of the crowd. She glanced at the stage and wondered how it would feel to know that every eye in the room was on you. For someone who preferred anonymity, being the focus of such intense public scrutiny must be excruciating.

Suddenly, a man walked on to the stage. He emerged from the wings with his head down, looking at the papers in his hand. He wore no jacket, only a waistcoat over his shirt, and his boots made a clicking sound on the wooden planks.

Joanna swallowed as her heart gave a lurch. 'Good afternoon, Mr Bretton.'

Laurence stopped, and raised his head in astonishment. 'Lady Joanna? What are you doing here?'

'I came with your sister. Did you not see her?'

'No, I've been in the green room.'

Having no idea what a green room was, Joanna said, 'She mentioned something about… going back to your uncle's office. I think she expected you to be there.'

'That would make sense since I told her I was here for a meeting with Theo,' Laurence concurred. 'But I have just been reviewing a few old plays for which I found scripts in the back office.'

It occurred to Joanna, as she drew closer to the stage, that Laurence could easily have been an actor. He was certainly handsome enough to be a leading man and, holding what might have been a script in his hands, he looked completely at ease on the stage, ready to deliver his lines.

'Are you going to perform for me?' she asked with a smile.

'I would, but the scene calls for two people. Rosalind and Duke Frederick.'

'As You Like It!' Joanna said. 'That was one of my governess's favourites.'

'Then perhaps you would care to come up and read it with me?' Laurence said. 'I have two copies.'

Joanna blanched. 'Oh, no, I couldn't!'

'Why not? You said it would be fun to pretend you were someone else.'

'Yes, but I never thought I actually *would*.'

'Come, come, Lady Joanna, what better opportunity than this to indulge in a bit of wickedness? There is no one around to see you break one of society's rules.' Laurence gazed down at her, every word a challenge. 'Why not take the opportunity to do something you might never do again? And that you might actually enjoy?'

Joanna felt her pulse begin to race, both from nervousness and from the thought of doing something she had never done before and that by rights she shouldn't be doing now!

Yet she wanted to, so very much. Laurence was right when he'd said there was no one else here—not a soul to watch her make a fool of herself. There was just the two of them. And it might, after all, be fun...

'Come on, Lady Joanna, where's your sense of adventure?' Laurence whispered. 'The theatre is a world of make believe. Here you can be Rosalind or Cleopatra. Lady Macbeth or Juliet. Or just...Lady Joanna Northrup pretending to be someone else.'

He was the devil in disguise, Joanna decided as she reluctantly walked on to the stage. Only the devil could make the doing of something immoral feel like it was anything but. 'If anyone finds out about this—'

'No one is going to find out,' Laurence assured her as he handed her one of the scripts. 'The only people in the building are my uncle, my sister and an elderly stage hand. If there *was* anyone who I thought might take note of your actions, I would tell you. You believe me, don't you?'

For whatever misguided reason Joanna did. 'Yes.'

'Good. Then let's give it a go, shall we?'

It all seemed harmless enough. Joanna glanced down at the script and saw that her part, or rather Rosalind's, was marked in red. Duke Frederick, the part Laurence was reading, was in black. 'Ready?' he asked.

At her nod, he took a few steps away. When he turned back, it was as though Duke Frederick stood in his place. He appeared straighter, stiffer, his shoulders thrown back, his head held high. '"You, cousin, within these ten days if that thou be'st found so near our public court as twenty miles, thou diest for it."'

Joanna stared at him in disbelief. Dear Lord, even his voice was different! It was stronger. Richer, imbued with the authority of a royal duke—

'Lady Joanna?' He was Laurence again.

'Hmm? Oh, yes.' Joanna glanced down at the page. Her hands were shaking and her heart was pounding. She'd never felt so self-conscious in her life. She took a deep breath, and began to read. '"I do beseech your grace, let me the knowledge of my fault bear with me—"'

'Slower, Joanna,' Laurence said, surprising her by the easy use of her first name. 'In speaking to thousands of people, you must not rush your words. Feel the richness of the language. The beauty of the Bard's words.'

Joanna nodded and, gripping the papers harder, began again. She wanted to do this well, if for no other reason than to look good in his eyes. '"I do beseech your grace, let me the knowledge of my fault bear with me. If with myself I hold intelligence or have acquaintance with mine own desires, if that I do not dream or be not frantic, as I do trust I am not, then, dear uncle, never so much as in a thought unborn did I offend your highness."'

'"Thus do all traitors,"' Laurence replied, striding back towards her, '"if their purgation did consist in words, they are as innocent as grace itself. Let it suffice thee that I trust thee not."'

'"Yet your mistrust cannot make me a traitor,"' Joanna said, hearing her voice echo in the emptiness of the theatre. '"Tell me whereon the likelihood depends."'

'"Thou art thy father's daughter,"' Laurence intoned, taking her chin in his hand and tipping it up so that their eyes met. '"There's enough."'

'"So was I when your highness took his dukedom."' Joanna trembled at the touch of Laurence's hand, yet it was as though she saw in his face, the face of her scheming uncle and all he stood for. "'So was I when your highness banished him. Treason is not inherited, my lord,'" she said proudly. "'Or if we did derive it from our friends, what is that to me? My father was no traitor. Then, good my liege, mistake me not so much to think my poverty is treacherous.'"

She went to pull free of Laurence's grip, but he held her firmly in place, his eyes burning into hers as he stared down at her.

Joanna met his gaze boldly, still viewing him as Rosalind to Duke Frederick, the tension between them causing her breath to quicken and her chest to rise and fall in the drama of the moment.

And then, abruptly, everything changed. It wasn't Duke Frederick's face she saw a heartbeat away from hers, but Laurence's—one that had become dearer to her than any other. She could feel the warmth of his breath on her face, smell the fresh citrus scent of his soap as he drew closer. In that moment, they were totally alone in that deserted theatre. No one else there…only the two of them.

'Joanna,' he whispered. His head bent towards hers, his lips drawing closer as she closed her eyes and reality slipped away—

She heard the applause first. A slow, steady clapping of hands. Then, 'Bravo, Lady Joanna, bravo! 'Pon my word, I have never seen such a compelling Rosalind these many years.'

Joanna gasped and jumped back, thrusting the script behind her. 'Mr Templeton!' To her horror, Laurence's uncle and sister were smiling up at her from the pit. 'I had no idea you were there!'

'I could tell,' Mr Templeton said. 'You were amazing! Totally consumed by the part. Laurence, why did you not tell me the young lady could act? I don't think I've ever seen a person with no experience step into a role so quickly.'

His words, though flattering, did nothing to lessen Joanna's mortification. She had been caught on a stage, with her chin clasped in Laurence's hand, staring up at him as though her life depended on it. And while Rosalind's had—hers most certainly had not!

'Yes, well, that was…quite thrilling,' she stammered, tugging self-consciously at her spencer. She thrust the script back at Laurence, aware that the wretched man was grinning from ear to ear. 'I really must be going.'

'Yes, of course,' Laurence said. 'Or we could, if you like, run through a scene from *Antony and Cleopatra*. I happen to have some pages from it here—'

'Thank you, Mr Bretton, but I have had quite enough performing for one day! Good afternoon, Mr Templeton.'

Her face burning, Joanna fled. She didn't wait
for either Laurence or his sister to join her. She
ran out to the waiting carriage, only to sit there
with her face in her hands, wondering if she
would ever recover from the humiliation.

What must they be thinking? It was bad
enough she had been heard reciting lines from
a Shakespearean play with a certain degree of...
enthusiasm, but to be caught staring at Laurence like some love-struck schoolgirl was beyond all explanation! Had they been enacting
Romeo and Juliet she might have been able to
put the look down to the part she was playing,
but there would have been no love in Rosalind's
eyes when she looked at her uncle. There would
have been antipathy. Hatred. Disgust.

None of which Joanna had felt—or communicated—during her last few minutes on stage
with Laurence. Her secret had been revealed by
a man who had been dead for centuries!

Truly, the gods were not smiling upon her
today!

It was a quiet ride home.

At least, Joanna was quiet. Laurence and his
sister chatted the entire way and though Joanna
knew they were trying to put her at ease, she
could not so easily be comforted.

'Please do not be embarrassed by what happened on stage. Lady Joanna,' Mrs Devlin said,

her warm eyes filled with compassion. 'My brother can be very persuasive when he sets his mind to it, and for what it's worth, I thought you made a superb Rosalind!'

'Indeed, you were exceptional,' Laurence said as the carriage drew to a halt in front of Joanna's home. 'You played the part splendidly.'

Somehow, Joanna managed to rouse a smile in the midst of her embarrassment, even though praise for her acting ability was not what she wanted to hear. 'Thank you.' She wanted to tell them it wasn't playing the part of Rosalind that she regretted, but *that look*. The one that had revealed far too much about her feelings for Laurence in front of both his uncle and his sister.

'Perhaps you could tell your father that I will call on him in the morning,' Laurence said, walking the short distance from the carriage to the door with her. 'If he has time.'

Joanna's eyes widened in disbelief. 'You wish to speak…to my father?'

'Yes. About the Rosetta Stone,' he said. 'I did make mention of that the other night.'

'Of course,' Joanna said, wishing a cataclysmic event would sweep her away like the eruption of Vesuvius had swept away Pompeii. Why else would he wish to speak to her father?

'I shall make mention of it to him over dinner this evening. If you do not receive word to the contrary, you will know that he has time.'

'Thank you.' Laurence bowed, but his eyes never left hers. 'And again, please do not regret what happened this afternoon, Lady Joanna,' he said softly. 'For what it's worth, I most certainly do not.'

Joanna's father was not otherwise engaged the following morning. When Quenton arrived to tell them that Mr Bretton was at the door, Bonnington instructed that he be shown in at once.

Joanna, sitting at her desk in front of the window, kept her head down and endeavoured to pay attention to her reading. Unfortunately, just knowing that Laurence was in the house made that all but impossible.

'Good morning, Mr Bretton,' her father said when the gentleman appeared. 'You look in fine fettle this morning.'

'It is a superb morning and I slept uncommonly well,' Laurence said. 'At least, I slept well when I did finally get to sleep. I have been up the last few nights working on a new play. Good morning, Lady Joanna.'

Joanna looked up, as though only just having become aware of his presence. 'Mr Bretton. How nice to see you again,' she said, moved to think that he did look uncommonly well for all the protestation of a late night. Casually dressed in a dark-blue jacket over buff-coloured breeches, and with that wicked sparkle in his eye, he was as dashing as she had ever seen him.

'So, you wish to talk to me about the Rosetta Stone,' her father said, thankfully drawing Laurence's attention away from her.

'Amongst other things. I have been reading about the deciphering of the hieroglyphic symbols at length this past six months and wondered what your thoughts on the validity of the stone were,' he said, his expression at ease, but the excitement in his voice palpable.

Joanna recognised that for what it was. She felt exactly the same way whenever an opportunity to talk about some aspect of Egyptian culture or history came up. But as the minutes passed and she listened to the conversation taking place, she couldn't help but again be impressed by the extent of Laurence's knowledge. His questions were intelligent and his opinions, when her father asked for them, were logical and made on the basis of knowledge rather than speculation.

'Well, Mr Bretton, I admit to being surprised,' Bonnington said when the maid arrived with a tea tray. 'Your knowledge of life during the reigns of Ramesses II and III is impressive. Tell me, if an opportunity came up for you to accompany us to Egypt, would you take it?'

Joanna's head snapped up. *Her father was inviting Laurence to come to Egypt with them?*

Oh, no, *no*, this was *not* good. Captain Sterne was going to be on that expedition. If she and Laurence went, she could only imagine how difficult life would be for all of them. Sterne would be there every day, watching what she and Laurence did. Listening to everything they said. Putting his own interpretation on every casual smile and every innocent gesture.

It would be torture! How could the three of them possibly exist in such close proximity for all that time? More importantly, how could she work so closely with Laurence for all those months and not give herself or her feelings for him away?

Please say no, Laurence! Joanna whispered silently. *Please do not make me go through this!*

Sadly, Laurence did not say no. After a brief hesitation, he leaned forwards in his chair and said in a voice of unmistakable pleasure, 'Yes, I most certainly would.'

And with those five words, Joanna saw her carefully mapped-out life begin to unravel. 'But…what about your plays?' she blurted out.

'I would still be able to write,' Laurence said, his gaze sharpening as it turned to rest on her. 'There would simply be more time between plays. But I wouldn't miss the chance to go to Egypt. It has long been an ambition of mine.'

'Then I think we must see about making it happen,' Bonnington said, a great deal happier with the outcome of the conversation than his daughter.

'But what would he *do*, Papa?' Joanna asked, hoping to find a solution in the practical aspect of the offer. 'You already have a full complement of workers.'

'*Had* a full complement,' her father said, reaching for a letter on his desk. 'This came from Mr Harkness yesterday. Apparently, his father is failing and, as eldest son, Mr Harkness feels obliged to take over the family business. He says he deeply regrets that he is unable to accompany me on any future expeditions and that he is tendering his resignation, effective immediately.'

Joanna's face fell. 'Oh, dear. That is most unfortunate.'

'Yes, it is and I am sorry to lose him. But his departure creates a vacancy and I need someone to fill it. Someone who is comfortable writing for hours on end.' He turned to look at Laurence. 'Is that a role you would be interested in filling, Mr Bretton?'

'I don't know, my lord. What exactly would I be required to do?'

'In a word, you would become my shadow,' Bonnington said. 'You would make notes about anything I find and keep track of our progress as we go along. I would expect you to take down questions and make detailed reports about everything we see, all transcribed neatly, accurately and in a timely manner. But I warn you, it isn't as easy as it sounds. Sometimes, so many things happen in a day you cannot write fast enough and on others nothing happens at all and you will likely be roped into doing something far more menial. And, of course, a lot of our dealings are done in Arabic so it would be necessary for you to work through an interpreter.'

'Actually, I have a good understanding of the language and speak it well enough to be understood.'

'So much the better.' Bonnington was clearly delighted with the information. 'I guarantee you would be an integral part of the team.'

It was easy to see how much the position appealed to Laurence and Joanna could only imagine how excited he was at being offered the post. But his accepting it would not be at all good for her. He would always be there, close by her father's side, writing down everything he said and asking questions, recording the exploits of the expedition as they happened. It would also be necessary that he spend time with her, making notes that corresponded to her drawings, the way she and Mr Harkness had.

And all the while, she would have to pretend that she had no special feelings for him. Pretend that her day didn't start until she saw him, or that when it was over, she would count the hours until she saw him again—

'Think about it for a few days, if you like,' her father said. 'Talk it over with your family and anyone else you need to. You are, as Joanna said, a very successful playwright. I'm sure there will be others who take a very different view of your accepting a position with me and traipsing off to the desert for eight months to a year.'

'I expect there will be,' Laurence acknowledged, 'but I really don't see why I cannot do both.' He looked across at Joanna and said, 'If anything, one should provide marvellous inspiration for the other.'

'You are the best judge of that, of course, but if it works to your advantage, so much the better.' Bonnington pulled out his pocket watch and swore. 'Damn. I'm late for lunch with Dustin and God knows I'll never hear the end of it. The man grows crustier with every passing year.' He got to his feet and brushed sand and other bits of debris from his jacket. 'I'll wait to hear from you, Mr Bretton. If you are not interested, I shall have to find someone who is.'

'You will have my answer by Friday,' Laurence promised.

'Good. If you have any questions, ask Joanna. She probably knows better than I do what is required, given how closely she worked with Mr Harkness.'

'Thank you, my lord.'

Joanna walked her father to the door and then came back to where Laurence was gazing at the large map of Egypt pinned to the wall. 'It is an incredible opportunity,' he said quietly

'Yes, it is,' Joanna agreed, knowing how much it meant to him and deeply sorry that she had to be the one to discourage it. 'But it is not easy work.'

'I didn't expect it would be. But it would have to be easier than drawing everything you see.'

'They are equally labour intensive, but require very different skills. But I do wonder how it will affect the writing of your plays,' Joanna said. 'You say the trip will serve as an inspiration, but I doubt you will have any time to turn your mind to fiction. You will be expected to focus on what is factual the biggest part of the time. And, of course, there are the inclement conditions.' She turned to look at him. 'Have you any experience with extreme heat?'

'None.'

'It can be debilitating. Quite apart from the intensity of the sun beating down on your head, the heat of the air can become oppressive and make it difficult to breathe. And, of course, disease spreads rapidly in the squalid conditions. A man in poor physical condition will suffer the effects very quickly.'

'Fortunately, I am in excellent health,' Laurence said. 'But I suspect there will be a period of acclimatisation.'

His casual use of the word made her smile. 'There is no question of that, but you must do so quickly if you are to be of any use to my father and the rest of the expedition. You must also be on the look out for poisonous snakes and scorpions. They seldom make any sound as they approach, but their bite is lethal.'

'I shall consider myself warned. Anything else?'

'Insects often carry disease. One must never go to sleep without ensuring that the netting around one's bed is secure. And, of course, stomach complaints and…other problems are quite common when one first arrives in Egypt,' Joanna said. 'One must take great care with the food and water.'

'Duly noted. What else?'

'A big issue is the people themselves. The incidents of violence against visitors can be quite high. The Turkish soldiers are without discipline and violent, the Arab tribes are often at war with each other, and one runs into Armenian mercenaries with alarming regularity. Somewhat less easy to learn is the ability to tell an honest Arab from a dishonest one.'

'That, I should imagine, is a skill acquired as a result of frequent dealings with both kinds,'

Laurence surmised. 'And one not to be learned overnight.'

'True, but it is imperative that you be able to recognise the signs quickly. One will be your greatest ally in the desert, the other, your greatest enemy.'

'Lady Joanna, is it my imagination or are you determined to discourage me from accompanying you and your father to Egypt?'

'That was not my intention at all,' Joanna said, blushing at the lie. 'But neither would I wish you to set off without being fully aware of the circumstances under which you will be required to work. The work is hard, the hours long and the conditions are not at all conducive to comfort. Then there is the question of your many followers.'

'My followers?'

'Yes. I am not at all sure the theatre-going public will be pleased when they learn of your intention to travel to Egypt,' Joanna said. 'Judging from what I saw at the theatre the other evening, you will be sorely missed.'

He waved his hand, as though to dismiss the seriousness of the statement. 'I am not the only one writing plays for the London stage.'

'No, but neither are you a run-of-the-mill playwright. You are Valentine Lawe.'

A muscle clenched in his jaw. 'I am Laurence Bretton…who writes plays as Valentine Lawe.'

'It is the same thing. It really doesn't matter who or what you call yourself. Only that you *are* the source of the stories.'

'But to be offered a place on your father's expedition means more to me than I can say,' Laurence said. 'You know that. I told you as much the first time we met!'

'I really don't understand you, Mr Bretton,' Joanna said in frustration. 'You have a God-given talent for creating stories, yet are determined to turn your back on it. What my father does is inspired by a love of history, but his knowledge comes from books. He has spent years studying and reading and researching. You just sit down and write. Surely to ignore that is a terrible waste.'

'A man must follow his heart,' Laurence said quietly. 'I never dreamt I would be offered an opportunity like this and now that I have, I cannot throw it away.'

'Yet you would risk your career as a playwright? Does it really mean so little to you?'

'No,' he said quietly. 'It means a great deal. But we have already agreed that a man can have more than one passion in his life.'

'A man may have many interests, but he can have only one true passion,' Joanna told him. 'Because a passion is all encompassing. An interest merely passes the time. Your passion *must* be writing or you would not have achieved the level of success you have. Please think very carefully about that before you give my father your answer, Mr Bretton. I would hate to see you make a commitment you will come to regret when it turns out the other opportunity wasn't all you thought it might be.'

At half past one in the morning, Laurence walked into the drawing room and pulled the stopper from one of the glass decanters. Splashing a generous measure of brandy into a glass, he tipped it back and drank deeply, his thoughts distracted for reasons he understood all too well.

He didn't like lying to Joanna and he was having to do it more and more every day.

He hadn't thought about any of this when he had taken up the role of Valentine Lawe. When Sir Michael Loftus had unexpectedly arrived at their home one day, demanding to know if the rumour about Victoria being Valentine Lawe was true, there hadn't been time to weigh the pluses or the minuses of telling the lie. Laurence had simply stepped forwards and claimed the role as his own.

He hadn't expected it to change his life. He had done it with a view to saving Victoria's reputation, indeed to saving the good name of his entire family. And in the beginning, things had gone very well indeed. Both of his sisters had been welcomed back into society and somehow or other, he had become its favourite. Much to his surprise, he was suddenly a sought-after guest, for where it was not the thing for a lady to write plays, it was perfectly all right for a gentleman to do so and he was celebrated for his achievements.

Nevertheless, there had been downsides. The sudden notoriety, the lack of privacy, the guilt he felt at having to lie to the people he cared about. None of those rested easily on his conscience, nor did he enjoy being praised for work that was not his. When glowing reviews of the play appeared in the papers, or when people came up to him and congratulated him on his success, Laurence was always quick to pass those kudos on to his sister.

Fortunately, Victoria didn't seem to mind. In her own words, she was far happier being out of the public eye than she was being in the centre of it. Nor was there any question that Winifred had benefited from his decision. Her association with Mr Fulton had blossomed and looked to be heading towards the long-awaited proposal.

Who could have foreseen that *he* would be the one to suffer for his actions? All because of a lady for whom he had developed the most intense and unfortunate attraction.

Now, for the first time, Laurence understood his sister's anguish at having to lie to the man she loved, because he knew how it felt to be deeply immersed in a deceit. Every time he opened his mouth he compounded his guilt.

How could he look Joanna in the face and know that what she saw was a lie?

He *was not* Valentine Lawe. He wasn't a playwright of any kind. But he was acting as though he was and Joanna believed him wholeheartedly.

Well, the time had come for it to end. He had to tell her the truth. It didn't matter that she was going to marry someone else; he didn't want her living with a belief about him that was false. He just couldn't do that any more—

'Laurence? What are you still doing up?'

'Winifred.' He glanced in the direction of her voice and was surprised to see his younger sister standing in the doorway, still dressed in her finery. 'Just enjoying a last glass of brandy before I turn in. Are you only now getting home?'

'Yes. I was at Lady Wayne's musicale. Mr Fulton gave me a ride home in his carriage.'

Laurence frowned. 'Not alone, I hope?'

Even in the dim light, he saw her blush. 'Yes, but there was a reason for it.' She started towards him and her face was glowing. 'He asked me to marry him, Laurie. And I said yes!'

'Well, thank God for that!' Laurence said, putting his glass down and walking across to embrace her. 'I am delighted for you. I suppose you're deliriously happy?'

'Over the moon!' she said, hugging him back.

'I wanted to tell you first because you are the one who made it happen.'

'Don't be silly, I had nothing to do with it.'

'You had *everything* to do with it! By pretending to be Valentine Lawe, you made all of us respectable again. Mr Fulton told me as much tonight,' Winifred said, dancing out of his arms and doing a little twirl in the middle of the floor. 'He said he wanted to ask me to marry him shortly after we met, but when the rumour about Victoria being Valentine Lawe came out, his family advised him against it. But once it was clearly established that you were actually the one writing the plays, his family withdrew their objections and everything was fine. If you hadn't done that, he would not have asked me to marry him and I would not now be the happiest girl in all England.'

Laurence wanted to be happy for her, and in some ways he was. But with every word she uttered, the possibility of his admitting the truth to Joanna slipped further and further away.

'I am happy for you, Win,' he said quietly. 'I know this is what you've been longing for and I wish both of you every happiness.'

'Thank you, Laurie. Mr Fulton is coming to see Papa in the morning and then we will tell the rest of the family. You won't let on, will you?' Winifred said, concern drawing a line across her brow. 'I know Mama would be terribly hurt if she thought she wasn't the first one to hear the news after Papa.'

'I shall be the very soul of discretion,' Laurence promised.

'Of course you will, because you really are the best of brothers. I know I haven't always told you that, but I am very grateful for what you've done for me…and for this family. We are all so terribly proud of you.'

In the silence that followed, Laurence stared into the dying embers of the fire and tossed back the rest of his brandy. Well, it was too late now. He *couldn't* tell Joanna the truth. To do so would be to put Winifred's forthcoming marriage at risk and there was no way he was going to do that. Not after everything she'd been through. He didn't know Joanna well enough to know if she would keep the information to herself or if she would spread it all over London. She certainly had no reason to keep his secrets and, given her situation, she couldn't be expected to hold anything he told her in confidence.

And *that*, he realised, raised another issue that required serious consideration. Could he realistically *be* a part of Bonnington's team if Joanna was married to Sterne and the two of them were there together?

To play a key role on an expedition to Abu Simbel was, undeniably, the opportunity of a lifetime—a chance he might never be offered again. But could he work with Joanna, day after day, knowing that she belonged to another man? Could he pretend not to see the glances they exchanged or act as though he didn't care when they retired to their tent or their hotel room together?

He wasn't made of stone, damn it! He couldn't pretend not to care that the woman was married to someone else—because he cared very much. Being in Egypt with Joanna would be both the culmination of a dream—and the beginning of a nightmare.

And that, Laurence realised with regret, was his answer. There was no way he could go to Egypt with Bonnington and his team if Joanna was there as Sterne's wife.

He might be willing to forfeit his fame for the chance to do something that really mattered. He was not prepared to sacrifice his sanity on the same altar.

Chapter Ten

'Mr Laurence Bretton,' the butler announced.

'Ah, good morning, Mr Bretton,' Lord Bonnington said, getting up from his desk. 'I was hoping to see you today. So, have you made up your mind to join us?'

Laurence walked slowly into the room, glancing at the pieces of pottery and bits of stone sculptures lying on the earl's desk with the fondness of a child gazing at a much-beloved pet. He had lain awake half the night thinking about what he was going to say to Joanna's father this morning, but now that the time had come, he found the words stuck in his throat like unspoken regrets. 'I have given your offer a great deal of thought, my lord, and believe me, I am grateful for the opportunity,' he said finally. 'But I'm afraid I cannot accept.'

'Not accept?' Bonnington said, astonished. 'I thought you were excited about the opportunity.'

'I was.'

'Then what made you change your mind? Did you not speak to my daughter about any concerns you might have had?'

'I did, and she answered all of my questions and raised a few issues I hadn't thought of. But for a number of reasons, I think it would be best if I do not accompany you,' Laurence said. 'I don't know that I am cut out to be both a playwright and an explorer.'

'But you said yourself there was no reason why you could not do both. It isn't as though you would be permanently removing to Egypt. If you wish to continue writing plays upon your return, there would be nothing to stop you.'

'Your daughter seems to think otherwise,' Laurence murmured.

'My daughter, bless her heart, is a woman and naturally views the situation through a woman's eyes. But you really shouldn't study what she says, Mr Bretton. I doubt she will even *be* on the next expedition.'

Laurence stared at the other man in bewilderment. 'Not be on it? Why?'

'Because I suspect she will not be allowed to go.'

'By Lady Cynthia?'

'My sister may have something to say about

it if Joanna hasn't made up her mind about marriage,' Bonnington said, 'but I suspect that decision will have been made by then, since Captain Sterne has already informed me of his desire to marry Joanna.'

Somehow, Laurence managed not to flinch. 'And did you give him your permission?'

The earl shrugged. 'I saw no reason not to. Sterne has much to recommend him, both as a husband and as a son-in-law,' Bonnington said. 'But he is well aware of what is and is not acceptable to society and allowing his wife to travel with him to Egypt will certainly fall into the latter category.'

'So even knowing what it would mean—what Lady Joanna would be forced to give up—you would let her marry him?' Laurence said.

'*Let* her marry him?' Bonnington said, frowning. 'My dear Mr Bretton, it would be in everyone's best interests for me to *encourage* her to do so. You must have heard the rumours about my...unfortunate circumstances.'

Laurence shook his head. 'No.'

'Really?' Bonnington's mouth twisted. 'I thought it was *the* topic of conversation in society drawing rooms.'

'Perhaps I do not frequent the right drawing rooms.'

'No, perhaps not. Still, you will hear about it sooner or later. The fact is, the estate I inherited is falling down around my ears. My late brother and nephew did an excellent job of going through a great deal of money with the end result being that I am now poised on the brink of ruin,' Bonnington said. 'As such, I have no choice but to pin my hopes on Joanna marrying an exceedingly wealthy man. And Captain Sterne *is* that wealthy.'

The news was astonishing...and devastating, Laurence acknowledged. Not only did his position in society—or lack thereof—preclude him from pursuing a more intimate relationship with Joanna, but his lack of the necessary wherewithal to support not only her but a bankrupt estate put him completely out of the running for her hand. 'I had...no idea.'

'It is not the kind of thing a man wishes to spread around,' the earl acknowledged in a heavy voice, 'but neither can I deny the fact that I am in dire straits. And while I would rather see Joanna marry a man for whom she feels the deepest affection, one cannot always have what one wishes. She must do what it best for the good of the family.'

So you never stood a chance, Laurence thought, the confirmation of his suspicions none the easier for having heard them spoken aloud. Being the son of a country gentleman who owned no property at all was not in the least distinguished. The house on Green Street belonged to his uncle, who kindly allowed Laurence and his family to use it while they were in London, and the house in Kent was owned by the local peer. What chance was there that Lord Bonnington would *ever* have considered him a suitable husband for his only daughter?

'It will be a bitter pill for Joanna to swallow, of course,' her father was saying, 'but she won't have any choice. Sterne will keep her in a fine house, several if I'm not mistaken, and she will have everything a young woman could wish for. But her place *will* be in the home.'

'Do you know that for a fact?'

'As good as, Mr Bretton, as good as,' Bonnington said with a sigh. 'Sterne accompanied me on an expedition a few years ago. We spent many a long hour talking into the night. He has quite rigid social and moral beliefs. I suspect he will have Joanna with child before the year is out and I venture to say she will never leave England again, which is a great pity, for my daughter has an exceptional mind and a natural flair for drawing. However, that is the way of the world. But you didn't come here to talk about Joanna,' Bonnington said, sitting down in his chair. 'Are you sure there is nothing I can say that will convince you to join us?'

Laurence glanced around the room, admiring the scrolls and the bits of jewellery the earl had collected during his travels, many of them thousands of years old, and realised that Bonnington was right. Everything in this room *was* what Laurence loved. He knew the language, he had studied the history, and it all came so easily to him...unlike writing plays, which until recently, had been an uphill battle.

Yes, he would be walking away from something that had brought him fame and turned his life around in a very short time, but he was convinced he could pick up the writing when he got back. This was a once-in-a-lifetime opportunity.

Besides, if what Bonnington said was true, Joanna wasn't even going to *be* on the expedition. He wouldn't have to see her, day after day, knowing that she went to Sterne's bed every night. He wouldn't have to watch her grow round with another man's child and pretend to be happy for her sake.

He wasn't that good an actor. The knowledge she wasn't going to be there was the one thing—the *only* thing—that made his going possible.

'I believe I've had a change of heart, my lord,' Laurence said quietly. 'In thinking over everything you've said, I realise I would very much like to be a part of your team.'

'Are you sure?'

'Quite sure.' Laurence glanced at Joanna's sketch of Ramesses I on the wall behind the earl's desk and knew she would be heartbroken at the thought of another artist taking her place.

But that was not his concern. He had to think of her welfare and of her future.

Her father had accepted the fact that Joanna was going to marry Captain Sterne. The sooner Laurence did the same, the better off they would all be.

Joanna had heard the news that Laurence would be joining the expedition when she got home later that morning. She had suspected he would come early and had gone out so as to avoid being at home when he arrived to give her father the news. But when she had learned that he had accepted the offer, it was all she could do not to go down on her knees and beg her father to revoke his acceptance. With all her heart, she had prayed that Laurence would turn it down.

'So, you've decided to give up your career as a playwright?' Joanna said as the two of them stood sipping champagne at Lord and Lady Kingston's soirée on the Monday evening following.

'Not at all.' Keeping his eyes on their hostess, Laurence raised an exquisite cut-crystal glass to his lips. 'It will simply not be my focus during the time I am away.'

Joanna likewise raised her glass and pretended to study the very select group of people sharing the elegant drawing room with them. With the exception of Laurence, they were all titled and wealthy, many of them sporting ancient titles and equally ancient fortunes. Yet they had all welcomed Laurence with open arms—an honour seldom accorded to one so closely associated with the theatre.

Still, why would they not accept him? Joanna mused. Laurence was as handsome, as charming, and as agreeable as any man in the room. His smile was sincere, his interest in what they were saying genuine, and no matter what manner of conversation he was invited to take part in, he was able to hold his own, whether it be about politics or the finer points of shooting.

He really was a remarkable man—and Joanna was glad she'd had the weekend to come to terms with the news that he would be accompanying them to Egypt. It had given her time to gather her thoughts and to figure out how she was going to cope with the problem of seeing him every day—because it was going to be a problem.

He had worked his way into her heart. Little by little, he had charmed her with his humility and beguiled her with his wit. Was it any wonder she had fallen head over heels in love with him?

Regretfully, it was an awareness that brought with it no pleasure. It did nothing to assuage her fears over the prospect of the three of them spending almost a year together in Egypt. If anything, for the first time, it made the idea of going to Egypt far *less* appealing. It was the reason she had purposely played up the hardships of the journey to Laurence and made no mention of the pleasures. She had tried to put him off by exaggerating the quantity of work and the endless hours he would be required to put in, but she had done it for her sake, not his.

Yet he had still decided to join them. Now she would be forced to work with him, day after day, to dine with him every night and to be amiable to both him and Sterne for as long as the expedition lasted. To pretend not to be in love with him.

How ever was she to bear it?

'By the way, I came across this while I was out yesterday,' Laurence said, taking a small velvet bag from his pocket and handing it to her. 'I thought you might like it.'

Joanna put down her glass and, taking the bag, undid the cord and tipped the contents of the bag into the palm of her hand.

An amulet slipped out, a golden disk suspended on a metal chain, and on the disk a raised image of the winged goddess Isis. Joanna's eyes widened in shock. 'Where did you get this?'

'From the same fellow who supplies me with books,' Laurence said. 'Apparently, he took it from a man who offered it in payment for an old manuscript. The shop owner thought it was a copy, but I believe it to be genuine.'

'I think you're right,' Joanna said, turning the disk over in her palm. 'But Papa would be the one to ask. The workmanship is incredible.'

'Yes, it is. That's why I want you to have it.'

'Me?' Joanna glanced at him in astonishment. 'I cannot accept this.'

'Why not? You said you liked it.'

'I do, but I couldn't possibly keep it. It would be highly inappropriate.'

'This from a young lady who prefers digging in the desert to attending fashionable soirées in Mayfair? What is that if not inappropriate?'

'That is a quirk of my nature,' Joanna said ruefully. 'But this…you know what society would say if I were to accept a gift from a man to whom I am neither related nor promised.'

'Society already frowns on you, Lady Joanna,' Laurence said, handing his empty glass to a passing waiter. 'I don't see that accepting a token like this from me is going to make it any worse. However, if it makes you feel better, you can say you found it on your father's last expedition.'

Joanna looked down at the exquisitely wrought piece of jewellery and waged a silent and desperate battle with her conscience. It was a beautiful piece of Egyptian handiwork, but it was also a gift from a man who, no matter what her feelings for him, could never be more than a friend. 'I am sorry, Mr Bretton, but I really cannot accept this. It wouldn't be right.'

She went to give it back to him, but Laurence closed her fingers around it and gently pushed it back. 'Please don't. This is something I know you, more than any woman of my acquaintance, would appreciate and I really would like you to have it. Perhaps it will remind you of me in the future.'

Yes, it would, Joanna thought painfully, and that was precisely the reason she did *not* wish to have it.

She gazed down at the figure of Isis, inlaid with tiny pieces of lapis and gold filigree, and marvelled at the delicacy of the work. Thousands of years ago, a goldsmith had sat over his fire, forging this piece of jewellery, carefully cutting the lapis into exactly the right shapes and painstakingly perfecting his image of the goddess. He might have made it for his wife...or for a queen. Now it was in her hands. 'I thought you did not approve of artefacts being taken from the tombs for personal use,' Joanna said, her voice husky.

'Perhaps I'm not as staunch in my beliefs as I thought.' Laurence laughed, but there was an echo of sadness in the sound. 'Or maybe, had I found it myself, I would have taken it to a museum, but because it came to me in the manner it did, I suffered no guilt about making a present of it to you.'

'Could you not return it to the man who gave it to you?'

'What would be the point? He would only sell it to the next customer who walked through the door. Someone who would never appreciate its value the way you would. That is why you are the one who should be wearing it.'

Joanna had no idea what else to say…and in truth, she didn't want to give it back. She wanted to keep it, knowing it would always be a very special and personal gift from the man she loved and would never be with.

'Thank you,' she said, slipping the amulet back into its velvet pouch. 'It is…exceedingly kind of you.'

'Kindness has nothing to do with it,' he muttered. 'Call it a peace offering, if you like. We didn't get off to the best of starts and it's been more of a rocky road than a smooth passage ever since. Or…' he said, his eyes back on the people around them, 'you could consider it…an early wedding present.'

Joanna stared at him, shock causing her to draw a quick, sharp breath. 'I beg your pardon?'

'Come, Lady Joanna, there is no reason to blush. Captain Sterne made his intentions very clear the night of your aunt's dinner party. Obviously he wanted to make sure I knew to stay well away from you and so said what he did when I was standing close enough to hear. Sadly, it comes as no surprise.'

'It doesn't?'

Laurence shook his head. 'I have recently been made aware of your need to marry a wealthy man.'

'I beg your pardon?' Her cheeks paled. 'Where did you hear that?'

'London is not so large that a gentleman's circumstances can go too long unnoticed,' Laurence said, avoiding her gaze. 'You must marry a rich man and it is clear Captain Sterne is that man. You could do a lot worse. You could end up leg-shackled to someone like Mr Rowe.'

'I would *never* marry Mr Rowe!' Joanna said, knowing it for the truth. 'Not even if not doing so meant my father and I would end up in the streets!'

'Fortunately, such drastic measures will not be called for. Sterne is wealthy, well bred and shares your interest in Egyptian archaeology. What more could you ask for?'

I could ask for you! Joanna cried silently. *I could tell you that I don't care about all those other things. That I love you, and that all that matters is being with you....*

'Mr Bretton, you really don't understand—'

'Yes, Lady Joanna, I do. More than you can possibly know.' His voice was soft, his eyes holding hers, the brilliant blue muted to co-balt. 'You must do everything you can…whatever is necessary…to save your home and your father's reputation. Indeed, your very way of life. Trust me, I know of what I speak. I could not stand by and see you throw it all away as a result of…a bad choice in husbands. Speaking of which,' Laurence said, grabbing another glass of champagne from the tray of a passing waiter, 'Winifred has at long last received a proposal from Mr Fulton and they are to be married. Naturally, my parents are delighted and a celebration is being planned. You will be sent an invitation, but I thought I would mention it in advance. Next Thursday is the date I believe they've settled upon.'

Joanna nodded, her throat growing tighter by the minute. 'Thank you.' How could she make him understand how painful this was for her? How much she wanted to be with him… 'If my aunt has not made other arrangements, I shall be…pleased to attend.'

'Good.' His smile, always attractive, seemed suddenly dazzling. 'It will be a good way to finish off the year. At least for her—'

'Ah, Mr Bretton, there you are,' Lady Kingston said. 'I wonder if you would be willing to lend your expertise to a discussion Lady Stanford and I are having about *A Midsummer Night's Dream*. We have a difference of opinion as to the point Mr Shakespeare was really trying to make.'

'I would be delighted, Lady Kingston.' Laurence's faint smile held a trace of sadness as he glanced at the velvet pouch in Joanna's hand. 'I have always had a particular fondness for Shakespeare's romantic works.'

It wasn't long before Laurence found out that Joanna was not the only one who harboured grave concerns about his going to Egypt.

The very next afternoon, Sir Michael Loftus called to see him.

'My apologies for troubling you, Mr Bretton, but I heard a bizarre rumour at my club last night that you were planning to go to Egypt,' the gentleman said. 'I told the fellow it was nonsense, of course, but he would have it that you were bound and determined to go.'

'It is not nonsense, Sir Michael,' Laurence said. 'I have agreed to accompany Lord Bonnington on his next expedition to Egypt and—'

'Egypt! Are you mad? You cannot leave now, and certainly not to go off to some God-forsaken country for months at a time. You have a commitment to finish a play!'

'Which I fully intend to honour,' Laurence said without raising his voice. 'But as I said, it will be on my schedule. This is the fulfilment of a dream—'

'Excuse me, but I thought your *dream* was to see one of your plays performed at the Theatre Royal, Drury Lane,' Sir Michael snapped. 'Damn it, man, you're a playwright, not an archaeologist!'

Laurence forced a smile. 'No one knows that better than I, Sir Michael, but I've told Lord Bonnington that I will accompany him to Egypt and I intend to stand by my word.'

'And what about your word to me, sir?' Sir Michael demanded. 'Have you forgotten that you said you would deliver your next play to me before the end of the Season?'

'I have not, but since we do not leave until the middle of February, I see no reason why the play will not be finished by then. I would also remind you that I did not promise that my next play *would* be written for Drury Lane. If my uncle and I feel the Gryphon is a more suitable venue, we must consider that as well.'

'I see. Well, this is very interesting,' Sir Michael said, rocking back and forth on his heels. 'I thought we had reached an accord, Mr Bretton. You were to write a play and I was to assist you in seeing it staged at Drury Lane. It was to have been a step forwards in your career; an opportunity presented you might never otherwise have had. It would be a pity to see that opportunity withdrawn and your career to fall back. Or to have your audience slip away altogether.'

Laurence's eyes narrowed. 'I'm not sure I understand.'

'I think you do,' Sir Michael said. 'The theatre is a highly competitive business, Mr Bretton. You know how it is. Conflicting scheduling of plays. Actors and actresses defecting to other companies. Bad reviews. They can all have a disastrous effect on a playwright's career. And on a theatre manager's, I might add. Consider yourself…warned.'

Laurence said nothing as Loftus walked out of the room. So, the man would stoop to blackmail. Now there was *no* doubt in his mind as to why his uncle had fallen out with him. The two had entirely different values when it came to the theatre.

Sir Michael wanted Valentine Lawe's next play to be staged at Drury Lane and if that didn't happen he was quite prepared to do whatever was necessary to destroy not only Valentine Lawe's career, but Theo Templeton's as well. It had happened before. Jealous theatre owners scheduling the opening of new plays on the same nights, ambitious managers stealing actors and actresses from the other company and critics making sure bad reviews greeted the opening night's performance. All guaranteed to bring about financial ruin and an early close to the play's run.

Clearly, the gloves were off. If Laurence

didn't produce a play that stood up to Sir Michael's expectations within the required time, he might as well go to Egypt and stay there—because he certainly wasn't going to have a career when he came back.

The invitation to Winifred Bretton's engagement celebration arrived the following morning.

Joanna prayed they were already engaged for the evening, but as it turned out, an unexpected cancellation had left them without any plans and Lady Cynthia said that of course they must go. If Mr Bretton was to become a member of her brother's expedition, it was only right that they take the opportunity to become better acquainted with his family and what better opportunity than the betrothal celebration for his youngest sister?

Not at all convinced that it was, Joanna had got dressed on the appointed evening, weighted down by guilt and suffering with a blinding megrim. She had been afflicted with these debilitating pains ever since she was a child, but it was years since she'd had one this bad.

Considering everything that was going on around her, it really wasn't all that surprising.

The engagement celebration was well underway by the time Joanna, her father and Lady Cynthia arrived. Guests crammed the hall and moved slowly through the receiving line, stopping to chat with the various family members as they passed. Mrs Devlin introduced Joanna and her family to her parents, both of whom were clearly delighted by their youngest daughter's good fortune, and then to Winifred and Mr Fulton, the latter appearing proud as punch of his beautiful bride-to-be.

Laurence was noticeable by his absence and, after offering her heartfelt congratulations to the happy couple, Joanna moved on, hoping to find him in the crowded reception room. She had given a great deal of thought to what she intended to say to him tonight. First and foremost was the absolute need to clear up the misunderstanding between them with regard to Captain Sterne and his intentions towards her. Joanna intended to make it very clear that she was not in love with Sterne and that she had no intention of marrying him. Her father might approve of the idea and her aunt wholeheartedly endorse it, but Joanna was the only one who could say yes and she had absolutely no intention of doing that. There *had* to be some other way of saving the estate, a way that did not necessitate her scarifying her soul.

Her father had said it of his own situation. It wasn't fair to go into a marriage when he had so little of his heart to give. Neither did Joanna.

She had given her heart to Laurence. There was nothing left for anyone else—

'I did suggest Mother stop at fifty,' said the familiar voice close to her ear, 'but she told me she could not possibly reduce the guest list to fewer than seventy-five, and as you can see, the house would have been crowded at thirty.'

Astonished by the pleasure she felt at hearing Laurence's voice again, Joanna turned to see him standing a few feet behind her, his dark good looks literally taking her breath away. Within the space of a few seconds, her heart was racing—which, unfortunately, did nothing to ease the pounding in her head.

'My aunt would not have done it any differently,' Joanna said, trying not to wince. 'A crush must have at least one poor lady fainting from the heat in order to be deemed a success.'

'A regrettable truth made even more so by the fact my mother subscribes to it.' He looked at her and, abruptly, his smile disappeared. 'You're in pain. What's wrong?'

Joanna sighed. So much for putting on a good face. 'I have a rather bad megrim,' she admitted. 'And as much as I want to be here celebrating your sister's good news, I would be far better off in a dark room with a cold cloth pressed over my eyes.'

'Poor thing, you shouldn't have come at all,'

he said. 'Would you like me to make your excuses? I'm sure no one would object.'

Joanna shook her head, not wishing to be deprived of a single moment of his company. 'No, though if you could lead me to a quiet spot in the house, I would be most grateful.'

'I'm not sure there *is* a quiet spot in the house tonight,' Laurence said ruefully. 'And even if there was, it would not be a good idea that I take you there.'

'Why not?'

There was a long moment of waiting before he said, in a voice of quiet resignation, 'Because I would be tempted to say things I should not and that I would no doubt come to regret later.'

His voice was calm, his eyes on the people moving around them, but when he turned to look at her, Joanna saw the fire smouldering in their depths and knew a moment of intense and passionate relief. He was *not* indifferent towards her. Despite what he'd said about Captain Sterne, Laurence *did* have feelings for her and if the situation presented itself, he would tell her how he felt.

Suddenly, Joanna knew how desperately she needed to hear those words. To know that he felt as passionately about her as she did about him. 'What would you say to me, Mr Bretton, that you feel you should not?'

He closed his eyes, shutting the fire away.

'Do not ask me to tell you what I have no right to say.'

'You have as much right as any man here.'

'No, I do not. I have neither wealth nor position, and even to be *considered* as a husband for you, a man must have both,' Laurence said. 'You would be damaging your reputation beyond repair for entering into what we both know would be a terrible *mésalliance.*'

'I don't care!' Joanna whispered. 'My heart is still my own, Mr Bretton, and I want very much to hear what you would say to me.'

'Lady Joanna—'

'Please!' she said, her voice beseeching. 'I do not know what the future holds, Mr Bretton, but if you would say only one thing to me tonight, I beg you say it now. What would you tell me if I was plain Joanna Northrup again, with no obligations to my name or responsibilities to my position?'

His eyes opened wide, his gaze returning to her face with a look of understanding mingled with hope, and just for a moment, Joanna caught a glimpse of something wonderful. Something she had only ever dreamt of finding before.

'I would tell you,' he said slowly, 'that I am not myself when I am around you. That I am like…a starving man who sees in you all he needs to stay alive. I would tell you that I have never seen a woman's complexion glow with such warmth that I wonder if I would burn were I to touch it. And I would tell you,' he murmured, moving closer, 'that you are, without question, the most beautiful and desirable woman I have ever known and that the thought of seeing you married to another man tears me apart.'

A hot ache grew in Joanna's throat; a shiver of longing making her lean towards him. His eyes dropped to her mouth and Joanna knew that if they had been anywhere else, he would have kissed her. And God help her, she wanted him to. 'Laurence—'

'No, there is something else I *must* say,' he interrupted. 'God knows I have no right, but I cannot let you continue on this path without knowing what lies in wait for you at the end.' He stopped and took a deep breath, closing his eyes as though trying to draw strength. 'I know Sterne intends to offer for you and while I suspect I know how you will answer, I beg you to think carefully before you do. Because if you do not give his proposal the consideration it deserves, you will be making a terrible mistake.'

It was the last thing Joanna expected. 'I don't understand. What kind of mistake?'

'One that will dictate how you spend the rest of your life.'

She smiled, because she knew what he didn't. 'But I know how I will be spending it—'

'No, you don't. *Ask* Sterne if he plans to allow

you to travel to Egypt after you are married!' Laurence said, cutting her off. 'Do not assume that because you've gone with your father in the past that Sterne will allow you to do so after you are his wife.'

'But…why would he not let me go?' Joanna asked, ignoring for a moment the fact that she had no intention of marrying Captain Sterne. 'He knows how important Papa's work is to me.'

'Perhaps, but he is more concerned with propriety than he is with your interests. Your father is of the same opinion—'

'My *father*?' Joanna said, wincing as the pain in her head intensified. 'You've *spoken* to him about this?'

'Yes, when I went to tell him I couldn't accept his offer.'

'But…you did accept it.'

'Only after he told me that in all likelihood *you* wouldn't be going.' Laurence took a step towards her, his voice low. 'Don't you understand? It was the only thing he *could* have said that would have made me change my mind, Joanna. Surely to God you know the reasons why—' He stopped abruptly. 'Winifred!'

Joanna whirled. Laurence's younger sister was standing behind her, her cheeks as red as summer poppies. Clearly, she had heard the end of their conversation and had no idea what to make of it.

'Yes, Win?' Laurence prompted. 'Did you have something to ask me?'

The girl blinked. 'I'm so sorry to have disturbed you.'

'It doesn't matter. What do you want?'

The brusqueness of Laurence's words caused the girl's colour to rise even higher. 'Mr Fulton asked me to…come and find you. He said he wanted to talk to you about something.'

'Can it wait?'

'I…don't know.' Winifred flicked an uncertain glance at Joanna. 'I didn't think you would be too busy to talk to him.'

A shadow of annoyance briefly darkened Laurence's face, but his voice, when he spoke, was uninflected. 'Tell Mr Fulton I shall be there directly.'

Winifred nodded and, with an uncertain smile for Joanna, fled.

Laurence stared at the floor, the muscles in his jaw working. 'I'm sorry,' he said finally. 'Maybe I had no right to say what I did about Sterne, but I did it out of a genuine concern for you.'

Numbly, Joanna nodded. She wished he had never brought the other man's name into the conversation. There was tension between them now that had never been there before and she hated it. 'I am grateful for your concern, Mr Bretton, but…it really isn't necessary.' She closed her eyes, pressing her fingers to her temples in an effort to ease the pain. 'That's what I wanted to tell you—'

'Whatever you wish to tell me can wait,' Laurence said firmly. 'You need to go home.'

'No, I'll be all right,' Joanna said, though the churning in her stomach suggested otherwise. 'Please, go and talk to Mr Fulton.'

'He can wait too. You need me more than he does.'

What she needed, Joanna thought wearily, was to sit in the darkness of her room and sort out what was going on in her life...*and* what she was going to do about it. But for now, she had to deal with the situation confronting her. 'Perhaps I do just need...a few minutes alone. You and I can talk later. For now, go to your sister and her fiancé. This is their night. Please don't spoil it because of me.'

'You could never spoil anything,' he said with infinite gentleness. 'But I *will* make arrangements for a carriage to take you home. We can talk when you are feeling better. In the interim, there is a room at the top of the stairs, second door on the right. Go there and wait for me to send word that the carriage is ready. You won't be disturbed and you will be able to get some much-needed peace and quiet.'

With that, he finally did leave and Joanna closed her eyes, massaging her aching temples.

She would have preferred to wait for the arrival
of the carriage down here, but when another
burst of laughter brought on a blinding stab of
pain that caused the bile to rise in her throat, she
realised it was better that she be alone.

She took a deep breath and stood up, waiting
for the room to stop spinning. Then, slowly, she
started towards the stairs, carefully putting one
foot in front of the other. She was jostled almost
every step of the way, until the pounding in her
head brought tears to her eyes and made it difficult to see, but she had to keep going. She desperately needed a few minutes alone, not only
because of her headache but because of what
Laurence had just said to her…

…it was the only thing he could *have said that
would have made me change my mind. Surely
to God you know the reason why….*

Joanna closed her eyes, one hand on the ban-
ister as she began to climb the stairs. Yes, she
knew why. How could she ignore the unspoken
message? Laurence wanted to go to Egypt more
than anything else in the world. More than he
wanted to stay here in London and write plays.
It didn't matter that he had no experience of the
desert conditions, or that Captain Sterne would
probably have made his life hell. He had been
willing to risk both for a chance to travel to a
place he had always wanted to see.

But he would *not* have gone if she had been

there as Sterne's wife. There was only one reason a man would say something like that. Only
one conclusion Joanna could draw—

'—hoped they would marry from our house,
of course, but if Winifred's heart is set on having the reception here, then here it must be…'

Joanna abruptly stopped. Opening her eyes,
she glanced at her surroundings in confusion.
Where had that voice come from? She had
reached the landing, but there was only one
door on the right, not two. Had she gone up one
flight too many or had she still one to go? She
had been so immersed in her thoughts she hadn't
paid any attention—

'…I'm sure you understand when I say that
her father and I wish to do everything we can
to see her safely married to Mr Fulton,' a different voice said. 'She came so close to losing
him over that wretched affair with Victoria, but
it all came right once Laurence told Sir Michael
that he was Valentine Lawe.'

Joanna's eyes opened wide. She knew *that*
voice. It belonged to Laurence's mother. But who
was the other woman? And why were they talking about Valentine Lawe—?

'…of course it did,' that lady replied. 'Main-
taining the story was the only logical thing to
do. We would all be in very different circumstances now had Laurence not stepped forwards
to claim the role.'

'Yes, well, I think the least said about that, the better,' Mrs Bretton said. 'I cannot bear to think what would have happened had Laurence kept silent and let Victoria tell Sir Michael the truth about Valentine Lawe...'

Joanna choked back a gasp. *The truth about Valentine Lawe?* What in heaven's name were they talking about? Everyone knew that Laurence was Valentine Lawe. She had been there in the theatre when his play had been performed. She had heard the audience calling his name and had watched him stand up and acknowledge their cheers. He even referred to himself by that name. He would *never* have done that if he wasn't Valentine Lawe!

But his mother had just inferred that Victoria had not told someone the truth about Valentine Lawe. Then what *was* the truth? Who really was Valentine Lawe?

More importantly, if it wasn't Laurence, why had he tried to fool everyone into believing that he was?

Chapter Eleven

In the dining room, Laurence stood and listened to his future brother-in-law's request that he be a groomsman at the wedding, and wondered why the man felt it necessary to make that particular request at this particular moment. There were far more important things both of them should be doing—and going upstairs and apologising to Joanna was most certainly at the top of his list!

He should *never* have told her that Sterne had no intention of letting her go to Egypt after they were married. Joanna's relationship with the other man was none of his business. If she wanted to marry him, let her! She had every right to do so.

But not to ruin her life! Not when you know something that could prevent her from doing that, the voice argued. If Sterne wasn't going

to tell her the truth, someone else had to. And
Laurence knew damn well that he had no choice.
That someone had to be him—

'Mr Bretton?'

Laurence looked up to see Henry Fulton staring at him and realised the man was still waiting for an answer to his question. A question
Laurence couldn't have cared less about. 'Yes,
yes, of course, I will play whatever part in the
wedding you wish. Now if you'll excuse me...'

He didn't wait for a response. The only thing
that mattered was finding Joanna and trying
to make her understand what was going on.
There were things that needed to be said. Things
he had to make clear between them. And he
needed to find out exactly how she felt about
him. Conflicting messages had been flying back
and forth all night. How was a man supposed
to know where he stood in a lady's affections
if he couldn't make any sense of what the lady
was trying to say—

'Joanna!' Laurence came to an abrupt halt.
She was standing at the foot of the stairs and he
could tell in a glance that she was in even more
pain than before. Her complexion was grey,
there were faint purple shadows under her eyes
and her beautiful mouth was compressed into a
thin white line. Whatever he wanted to say was
going to have to wait. 'Stay here,' he said. 'I'll
go and see if the carriage has arrived—'

'No, wait. Please,' she said, whispering the words as though speaking in a normal voice would only cause her more pain. 'I must ask you a question.'

'You may ask me anything you wish,' Laurence said, hating to see her in such misery. 'But can it not wait until tomorrow?'

'No, it must be now.' Joanna closed her eyes, her lashes casting dark shadows on her cheeks. 'I heard something…just now. Something I was… not meant to hear and that I don't know whether to believe or not. But I have to know the truth and you must be the one to tell me.'

'I will tell you anything you wish,' he said. 'You have only to ask.'

He waited as she opened her eyes, watched her stare for a moment at the floor before slowly lifting her head and then raising her eyes to look at him.

'Are you or are you not Valentine Lawe?'

So, this was how it began. With a simple question that had a far from simple answer. Laurence heard the drumming of his heart as everything else faded into the background. 'Why would you ask me that?'

'Because I heard someone say it. They claimed that…your sister didn't tell the truth about Valentine Lawe,' Joanna said. 'That you… stepped forward to *claim* the role. Is it true?'

Thoughts raced wildly through Laurence's mind: the ease of telling a lie versus the difficulty of telling the truth. The safety in keeping quiet versus the danger of revealing all. The consequences of what would happen—of what he stood to lose—either way.

'I once told you that Valentine Lawe was a character in name only,' he said.

'You told me Valentine Lawe was your pseudonym,' Joanna replied. 'You led me to believe you were the author of those plays. But are you really or is your sister the one to whom all the credit *should* be going?'

The silence stretched long as Laurence waged a silent battle with his conscience.

Tell her the truth! whispered the voice of his heart.

No! Don't tell her anything! argued the one in his head. *The welfare of your family depends on you keeping silent. Besides, she is going to marry someone else. Why should she be the one in whom you confide?*

It was a persuasive argument. Joanna owed him nothing. Not loyalty, not a promise of confidentiality, not even her trust—

'Oh, God, you're not him, are you?' Joanna said, her eyes growing wide in horror. 'You didn't write any of those plays.'

'You would take my silence as consent?'

'I think I must. If the accusation were false,

you would tell me, but you cannot.' She slowly backed away from him, shock and disillusionment written all over her face. 'Why did you do it, Laurence? Why did you pretend to be someone you were not?'

He felt as though the weight of the world had suddenly dropped on to his shoulders. How did he respond to a question like that? What words did he use when there were no easy or straightforward answers?

He tried putting himself in her place. Tried to imagine what it would be like to hear a revelation like that from someone about whom he cared so deeply. Would he feel betrayed the way she so obviously did? Feel as though everything he believed in had been blown apart by a lie?

She would never have cause to trust or believe him again.

And yet, what were his alternatives? How could he put Winifred's happiness at risk and Victoria's reputation in jeopardy? How could he humiliate his mother, and hold his father and uncle up to ridicule? How could he do any of those things, when telling a small untruth prevented it all?

'There are things I cannot tell you,' he said finally. 'Things that, were they to be made public, would be damaging to others.'

'But surely you can be honest with me? I thought we were friends,' Joanna whispered, her eyes begging him to tell her what she wanted to hear. 'Indeed, given what you told me tonight, I hoped we were…more than that. Or was that just a lie too?'

'No!' Laurence snapped, his voice raw with emotion. 'I would *never* lie about my feelings for you.'

'Yet you would lie to me, and to all who know you, about being Valentine Lawe,' she said. 'You would accept our adoration and not feel guilty about deceiving us—'

'Joanna, it wasn't like that!'

'No? Then what was it like?' she flung at him. 'It obviously isn't enough that you are a gentleman and a scholar. You had to lie to your friends…to me…in order to make yourself look better in the eyes of the world. Is your ego so inflated that you need set yourself up as someone you're not? Does the public's adulation really mean so much?'

Laurence reeled as accusation after accusation slammed into him, cutting him to the bone and laying bare his soul. She didn't understand anything about him—yet she was judging him regardless. 'You believe I would do something like that just to gain notoriety?'

'What other reason could there be? I have seen the evidence of your popularity with my own eyes,' Joanna said. 'Marriageable young girls follow you wherever you go. You mingle with the best in society and dine at the homes of viscounts and earls. It must be a heady feeling for a man who actually has so little to his name.'

Her disgust was evident—and it tore a hole in Laurence's heart. 'If that is what you believe, perhaps it is just as well we are having this conversation now. It has allowed me to see what you really think of me and to learn what your feelings towards me truly are. Because if you believe in your heart that I need the validation of others to make me feel better about myself,' Laurence said, 'you really don't know me at all.'

'No, Mr Bretton, I do not…and I am sorry to say that because I have come to like you very much. Indeed, far more than I should,' Joanna said as tears pooled in her eyes. 'But you have corrected my misconceptions and I shall not make the mistake again. I know now what you are and it is not a man to be admired.' She turned to go, pausing only long enough to say, 'For all your criticism of Captain Sterne, at least *he* hasn't lied to me.'

Laurence made no move to stop her. Furious with himself and the situation, he walked back to the drawing room where he stayed only long enough to hear the speeches given by Mr Fulton and his father, before escaping to the privacy of his study and reaching for the decanter of brandy. He was in no mood for company and no one was likely to want his. Not after what had happened tonight.

He had fought for Joanna's love, but not won it, and had won her respect, only to lose it.

It was a greater tragedy than even the Bard himself could have written.

He was on his fourth glass of brandy when Victoria found him.

'There you are, Laurence!' she said, walking into the room. 'I've been looking for you everywhere. The Northrups are ready to leave, but they cannot find Joanna.'

'She left.' Laurence raised the glass to his lips, surprised at how steady his hand was. 'Hours ago.'

'On her own?' Victoria frowned. 'Why would she do that?'

'Because she found out something that made it impossible for her to stay.'

'Found out? What could she have found out that would—' Victoria looked more closely at his face, and then glanced at the empty decanter. 'Oh, *no*! Please don't tell me she knows about—'

'My not really being Valentine Lawe?' Laurence said. 'Yes, I'm afraid she does. And she was none too pleased about it, I can tell you.'

'But how on earth did she find out? Surely *you* didn't tell her?'

'Do you think me mad?' Laurence snapped. 'Apparently, she overheard a conversation.'

'Between whom?'

'Who knows, though it had to be someone in the family. No one else knows.'

Victoria abruptly sat down. 'Mama and Aunt Tandy went upstairs for a while. It's possible they may have said something that Lady Joanna overheard. But…what did *you* say to her when she confronted you with it?'

'Nothing.'

'Nothing?'

'She asked me if I was the author of those plays and I refused to answer,' Laurence said. 'She drew her own conclusions.'

'Oh, Laurence. Was she very angry?'

'Let's just say that whatever hopes I might have had in the lady's direction no longer exist.'

'Oh, my dear, I am so very sorry. Why didn't you tell her the truth?'

'Because telling her the truth would have put everyone else's happiness at risk and I wasn't in a position to do that,' Laurence said. 'Winifred told me the other night that the *only* reason Fulton had proposed to her was because I had stepped forwards to claim the role of Valentine Lawe. Had I not done that, we would not now be celebrating their engagement. What do you think Fulton would do if he were to find out the truth now?'

'I don't know. But surely it will not come to that? You cannot be certain Lady Joanna will tell anyone.'

'No, but neither can I be certain that she will not and therein lies the problem. She doesn't owe me her loyalty. She's going to marry Captain Sterne.'

Victoria's eyes widened. 'Did she tell you that?'

'No, but I know he intends to ask and circumstances demand that she marry a wealthy man. Sterne fits the bill.'

'Oh, Laurie, I don't know what to say,' Victoria said. 'I was much more inclined to go along with the story when it was only my own happiness that was at stake, but now to see the lie become the source of so much heartache for you—'

'Don't, Tory,' Laurence said, though his voice was gentle. 'None of this is your fault and recriminations won't do us any good. We knew the risks when we made the choice to continue with the charade.'

'So what are we going to do?'

'*We* aren't going to do anything,' Laurence said, putting his empty glass on the table. 'Winifred is going to marry Mr Fulton, you are going to carry on exactly as you are and I am going to continue playing the role of Valentine Lawe. That is what we, as a family, decided to do. I do not intend that everyone should be called together again for a change in direction.'

'But what if Lady Joanna says something?'

Laurence felt a stabbing pain in the middle of his chest, as though his heart was being cut out by a dull knife. 'I would call her story false. As much as I would hate to do it, I would stand by the story we have been telling all along and let society make up its own mind.'

'Oh, Laurence, I cannot bear to think that this might all fall down around us,' Victoria whispered. 'Everything was going along so well.'

'Everything still is. We just have to carry on.'

'Do you really think Lady Joanna would be so vengeful?'

'I have no idea,' Laurence said in a voice of deep regret. 'Before tonight, I thought I knew the lady. As it turns out, I really didn't know her at all.'

The megrim did not go away. Joanna stayed to her room and suffered with it through two more days before the throbbing finally began to subside. But even as the pain in her head eased, the crushing ache in her heart took over.

How could this have happened to her? How could she have fallen in love with a man who had to lie in order to make himself look better in the eyes of the world? A man who would pretend to be someone he was not?

It was hard to believe she had let herself be so thoroughly taken in.

Laurence was *not* Valentine Lawe. He had lied to her outright and hadn't even had the decency to admit it. Maybe he did have a good reason for claiming to be someone he was not, but if he cared about her the way he said he did, surely he would have found some way of telling her what she needed to know. By refusing to answer, all he had done was make it painfully obvious that he didn't trust her with the truth.

Then he had turned everything back on her by trying to blame *her* for not having enough faith in him! What kind of a man did that?

Clearly, one with no conscience. One who didn't care that he destroyed other people's lives in the pursuit of his own happiness.

A man she did not wish to know.

Unfortunately, the situation with Laurence was not the only bleak spot in Joanna's life. While she had been shut away in the dark cocoon of her room, her father and aunt had been having conversations and the results, made known to her over breakfast that morning, had done nothing to raise her spirits.

She was not allowed to go to Egypt. It seemed that with the addition of Laurence to the expedition, the potential for scandal was simply too great. Her aunt had informed her that she had to consider Joanna's reputation in light of the altered circumstances, and that unless she was *married* to Captain Sterne by the date the expedition set sail, she would not be allowed to go and there would be no more trips for her in the foreseeable future.

Was it any wonder there was no joy in her heart as she stood beside Mrs Gavin at the Barker-Howards' musicale that evening?

'You need to get out in the fresh air, Joanna,' Mrs Gavin said. 'You are looking decidedly pale and unbecomingly drawn.'

Dragged from the murkiness of her thoughts, Joanna managed a cynical smile. 'Thank you, Aunt Florence. It is always nice to know that one looks as dreadful as one feels.'

'I'm sorry, my dear, but you know I have always been one for speaking the truth, and if it is of any consolation, I do know what you are going through. I have suffered with megrims for most of my life and know how debilitating they can be. No doubt you inherited them from our side of the family.'

'Yes, no doubt,' Joanna said listlessly

Her aunt cast a worried glance in her direction, and then said after a sigh, 'Lady Cynthia told me about the conversation the two of you had this morning, about your going to Egypt in the spring.'

'You mean about my *not* going to Egypt,' Joanna muttered, the knowledge twisting inside her like so many snakes.

'Well, I cannot say I am all that surprised. You cannot expect her to be happy at the thought of her unmarried niece living under the same roof, so to speak, as two single gentlemen. I certainly wouldn't allow Jane to do such a thing.'

'Jane and I are entirely different people.'

'On the contrary, you are both unmarried females in need of husbands,' Mrs Gavin said. 'The similarities need be no greater than that.'

'I still don't see what all the fuss is about,' Joanna said. 'It is not as though I would be alone with Captain Sterne or with Mr Bretton. Papa would be there the entire time.'

'Yes, but men don't look at these things the same way we do. Everyone knows how distracted your father gets when he is working. I dare say you could be having a torrid affair with *both* gentlemen and he wouldn't even notice.'

'Aunt Florence!'

'Now, now, child, I'm not saying you would,' her aunt said. 'But there is a reason why chaperons are usually women. And you really must try to see the situation from your aunt's point of view. It was bad enough when only Captain Sterne was going. He, at least, has an interest in archaeological explorations and a pre-established connection with your father. But Mr Bretton is a handsome and eligible bachelor who has made his interest in you plain, but who cannot be viewed as a potential husband because of who and what he is. It was only to be expected that when word of his accompanying you and your father got out, eyebrows would be raised.'

The knowledge that people were whispering about them did not make for welcome news, but Joanna knew better than to doubt it. Society lived for gossip—even the possibility of a scandal was music to its ears.

'Still, I really do not see why you are so downcast,' Mrs Gavin continued more briskly. 'You have said all along that you are not interested in Mr Bretton, and if you marry Captain Sterne, you will be able to go on the expedition as his wife. Plus he has the wherewithal to pay off your father's debts and, from what I understand, has expressed a willingness to do so. So why should you not marry him when doing so will take care of everyone's problems?'

Because I don't love him, Joanna raged silently. *Because I cannot think of any man when I am still so desperately in love with Laurence*—

'Good evening, Lady Joanna, Mrs Gavin.'

The arrival of Captain Sterne did not come as a surprise. Joanna had noticed him talking to Mrs Barker-Howard shortly after her arrival, but had not sought him out, even though he had smiled warmly in her direction. She was not in the frame of mind to see him, especially when she knew how matters stood between them. 'Captain Sterne.'

'I was beginning to think you were avoiding me, Lady Joanna,' the gentleman said. 'You have not been at home the last three times I called.'

'Only because there has been much to keep me occupied elsewhere,' Joanna said, guiltily aware that on two of the three occasions, she had stayed upstairs in her room.

'Indeed, but it is a pleasure to see you here at last.'

'Well, I think I shall go and have a word with Mrs Taylor,' Mrs Gavin said. 'I am finding her to be quite delightful company. Your father would do well to spend some time with the lady.'

'I hope you do not think to promote a match, Aunt,' Joanna said. 'You know how Papa feels about the subject.'

'I do, but it will not hurt him to spend a little time in conversation with her. If he does not, he will forget the art altogether and end up a dried-up recluse with whom no one wishes to associate.' Having made that dire prognostication, Mrs Gavin left them to seek out the lovely and very wealthy young widow.

'I take it your father has no wish to remarry?' Sterne commented.

'He is resistant to the idea,' Joanna said.

'Then you cannot afford to be.' His glance

moved in her direction. 'Have you given any more thought to what we talked about?'

Joanna's lips compressed. She didn't want to think about this right now, let alone to talk about it in a room filled with hundreds of people. 'No, but neither am I in a hurry to marry.'

'You should be.' Sterne lifted the glass to his lips. 'From what I hear, your father's creditors are growing anxious and money lenders can become very unfriendly in such cases. The sooner you marry me, the sooner I can start taking care of things.'

'Why me?' Joanna asked in confusion. 'Why marry someone as penniless as me? You could have your pick of any woman here. Any woman you desire.'

'Yes, but I *desire* you,' Sterne said, his eyes darkening as he stared down at her. 'Does that come as such a surprise? You must know how beautiful you are.'

Joanna closed her eyes as the memory of Laurence's words washed over her.

...I would tell you that you are, without question, the most beautiful and desirable woman I have ever known and that the thought of seeing you married to another man tears me apart...

Beautiful words, Joanna reflected sadly, but meaningless. Laurence's feelings for her had not persuaded him to tell her the truth. She still didn't know who he really was or why he had entered into the lie. And the acceptance of that truth made her realise that she no longer had a choice. Whatever she had once felt for Laurence must now be put aside. He had shown himself for who he really was. A man without conscience. One who could pretend to be someone else in order to give meaning to his life.

A man like that had no place in her heart… or in her future. Life was about practical matters, like marrying and setting up a home. It was about having children and watching them grow up, because now more than ever Joanna *needed* something to give meaning to her life.

A heart grew old and tired with nothing but memories to sustain it…

'Lady Joanna?'

Sterne's voice brought her back…and Joanna knew what she had to do. What answer she had to give him. But she couldn't do it tonight. She needed time to come to terms with what her future was going to be—and the fact that Laurence was never going to play a part in it.

'I will not give you an answer here, Captain Sterne,' she said in a low voice. 'But I will answer you before the week is out.'

'Have I your word on that?'

'Yes.' She looked up at him, praying that, in time, she might find something about him to love. 'But there is something I need to ask you first.'

'Of course.'

'*If* I were to agree to become your wife, would you allow me to travel to Egypt with you in the spring?' Joanna asked. 'And to continue allowing me to travel with my father on any expeditions he might undertake in the future?'

She saw a slight arching of one eyebrow. 'Aren't you getting a little ahead of yourself? The trip is still months away. You may feel differently when the time comes. After all, you will be a married woman by then and may have developed other interests.'

'I may have developed other interests, but being your wife will not lessen my desire to go to Egypt,' Joanna said. 'You know how much the work means to me.'

Nothing changed in Sterne's expression; neither surprise nor disappointment registered on his face. But his voice was thoughtful when he said, 'Yes, I do. Indeed, I have never known a woman so passionate about a field so far removed from those normally associated with female endeavours. However, since my only goal is to make you happy, I wouldn't dream of standing in the way of you achieving your desires, or force you to remain here in London.' He smiled at her with practised charm. 'And on that, Lady Joanna, you have *my* word.'

If there was one thing Laurence learned over the next few weeks, it was that work was a great panacea for heartache. The morning after Winifred's engagement celebration, he sat down to work on his new play and scarcely looked up until it was finished. In all of that time, he hardly slept, took most of his meals in his room and only went out to buy more paper.

And he steadfastly and resolutely refused to think about Joanna.

What was the point? She obviously wasn't thinking about him. No letters had arrived, asking him to call upon her, nor had she come to see him with a view to clarifying the situation between them. Clearly, in her mind, he was a liar and a fraud. That was all she needed to know.

Besides, it was entirely possible that her own circumstances had changed. Though no news of an engagement had been made public, Laurence had no reason to assume she was not now betrothed to Captain Sterne. She would become his wife and even though she *knew* how much he cared for her, she hadn't had the decency to send him a letter informing him of her status as a newly engaged woman.

By God, she must truly despise him.

Either that or she didn't care, Laurence reflected as he sat with his uncle over lunch a week later. Maybe she hadn't wasted a moment's thought on him after they had parted company that night. To his knowledge, no questions about his being Valentine Lawe had been raised, nor had any rumours or gossip made its way back to anyone else in the family.

Did that mean the danger of exposure was past? Surely if Joanna had intended to strike back at him, she would have done so by now.

His uncle certainly seemed to think so.

'After all, what would be the point in waiting?' Theo asked. 'Any woman that angry would naturally lash out before she had a chance to calm down and change her mind. But there has been no word to that effect. Indeed, Lady Joanna hasn't been seen much in society at all.'

It should have made Laurence feel better, but if anything, it only exacerbated his feelings of guilt. She had not exposed him. Despite the disgust in which she must surely hold him, she had not said anything to threaten his reputation or to tarnish the good name of his family. She had simply slipped back into the shadows of his life…

'So, the play is finished.'

Laurence looked up to see his uncle thumbing through the pages of his completed manuscript. 'Yes, such as it is. I'll be interested in hearing what you think.'

'I like the opening scenes very much,' Theo said. 'But I have to say it's not what I was expecting.'

'Is that a kind way of saying it's not worthy of being published?'

'Good God, no! It's off to a fine start and the writing is excellent. But if the story continues in this vein, I'm not sure Loftus is going to approve.'

'I didn't write it for Loftus,' Laurence said quietly. 'I wrote it because I was inspired to do so.'

Theo chuckled. 'So the muse spoke to you, did she?'

Laurence thought about Joanna, remembering how she had advised him to combine his two great passions and write a story set in the distant past. If that made her his muse, so be it. 'You could say that, yes.'

'Well, I promise I'll read it as soon as I can and let you know what I think. Then, I'll either pass it on to Loftus or give it back to you. Either way, I'm proud of you, Laurence. I wasn't sure you had it in you to finish a full-length work, but this more than proves that you can.'

'I'll wait to hear what you think about the entire piece before I let the compliment go to my head,' Laurence said, not about to get his hopes up. 'Just because I'm able to finish something doesn't mean it's worthy of being shown to anyone else. It may end up in the grate, where all bad manuscripts go to die.'

'And what will you do then?'

'Carry on with my life.'

'What about your plans to go to Egypt?'

'Uncertain.'

'Why? Because of Valentine Lawe…or Lady Joanna Northrup?'

Laurence's mouth tightened. 'Lady Joanna has nothing to do with it.'

'Rubbish! Lady Joanna has *everything* to do with it and if you want my advice—'

'I don't.'

'—you will sit down with her and patch things up.'

'That is not my decision to make. *She* was the one who walked out.'

'Of course, because *you* were the one who told the lie.'

'*I* told the lie?' Laurence couldn't believe his ears. '*You* were the one who said it was the right thing to do! The one who's said all along that we have to perpetuate the myth.'

'Yes, because it was the best way to avoid society's scorn and the fallout that would naturally occur. But *you* have to decide to whom you tell the truth and who you leave in ignorance,' Theo said. 'Victoria told Devlin because she loved him. She didn't know how he was going to react, but she took the risk because she felt he deserved to know.'

'So now you're questioning my love for Joanna?'

'No. I'm questioning your faith in her.'

'She's going to marry someone else!' Laurence all but shouted. 'How much faith am I *supposed* to have in her?'

'I admit that does make things a little more difficult,' Theo acknowledged, 'but all is not lost. Until the minister pronounces them husband and wife, there is still hope.'

Laurence shook his head. 'Your perception of faith and mine are very different, Uncle. I gave up all hope of Joanna choosing me when she accused me of playing Valentine Lawe in order to satisfy my need for public adoration. Any woman who believes *that* cannot have much faith or affection for me to begin with.'

It was a couple of weeks before Joanna saw Laurence again, and when she did, it was in the very shop where they first met. She was browsing through a selection of books when she heard the bell over the front door ring and looked up to see Laurence and his sister walk in. They were talking quietly and did not notice her. But when the young lady standing next to Joanna dropped a book that landed with a resounding thud, they both turned to glance in her direction.

Joanna held her breath, afraid to look, but unable to resist the temptation.

Laurence was staring at her, but he did not smile. He just stood there unmoving, his expression remote, his manner as cold as that of a marble statue.

Sick at heart, Joanna went back to her browsing. So, nothing had changed. He obviously still thought she was in the wrong and intended to continue his avoidance of her.

How far they had come over the past few weeks. It was impossible now to equate the distant, aloof man with the one who had gazed at her so warmly on the night of the theatre outing. His indifference lodged like a steel weight in her chest and her throat burned with the effort of holding back tears.

But she would not let him see her desolation. It could no longer be of any concern what Laurence Bretton thought of her. He had communicated very clearly his lack of feelings when he had made the decision not to tell her the truth about Valentine Lawe—

'Lady Joanna.'

Her fingers froze on the spine of the book at hand. 'Mr Bretton.'

'Forgive me for having interrupted your browsing.'

'You did not.' Joanna pulled out the book and dropped it into her basket. 'I found what I was looking for.' She had no idea what the book was, nor did she care. All she wanted was for him to go away and leave her alone. She wasn't ready to deal with this…with him…

'I trust you are well?' he asked in a polite, remote voice.

'I am, thank you.'

'And your father?'

'Fine.' Her face felt as stiff as a board, but she forced herself to continue the conversation. 'He was wondering why you have not been around to see him. He thought perhaps you had…changed your mind about going on the expedition.'

'I have been busy with other things.'

'Writing a new play, perhaps?'

Joanna could have bitten her tongue. The words, sarcastic and judgemental, caused a blind to drop down over Laurence's eyes. 'As a matter of fact, I have, though I don't expect you to believe that.'

'If you say you are writing, it is not for me to question your word.'

'You did before.'

Unwelcome heat burned and she glanced away. 'That was in the past. I really don't care what you do now, Mr Bretton.'

'Yes, you made that perfectly clear when last we spoke,' he said quietly. 'But I had hoped that with time your thoughts might have taken a more forgiving turn.'

'Forgiving?' Surprised, Joanna looked back at him. 'Why would you think that? Nothing has changed. You are still playing the part of the playwright and deceiving everyone you know. How am I to see that as an admirable quality or one deserving of my respect?'

His expression was briefly one of pain before his cheeks darkened and he said, 'We all do things for a reason, Lady Joanna. The fact we do not choose to divulge those reasons should not be held against us. However, I did not come over here to rake up past grievances. I came to ask if I am to wish you happy.'

'Happy?' Joanna knew exactly what he was referring to, but if he could pretend ignorance, so could she. 'In what regard?'

'Your engagement to Captain Sterne. I thought a decision might have been reached.'

'I see no reason why that should be of concern to you.'

'Nevertheless, it is,' Laurence said. 'And I would ask, for the sake of a friendship I believe we once had, whether or not you have agreed to marry him.'

Part of her wanted to lie—that small spiteful part, desperate to inflict the same kind of pain he had inflicted on her. But what would be the point? She would feel no better walking away as a result of having been dishonest with him. Two wrongs did not make a right. 'No, Mr Bretton, I have not,' she said finally.

His brows flickered. 'You turned him down?'

'No. I have not yet given him an answer.'

'But he has asked.'

'Yes.'

'Then why have you not answered him?'

'The reasons don't matter.'

'They do to me,' Laurence said.

'Unfortunately, as you said yourself, we all do things for a reason, but we do not always choose to make those reasons known.'

'So because I have not been honest with you, you have no intention of being honest with me.'

Joanna raised her chin. She wasn't about to tell him she hadn't agreed to marry Captain Sterne because the sight of him failed to cause even the slightest quickening of her pulse. Or that she didn't count the hours until they were together again, or wish that the hours they had together might last for ever, the way she did with Laurence. He didn't deserve to know any of that. It was bad enough she couldn't shake the awareness of it herself. 'I think that only fair.'

Laurence glanced at the book in her basket, then at the young lady standing further along the row. Anywhere, it seemed, but at her. 'I see.'

'No, you don't see,' Joanna said, suddenly feeling as brittle as glass, knowing that if he touched her, she would shatter. 'If I was with you, my life would become as much of a lie as yours is. I would be forced to listen to people talk about how talented you are, and about what a great man you are, all the while knowing that none of it was true. I would feel compelled to keep your secret from my father because I would not wish to see you humiliated in the eyes of someone who knew and respected you.' *And it would tear me apart in the process.*

It was a wretched situation and as the tears spilled over, Joanna wondered how this could all have gone so terribly wrong—

'Forgive me,' Laurence said, his voice as tortured as her thoughts. 'It was not my intention to hurt you. I only wanted to talk to you in the hopes…'

Joanna gazed up at him through her tears. 'Yes?'

His eyes burned into hers, but in the end, he only shook his head. 'Nothing. It doesn't matter any more. I've done too many things wrong to hope things could ever be right between us again and for that I am truly sorry. Good afternoon, Lady Joanna.'

Laurence bowed and returned to his sister's side. Joanna saw Victoria cast a regretful look in her direction, then brother and sister left the shop together. As they did, she closed her eyes and let the tears fall unchecked.

Oh, *why* couldn't she just get on with her life! Laurence didn't deserve her tears. A woman needed to know that the man she loved was being open and honest with her. Otherwise, it was just a case of him telling her what she wanted to hear—or, worse, what he wanted her to hear.

But, what was the *truth*? She still didn't know

because Laurence wasn't willing to tell her and she knew better than to ask his sister. The two were as thick as thieves and if Victoria *was* the famous playwright, there was no way on earth she would reveal that and risk exposing her brother to criticism and censure.

So who did that leave? Who else was there that might know the truth about Valentine Lawe—and not be afraid to tell her?

Chapter Twelve

The disparaging article appeared in *The Times* two days later.

Joanna found the newspaper on the corner of her father's desk. The fact it was open to the society pages was, in itself, unusual, but when the name Valentine Lawe jumped out at her, she couldn't help but pick it up and read the article all the way through.

It was not kind. It set out the intention of one Famous Playwright, never mentioned by name, to accompany Lord Bonnington and his team on an expedition to Egypt. The lack of experience on the part of the Famous Playwright was mentioned, as was the fact that he was abandoning his highly successful profession in order to take part in an expedition that, in the writer's opinion, could hardly be benefited by his presence.

'After all...' the author wrote, *'...what can a man whose claim to fame is writing satirical plays hope to offer a man who has dedicated his life to uncovering the secrets of the past?'*

Heavy at heart, Joanna put the paper down. For all her anger at Laurence, she hated to see him vilified like this. Clearly the author of the article didn't agree with his plans to travel to Egypt and was not afraid to say so in a very public forum.

She picked up the paper and continued reading, only to discover that Laurence's uncle had also been included in the attack.

'One would think...' the writer continued, *'that the charismatic Mr Templeton, a man possessed of considerable knowledge and expertise in matters theatrical, would have advised his nephew to think twice before abandoning what can only be viewed as a wildly successful career to go and dig in the dirt like a common labourer...'*

Again, Joanna put the paper down, but this time, her thoughts turned in an entirely different direction. Theo Templeton had produced all four of Valentine Lawe's plays. As such, he had as much to win...or to lose...as Laurence did. So if, in fact, Laurence was *not* the author of those plays and Victoria Bretton was, surely it was in Mr Templeton's best interests to see his niece revealed as the author so that Laurence's actions would not impact negatively upon her success.

Surely he could be made to see that making the truth about Valentine Lawe known was the only right thing to do.

'Mrs Templeton will see you now, Lady Joanna,' the butler said. 'If you would be so good as to come this way.'

With a brief nod, Joanna followed the servant up a wide marble staircase. Large portraits of exquisitely dressed ladies and dashing gentlemen in Elizabethan costume hung from pale-gold walls, their eyes seeming to follow Joanna as she climbed.

Her decision to approach the Templetons with regard to Valentine Lawe had been reached after a number of sleepless hours during which she tried to work out the best way of finding out the answers she needed. Now, as she followed the butler into a lavishly decorated drawing room that, while somewhat out of date, seemed perfectly in keeping with the eccentricities of a theatre producer and his decidedly flamboyant wife, she hoped she would not come to regret it.

'Lady Joanna, how delightful to see you again,' Mrs Templeton said, rising to greet her. She was garbed in a gown of deep-violet silk that looked marvellous against her flaming red hair. Diamonds flashed at her ears and throat, as though she was off to a midnight gala rather than welcoming a visitor to her drawing room in the middle of the day. 'I am so sorry we did not have more of an opportunity to chat at Winifred's engagement celebration.'

'No apology is necessary, Mrs Templeton, there were a lot of people there,' Joanna said, remembering what she *had* heard of the lady's conversation and exceedingly grateful they had *not* had an opportunity to spend any more time together.

'Yes, celebratory parties are always so busy, are they not? But now that you are here, we will be able to make up for it.'

'Mrs Templeton,' Joanna began, hoping that what she was about to say would not sound terribly rude. 'Would it be possible to speak to your husband?'

There was a very brief pause. 'My husband?'

'Yes. I would like to ask him about…a play. Several plays, in fact, with which he has been intimately involved.'

The lady blinked large, emerald eyes. 'I see. Well, yes, if that is what you wish, I will see if he is available.' She nodded at the footman standing discreetly in one corner, who left immediately. 'Laurence tells me you are an exceedingly talented artist, Lady Joanna,' Mrs Templeton continued after the door closed. 'And that your sketches of a particular place in Egypt, the name of which I cannot remember, were quite stunning.'

'It was good of him to say so,' Joanna murmured, uncomfortable at the mention of Laurence's name given her reasons for coming here today.

Fortunately, Mrs Templeton didn't seem to notice. 'I do so envy you the experience of travelling to foreign places. I too had quite an adventurous streak when I was a younger woman. I was forever making up stories about being a queen in a faraway land. Indeed, as a little girl I used to dress up in my mother's clothes and stage amateur theatricals for my family. They were all very kind, of course, and put up with me asking for the strangest things, but I did so love performing. And I was very good at memorising lines. No doubt that is why I ended up on the stage.'

'Where you turned your youthful exuberance for play acting into a true talent for performance,' Theo Templeton said, walking into the room. 'And delighted a great many more people than just those who were obliged to watch your performances for free.'

'Thank you, darling,' his wife said, offering up her cheek for his kiss.

'And good afternoon to you, Lady Joanna,' the gentleman said, straightening.

'Mr Templeton.' Joanna abruptly stood up.

'I hope you will forgive my disturbing you like this.'

'Not at all, I was getting rather tired of totting up figures. Please sit down. I never like to keep a lady standing on my account.'

'I know this is somewhat unusual,' Joanna said, resuming her seat, 'but I was hoping you might be able to clarify a very confusing situation for me. One that concerns some of the plays you produced at the Gryphon.'

'Of course, if it is within my power,' Mr Templeton said.

They were interrupted by a knock at the door and by the appearance of a young maid, asking if Mrs Templeton might have a moment to speak to Cook.

'Certainly,' Mrs Templeton said, rising. 'Forgive me, Lady Joanna, but we are having a large dinner party tomorrow evening and I asked Cook to try something new. No doubt the poor woman is finding some of my instructions difficult to follow. That is what comes of trying to teach an English cook to prepare a French soufflé! I shan't be long.'

Mrs Templeton departed in a rustle of silk and a flash of diamonds, leaving behind the delicate fragrance of lily of the valley. Joanne could have kissed the unknown Cook for the excellence of her timing.

'Now, Lady Joanna,' Mr Templeton said

when they were alone, 'what is it you wish to—gracious, what now?' he said as the door opened again and his butler appeared. 'Yes, Trehorn?'

'Pardon me, Mr Templeton, but Sir Michael Loftus has called and is asking if he might have a word with you.'

'Goodness, what a busy day. Show him into my study,' Mr Templeton said, 'and tell him I shall join him in a few minutes.'

'Very good, sir.'

The butler withdrew and Mr Templeton turned to Joanna with a smile. 'Forgive me, Lady Joanna. The house is more like a coaching stop this morning, with all this coming and going. But we shall try again and hopefully without any further interruptions. Now, what was it you wished to ask me?'

The intensity of his gaze brought a flush to Joanna's cheeks, but she forced herself to say what she knew she must. 'You will no doubt find this strange, Mr Templeton, but a little while ago, I came into possession of some information. It was not by the most honest of means, I admit, but the conversation I overheard has left me feeling extremely concerned and deeply confused.'

'I see. And you believe I am in a position to relieve your concern and confusion?'

'I do…because the confusion involves your nephew Mr Bretton, and his sister Mrs Devlin.'

Joanna watched the gentleman's face intently

for any signs of dismay or embarrassment, but beyond an expression of mild curiosity, she saw nothing. 'Really? What exactly did you overhear?'

'First, let me say that I was somewhere I should not have been and that the conversation I heard was not meant to go beyond the walls of the room in which it took place,' Joanna said, wishing to be very clear on that point. 'But rightly or wrongly, I *was* in the vicinity and I heard Mrs Bretton speaking to your wife about this "wretched affair with Victoria".'

Mr Templeton's eyebrows rose ever so slightly. 'Did you indeed.'

'I had no idea it meant anything until I heard Mrs Bretton say that it all came right when Laurence told Sir Michael that *he* was Valentine Lawe, and then Mrs Templeton replied that matters would have been very different had Mr Bretton not stepped forwards to claim the role.'

'How interesting.' Mr Templeton got to his feet and crossing to the wall, pulled on a slender tapestry panel. 'Anything else?'

'Mrs Bretton then said it had all come far too close to crashing down for her liking and that she hated to think what would have happened had Mr Bretton let his sister tell the truth about Valentine Lawe. And it is that remark which has prompted me to call upon you today, Mr Templeton. I would very much like to know what she meant by that.'

'I really cannot say,' Mr Templeton replied with every appearance of sincerity. 'Are you sure that is what you heard?'

'I was all but standing outside the door,' Joanna said. 'I admit, there were a few times when the voices grew muffled, but I thought I heard the rest of it quite clearly.'

'And I suspect, Lady Joanna, that you may have missed more than you thought. Ah, Trehorn, good. Would you be so kind as to bring Sir Michael up?'

'Right away, Mr Templeton.'

Joanna blinked her surprise. Sir Michael Loftus was to join them? Without her being given an opportunity to finish what she had come to say?

'Do not fear, Lady Joanna, I am not trying to rush you out of the house,' Mr Templeton assured her with a genial smile. 'But I believe Sir Michael will be able to add something of value to the conversation. I know for a fact that when he originally called at Green Street to enquire after the identity of Valentine Lawe, he was informed by my nephew that he *was* Valentine Lawe, and that he did so in front of his father, his sister and her then soon-to-be husband. I can assure you that no voices were raised to the contrary, but I shall ask Sir Michael to corroborate that when he arrives.'

'But *is* Mr Bretton truly a playwright? Or is this all a great hoax?'

Joanna heard the drawing door open and, expecting it to be Sir Michael Loftus, did not immediately turn around. As such, she was totally unprepared to hear Laurence say, 'I would prefer to answer that myself, if you don't mind, Uncle.'

Joanna whirled. 'Mr Bretton!'

'Good day, Lady Joanna.' Laurence walked into the room with, of all people, Mrs Devlin a step behind. 'Pardon the interruption, Uncle, but Victoria and I came to see you about an article that appeared in the morning paper. I had not thought to see Lady Joanna here as well.'

'No, I suspect not,' Mr Templeton said, getting to his feet. 'But it seems she has some concerns about your ability to write plays and I was about to give her an answer when you arrived. Ah, Sir Michael, excellent timing,' he said as a well-dressed gentleman walked into the room. 'I think you know everyone here, with the exception, perhaps, of Lady Joanna.'

'Indeed. Good afternoon, Lady Joanna, Mrs Devlin,' Sir Michael said with a bow. 'And Mr Bretton, how fortuitous. I had planned on calling to see you later in the day about your new play, but your arrival here now saves me the trip.'

'His new play?' Joanna said, glancing at Laurence.

'Indeed, as brilliant a piece of writing as I

have ever seen, as I told Templeton yesterday,' Sir Michael said. 'Did you not think so, Mrs Devlin? You must have read it.'

Mrs Devlin glanced at her brother with a look of incredulity. 'As a matter of fact, I have not, Sir Michael. I wasn't even aware Laurence had finished it.'

'I did, barely a week ago,' Laurence said slowly, 'but I decided to show it to Uncle Theo first because I thought he would be the best judge of whether or not it was good enough to show anyone else.'

'Sound thinking,' Mr Templeton commented. 'And I shouldn't be offended, Victoria. Laurence knew how busy you were with Isabelle's wedding and probably felt you wouldn't have time to give it the consideration it deserved. But I was delighted to read it because it is, in a word, outstanding.'

'Yes, it is,' Sir Michael agreed. 'And I admit to being surprised because it is a complete departure from any of Lawe's previous works, but I predict it will be just as big a success. Why don't you tell the ladies a little bit about it, Mr Bretton?'

Laurence stared in disbelief at the two men standing opposite him, waiting for him to deliver a précis of his play. His uncle thought the work *outstanding*? Sir Michael thought it a *brilliant piece of writing*? Never in his wildest dreams had he imagined that something he had pulled together in less than three weeks would merit such superlatives.

It was all he could do not to take Joanna in his arms and dance her around the room.

He did not, of course, because this was supposed to be his fifth play, not his first, and the thrill of hearing that he had written something good enough to be produced for the stage should have lessened considerably by now. Nevertheless, it was difficult to maintain a convincing level of sang-froid when the knowledge he had produced a work to the standard of Valentine Lawe had been pointed out to everyone in the room…especially Joanna.

'Yes, of course,' he said, clearing his throat. 'The play is entitled *The Silver Chalice* and it is the story of two warring nations, one ruled by a despotic pharaoh, the other by a clever but humble woman who is determined to defeat him and to gain freedom for her people.'

'A noble premise,' Victoria said. 'When and where is it set?'

'Egypt, 1280 BC.'

Joanna gasped. 'But that is the time of Seti the First!'

'That's right, and it was you who inspired the story, Lady Joanna.'

'*Me?*'

'Yes. The day you told me I should combine my passion for ancient Egypt with my love of telling stories,' Laurence said quietly. 'For some reason, the thought of doing so had never occurred to me before, but once I sat down to rework the story along those lines, it all fell perfectly into place.'

'As I said, it is a departure from the Valentine Lawe plays we are used to seeing,' Theo said, 'but I agree with Sir Michael that the story is riveting and I predict it will attract an even wider audience than did his first four plays, especially if it is produced at Drury Lane.'

'I still have to get Elliston's approval on that,' Sir Michael said, 'but based on the strength of Valentine Lawe's name, I don't anticipate any problems. I'll get back to you in a few days, Templeton. Well done, Mr Bretton. Well done indeed!'

'My goodness, this *is* exciting news,' Victoria said as that gentleman left the room. 'You were very naughty not to tell me you had finished the play, Laurence, but I am thrilled to hear it has been so well received.'

'No more than I, I can assure you,' Laurence admitted with a rueful smile.

His sister's eyes sparkled with mirth. 'Yes, I'm sure. But now I really must run. I promised to meet Mr Devlin at the orphanage and I do not like to keep him waiting. Shall I wait for you in the carriage, Laurence?'

Laurence could see that his sister was bursting with curiosity and knew she would have a thing or two to say to him when they were alone. But he said only, 'No, you go on ahead. I shall make my own way home. I'd like to have a word with Lady Joanna first.'

'Very well, then, I shall see you at Mama's later. She has invited Mr Devlin and myself for dinner, so you may tell me all about your new play then. As for you, Uncle,' Victoria said, crossing the room to kiss him affectionately on the cheek. 'Thank you for giving us such splendid news. It could not have come at a better time.'

'I am inclined to think the same,' Theo murmured. 'I shall see you after dinner. I need to have a word with your father.'

Joanna, who had said very little during the last few minutes, abruptly stood up. 'I must be going too—'

'Lady Joanna...' Laurence said. 'If I could have a moment—'

'Thank you for agreeing to see me, Mr Templeton,' Joanna said, directing her comment to his uncle and sparing not so much as a glance for Laurence. 'Please accept my apologies for having taken up so much of your time.'

'You took up no time and no apologies are

necessary,' Theo assured her in a gentle voice. 'It was a pleasure to see you again, Lady Joanna.'

'Lady Joanna,' Laurence said, stepping in front of her. 'I really *must* speak with you.'

'I'm afraid I have no time, Mr Bretton.' Joanna smoothed her gown and tucked an errant curl under the brim of her bonnet. 'I have a very busy afternoon.'

'Have you no word for me at all?' Laurence said, desperate to know how she felt. But though the lady looked as though she might say something, in the end, she merely pressed her lips together and shook her head before walking quickly out of the room.

Laurence went to follow, but was stayed by the pressure of his uncle's hand. 'Let her go, Laurence,' Theo said.

'But I have to explain—'

'She will not hear what you have to say, nor will she thank you for following her out,' Theo said. 'She came here today, expecting to hear one thing, only to be told another. And it was made worse by the fact that Sir Michael Loftus said what he did in front of both of you.'

Laurence paused, torn between what he wanted to do and what his uncle believed to be the right thing. 'Did you say what you did about my play for her benefit?'

'Good God, no! I said what I did because the play is excellent. And you know Loftus wouldn't have said it was exceptional unless it damn well was. I had no idea you could write so well.'

'Perhaps I've been lacking the right motivation,' Laurence murmured. 'As regards Joanna, you were right to tell me I was the one who had to patch things up with her. I know now that it is my responsibility and I intend to take care of it. But if I let her leave here today without making at least *some* attempt to speak to her after what Sir Michael said, I fear it will only make matters worse.'

Theo nodded and removed his hand. 'In that case, I will see you at the house later. It appears that we *all* have a great deal to talk about.'

Laurence caught up with Joanna as she was climbing into her carriage. 'Lady Joanna, wait! I must speak with you.'

'There is nothing to say,' she said. 'Can you not see how difficult this is for me? How mortified I am?'

'But you have no reason to be mortified.'

'Of course I do. Why do you think I came here today?'

'I really don't care—'

'Well, I do,' Joanna said unhappily. 'I came because I didn't believe you and because I wanted to find out the truth about Valentine Lawe. When I read that article in the paper this morning, I thought talking to Mr Templeton might give me the answer I needed…and it did. It gave me irrefutable evidence that you are *exactly* who you claim to be and that I have been wrong all along.'

'Damn it, Joanna, you're not wrong!'

'Yes, I am,' she said with quiet conviction. 'Ever since we met in the Temple of the Muses, I have doubted you. I've questioned your integrity, challenged your commitment to archaeology and, worse, called you a liar to your face. Were I a man you could demand satisfaction, but as a woman, I can offer nothing but the most heartfelt apology. I should have known that a man as honourable and as honest as you would *never* pretend to be someone he was not.'

'Joanna, please *listen* to me!' Laurence said, needing to stem the flow of words in an effort to make her understand. 'I know this isn't a good time—'

'Nor will there ever be a better one. It was bad enough your uncle and sister saw me with you on stage that day, behaving in a way no well-bred young lady would ever consider behaving,' Joanna said, blushing furiously. 'But to have them find me here today, knowing I came because I did not believe you, is too much to be borne. It is best we say our goodbyes now and let that be an end of it.'

'Joanna, for God's sake—'

'Good afternoon, Mr Bretton. Drive on, James!'

The reins jangled and the carriage pulled away, forcing Laurence to jump back to avoid being run over by the wheels. Muttering a string of expletives, he shoved his hands into his pockets and stood staring after it.

What was he supposed to do now? Rather than having assured Joanna that her doubts about his being Valentine Lawe were justified, she was more convinced than ever that *she* was the one in the wrong. He had been spared yet again; the deception played out to the benefit of himself and his family.

Yet nothing his uncle or Sir Michael had said this afternoon was a lie. *The Silver Chalice* was his own work. He had written it without help from anyone else and if it did turn out to be the success both men predicted, it would only be because the story and the writing were strong enough to stand on their own merit.

He no longer had to *pretend* to be Valentine Lawe. He could truthfully claim the role as his own. Then why did he still feel so utterly wretched? Why, at the very moment he had achieved all that he needed to turn the lie into a fact, did he feel it was more of a lie than ever before?

Joanna scarcely remembered the drive home. She was weighted down with guilt, unable to think about anything beyond the conversation that had just taken place and about how horribly wrong she had been about everything.

Laurence Bretton was indeed Valentine Lawe! His uncle *and* Sir Michael Loftus had confirmed it. The latter had held up Laurence's latest play—a play Laurence had credited *her* with having inspired—and said it was a brilliant piece of writing, while Mr Templeton had said it promised to be as big a success as any of Laurence's other plays.

Clearly she had been mistaken as to the nature of the conversation she had overheard between Mrs Bretton and her sister-in-law the night of Winifred's engagement party. Or, as Mr Templeton had pointed out, she had missed some of the more salient parts.

Clearly, the *most* salient ones, Joanna reflected, and she deserved to lose Laurence's good opinion as a result.

But, the awareness that she had made one terrible mistake only strengthened her resolve not to make another. Until a few minutes ago, she'd had every intention of accepting Captain Sterne's proposal and of moving on with her life. But now, in light of her astonishing discovery, Joanna knew that was impossible. She *would not* marry a man she did not love and turn her own life into a lie as a result.

'James,' she called to the driver. 'Do you know where Captain Sterne lives?'

'I do, my lady.'

'Then take me there now,' she said, staring blindly at the row of fine houses lining either side of the street. There had to be some other way of raising the money necessary to pay off the estate's debts, some way that did not necessitate her sacrificing her pride and, more importantly, her heart in the securing of that goal. She was just going to have to find it—and pray her father and the rest of her family would understand and forgive her for it.

'I'm sorry, Lady Joanna, but Captain Sterne is presently engaged,' the gentleman's butler informed Joanna when she handed him her card. 'If you would care to wait in the drawing room—'

'Thank you, but I would rather wait here,' she said, and promptly sat down in the chair by the large palm.

The butler inclined his head and turned to carry her card upstairs to his master.

In the minutes that followed, Joanna tried to calm the frantic beating of her heart. There was no point in putting off what she had to do. She was not going to marry Captain Sterne. It was only fair that she tell him sooner rather than later.

She looked up at the sound of footsteps on the stairs. It was not the Captain she saw coming down, but a young man carrying a collection of drawings under his arm. He was not dressed like a gentleman of means. His jacket showed signs of wear, his boots were in need of a polish and, when he drew closer, Joanna noticed a stain on the collar of his shirt. But he smiled gamely as he passed and Joanna—upon noticing that the uppermost sketch under his arm was a very good rendering of an Egyptian temple—put out her hand and said, 'I beg your pardon, but is that the Temple of Luxor?'

The young man stopped, a surprised blush darkening his already ruddy cheeks. 'Yes, it is. How did you know?'

Joanna managed a tight smile. 'I have an interest in the subject.'

'It's not a very good replica,' the man acknowledged self-consciously, 'but it was the best I could do from Mr de Forbin's painting. Are you here for the interview?'

Joanna pulled her eyes from the drawing. 'The interview?'

'Yes. For the illustrator's position. Apparently Lord Bonnington is planning an expedition to Abu Simbel next spring and is looking for an artist.'

'Lord *Bonnington's* expedition?' Joanna said, a hard knot forming in the pit of her stomach. 'Are you sure you have the right gentleman?'

'I believe so. Captain Sterne told me about it

last week,' the gentleman said. 'He came to pay a call on my father and happened to see a sketch I had done of St. Paul's Cathedral. When he asked me if I was able to draw something Egyptian, I told him I probably could and he said if it was good enough, I should come and talk to him about the possibility of my going on the expedition with him.'

'Really.' Joanna stared at the drawing as the dreadful awakening sunk in.

Captain Sterne had lied to her. He had spoken to this young man *after* he had proposed to her and had interviewed him about taking her place on the expedition before she had given him her answer. Obviously, he had never intended that she should go with him to Egypt at all!

'Lady Joanna! What a delightful surprise,' Sterne said, appearing at the top of the stairs. 'I wasn't expecting you to call.'

'No, I'm sure you weren't,' Joanna said, still trying to come to terms with what she had just learned. 'But in the interim, I have been speaking with this gentleman, who told me he came to apply for the position of artist on Lord Bonnington's expedition to Abu Simbel.' She forced herself to smile. 'I wasn't aware there was a vacancy. Have you spoken to my…to his lordship about this yet?'

Please say no, Joanna thought, praying her

father had no knowledge of this underhanded endeavour.

Thankfully, the rush of colour into Sterne's face betrayed him. 'On your way, Mr Stocks,' he barked at the young man.

Not surprisingly, the young man went.

Joanna took a few moments to gather her thoughts, afraid of what she might say if she did not. 'Would you care to explain what's going on, Captain Sterne? Or shall I just assume that Mr Stocks was to be my replacement on the expedition?'

'Not at all. I simply thought it would be a good idea to have a back-up plan in case you decided, once we were married, that you did not wish to accompany us to Egypt,' he said smoothly.

'So it was already a foregone conclusion in your mind that I *was* going to accept your proposal.'

'I saw no reason why you would not. Your father is in desperate need of financial assistance and I am in a position to give him that. I also expected that because you and I *would* be married by the time the expedition set off, you might have a change of heart and prefer to stay in London. That would have left the expedition in the lurch and you know as well as I do how difficult it is to find competent artists, never mind one of your calibre.'

'Thank you,' Joanna said coldly, 'but if we were married and I changed my mind about going on the expedition, I would have told my father in enough time that he could have found someone else. He is not without connections. But that was never the case, was it, Captain Sterne? You had no intention of letting me go regardless of what I wanted.'

'Does it really matter?' His smile was suddenly hard. 'Lady Cynthia told me you were not to be allowed to go unless you *were* married, so if you don't agree to marry me, there is absolutely no chance of your going to Egypt. Either way, we both know it is in everyone's best interests for you to accept my proposal.'

Joanna nodded, an equally cold smile forming on her lips. 'I did feel that way. Briefly. But your conduct today has more than convinced me that I would have been making a bigger mistake by agreeing to do so than by refusing. I have no intention of marrying you, Captain Sterne, and there is nothing you can say that will make me change my mind.'

He didn't look surprised...or particularly troubled by her answer. 'I wouldn't be so sure. I suspect your father will have something to say about all this.'

'I suspect he will, but I doubt it will be what you think,' Joanna said quietly. 'He will not be pleased that you have taken the liberty of interviewing someone for a position on his expedition without his knowledge or permission beforehand, and he would *never* expect me to enter into an engagement with a man who had lied to me without compunction. We will manage just fine without your help, Captain Sterne,' she said, starting for the door. 'Of that, you can be very sure!'

Chapter Thirteen

Laurence was glad *The Silver Chalice* was finished. Had it not been, it would have languished in a drawer for months before he rounded up the energy or the inclination to finish it. His brief spurt of creativity had exhausted itself and he had no desire to write another word until this matter with Joanna was settled once and for all. He had written to her, several times, but each note had been returned unopened. He had even called at Eaton Place, only to be told that she was not receiving visitors.

And so he resorted to his last option. One he would never have considered had the circumstances been different.

'My dear Mr Bretton,' Mrs Gavin greeted him as he walked into her drawing room. 'I cannot tell you how pleased I was to receive your note asking if you might call.'

'I hope you will be as pleased when I tell you why I have come,' Laurence said.

'I see no reason why I should not. I suspect you wish to speak to me about Jane.'

'Actually, no.' His smile was strained. 'As delightful as your daughter is, it is your niece I have come to talk about.'

'Joanna?' Mrs Gavin repeated in surprise. 'Is there some reason you cannot apply to the lady yourself?'

'I fear that on the occasion of our last meeting, we had a slight…misunderstanding,' Laurence said, careful with his words. Joanna's aunt was no fool. She would see through him in an instant if he told her too much. 'As a result, she is reluctant to see me.'

'I see.' Mrs Gavin's eyes narrowed. 'So you have come to plead your case to me?'

'I hoped you might be willing to help me, yes.'

'I hardly think it my business, Mr Bretton. If my niece has no wish to see you, you can hardly expect me to intervene on your behalf.'

'I understand that. But the reasons behind the misunderstanding are what I wish to explain to her and she is reluctant to hear them.'

'Why don't you send her a note?'

'I have written several, all of which have been returned unopened.'

'Hmm.' Mrs Gavin's observant eyes focused

in on him like a hunter on its prey. Then, finally, 'Very well, Mr Bretton, I will give you the opportunity you seek, though it goes against the grain to do so. I will make arrangements for my niece to be here and will advise you in advance of the day and time. I will then give you five minutes alone with her, but five minutes only. Do I make myself clear?'

Laurence assured her that she had, and when he left her house, it was in a mood of cautious optimism. If he could sit Joanna down and make her listen to what he had to say, hopefully five minutes would be all he needed. But first, he had to get through his next meeting. One that was going to be a great deal harder than the one he had just left.

One that no matter how it turned out was going to affect the rest of his life and that might make his five minutes with Joanna a complete waste of time.

'Mr Laurence Bretton,' the butler informed the gentleman seated behind the huge mahogany desk.

As the doors closed behind him, Laurence walked into Sir Michael Loftus's exquisitely appointed library and waited for the man to look up.

'Mr Bretton,' Sir Michael said, finally doing so. 'This is a surprise.'

'I hope I haven't called at an inconvenient time.'

'Not at all. I was just finishing up some correspondence. Sit down,' Sir Michael said, indicating the deeply padded armchairs in front of the fireplace. 'I'd not thought to see you so soon after our encounter at your uncle's house.'

'It is partially because of that encounter I'm here,' Laurence said. 'You left before I was able to tell you something that I have decided you need to hear.'

'Oh? Has it to do with your new play?'

'Not exactly,' Laurence said, sitting down in one of the two high-back leather chairs. 'It has to do with the last four Valentine Lawe plays, all of which I know you're familiar with.'

'I am indeed, Mr Bretton,' Sir Michael said, settling into the vacant chair beside Laurence's and stretching out his legs. 'So, what is it you wish to tell me?'

Laurence took a moment to gather his thoughts. He was well aware that what he said next was going to change everything, but he had thought long and hard about this and he knew it was what he had to do. Joanna was right. As long as the truth remained hidden, there could never be honesty between them. And without honesty, there could never be respect. A man might lie for what he perceived to be a good and valid reason, but in the end, it was still a lie.

'I came here to tell you,' Laurence began quietly, 'that I am not now, nor have I ever been, Valentine Lawe. I assumed the role for reasons I intend to make clear, but it is my sister Victoria who is the author of those four plays and it is she who deserves to be acknowledged as such.'

Laurence waited for the news to sink in. He wasn't surprised to see the expression on Sir Michael's face change, but he was surprised when all the other man said was, 'Go on.'

And so, Laurence did, explaining in detail how Victoria had started out writing and how it had been necessary to conceal that fact from their mother, who viewed the theatrical world with abhorrence. He explained how his uncle, Theodore Templeton, had been instrumental in encouraging Victoria's skills, and how, when she had written something worthy of production, Theo had suggested that she do so under an assumed name so that their mother would not learn of her occupation and be disgraced by it.

Finally, Laurence admitted that he had assumed the role of Valentine Lawe in the hopes of protecting his sisters' reputations after they both fell in love with men whose families would not have approved of their association with the theatre. He admitted to having done so without the prior consent or knowledge of his family, and that he had then done everything he could to make sure society believed he truly was Valentine Lawe.

In the end, there was nothing left to say. The truth was out and as Laurence waited for Sir Michael to respond, he knew the man had every right to call him a liar and a cheat. To demand that he leave his house and be prepared to face whatever consequences might result.

To his surprise, however, none of that happened. Sir Michael stood up and locked his hands behind his back. He began to pace, his head down, his brows pulled together in a dark line. Finally, he stopped and fired an abrupt question at Laurence. 'Are you the author of *The Silver Chalice*?'

Surprised, Laurence nodded. 'I am.'

'And did you write it entirely on your own, unaided by your sister, your uncle or anyone else?'

'I did.'

'And is anyone, other than myself and your family, aware of what you've just told me?'

'Yes. Lady Joanna Northrup by virtue of having overheard a conversation between my mother and my aunt a few weeks ago,' Laurence said. 'Validating that conversation was the reason she was at my uncle's house the day you also happened to be there.'

'Then you did not tell her of the charade yourself.'

'No.' The comment shamed him, though Laurence suspected that wasn't Sir Michael's intent. 'I wanted to, but out of a concern for my family, I said nothing. I went to my uncle's house that day for another reason entirely and found her there. Then you arrived and, by praising my work, inadvertently confirmed my role as Valentine Lawe.'

'Ah. So the lady still believes you to be the playwright?'

'Yes, though I have every intention of setting her straight,' Laurence said. 'Coming here and telling you the truth was the first step in being honest with her.'

'Because you love her.'

'Very much.'

'Fine. Then tell her what you must and let that be an end of it,' Sir Michael said, abruptly sitting down again.

Laurence stared at him in confusion. 'I don't understand. I've just told you it was all a lie. That I'm not Valentine Lawe.'

'Of course you're not Valentine Lawe. I knew that as soon as I read your play.'

It was a stunning revelation and one Laurence wasn't sure whether to believe or not. 'How?'

'Your voice. Every writer has his own unique voice, Mr Bretton. A tone, if you will, that sets his apart from every other writer's,' Sir Michael said. 'Valentine Lawe's is quite distinctive and was consistent throughout all of the first four plays. The moment I read yours, I knew it was not the same voice and, therefore, could not be the same author.'

'Then why didn't you say something that day at my uncle's house?' Laurence asked. 'From what I understand, you and my uncle have not always seen eye to eye. It would have been an excellent opportunity for you to even the score.'

'Yes, it would, but revenge is a dish best served cold and I have no desire to make an enemy of Templeton. As it happens, I think he's a damn fine producer, though I'll deny it if you ever say as much. Besides, I know *why* you did what you did, Mr Bretton,' Sir Michael said, 'and even a hard-hearted critic like myself would find it difficult to find fault with your motives. But tell me, does your sister intend to write any more plays?'

'I honestly don't know,' Laurence said, still reeling from the shock of finding out that Loftus already knew he wasn't Valentine Lawe. 'She has taken to writing children's stories and seems to enjoy that very much.'

'Pity. Writing for children may be rewarding for the soul, but I doubt she will find it particularly lucrative. However, married to Alistair Devlin, that won't be a consideration. Still, it is not the end of the world. If *you* are able to continue writing plays the calibre of *The Silver Chalice*, Valentine Lawe needn't die.'

'But I've just told you I'm not him.'

'And I'm telling you it doesn't matter *who* Valentine Lawe really is,' Sir Michael said. 'Only that he is *perceived* to be the playwright. It may surprise you to learn that some believe William Shakespeare was only a pseudonym. This is no different.'

'I cannot lie to the people I care about,' Laurence said. 'Not any more.'

'Fine. Then be honest with those you love and lie to everyone else. The theatre is not meant to be taken seriously, Mr Bretton. It isn't a place of law or punishment. It is a place of entertainment and farce. A place where a man goes to forget about his troubles for an evening. What does it matter if you are truly the author of plays that in a few years' time society will have forgotten all about?'

Laurence got to his feet. 'It matters to me.'

'Yes, I'm sure it does, but what of your family? Do you not care about them any longer? Your eldest sister is part of a noble family now and your younger sister is not yet married. Are you prepared to see them suffer so that your conscience can be clear?'

It was the question he still battled with, Laurence acknowledged, the question for which he did not have an answer.

'No, I thought not,' Sir Michael said quietly. 'And that is not a bad thing. A man should care about his family and wish to protect them. For that reason, I suggest we strike a bargain.'

Laurence raised an eyebrow. 'What kind of bargain?'

'One that works to the benefit of everyone involved. I respect what you did today, Mr Bretton. It took courage to tell me the truth and I understand your desire to acquaint Lady Joanna with the facts given that you're in love with her and likely hopeful of marrying her. But beyond that, I suggest you make no further declarations of the truth,' Sir Michael said. 'The fact your plays are going in an entirely different direction from those of your sister will be a sufficient point of differentiation. Even if you suddenly start writing plays as Laurence Bretton, society will still think of you as Valentine Lawe. And while there will be those who don't like your new plays as much as your old, there will be just as many who like them even better.' Sir Michael crossed the short distance between them and held out his hand. 'The main thing is that we continue to produce plays that continue to be profitable. Are we in accord?'

It made sense, Laurence admitted. While still not being entirely honest, it did protect those he loved from censure and he had Sir Michael's assurance that any new works would be published under his own name. More importantly, it allowed him to go to Joanna now and tell her that the identity of Valentine Lawe was no longer a secret.

But would it be enough? Would she be able to forgive him for the lies he had told, or was it too late to regain her respect? Because without her respect, there wasn't a hope in hell of winning her heart.

Joanna had no desire to go shopping with her aunt. The days following her unhappy meeting with Laurence and her unpleasant argument with Captain Sterne were far from cheerful and the last thing she felt like doing was making frivolous fashion decisions. But after being told that her complexion was the colour of uncooked pastry and that the circles under her eyes were making her look like a street waif, she decided an outing might not be a bad idea.

If nothing else, it would be better than sitting in her room, brooding.

The arrangements were made for her to call at her aunt's house on a day suitable to her, at which time the three of them—Jane being included on the expedition—would set out for the shops.

Joanna dressed and arrived at her aunt's house on the prearranged day and at the requested time, and was informed by the butler that Mrs Gavin and her daughter would be down shortly. But when she was shown into the drawing room to wait for them, it was to find the room already occupied.

Laurence Bretton was there, standing with his back to the fireplace.

'What are you doing here?' Joanna demanded.

'Waiting for you,' he said quietly. 'Since you refused to meet with me or to read any of my letters, I was left with no other choice.'

'You *planned* this?'

'I'm afraid so.'

'With my aunt's help.'

'I could not do it without.'

'How dare you!' Joanna said, her embarrassment turning to anger. 'I don't know who to be the more upset with.'

'Please do not blame your aunt, the idea was entirely mine,' Laurence admitted. 'I asked Mrs Gavin if she would be willing to allow a meeting to take place and, against her better judgement, she granted me five minutes to state my purpose. If, at the end of that time, I have not managed to change your mind, I will leave and not bother you again. But I wasn't about to let you go on with your life without telling you how I felt, or assuring you that the guilt you are feeling is entirely misplaced.'

'On the contrary, it is entirely justified,' Joanna said, turning away from him. 'I have sullied your reputation. You have no reason to be so tolerant or so forgiving.'

'If I am forgiving it is only because the circumstances demand it. And before another day goes by, I *will* have honesty between us, Joanna,' Laurence said. 'And the truth is I am not Valentine Lawe.'

Joanna briefly closed her eyes, torn between frustration and anger. 'Mr Bretton, there really is no need to maintain this pretence. Sir Michael Loftus told me who you were the day I called at your uncle's house. You were there. He held up your play and said it was exceptional. As good as anything you had previously written. Or are you going to tell me now that *The Silver Chalice* is not your play?'

'No, it is mine,' Laurence said. 'But it is my first play rather than my fifth. Victoria wrote the first four because she *is* Valentine Lawe.'

'But you *talked* to me about those plays,' Joanna said, turning back to face him. 'You knew everything there was to know about them.'

'I *had* to in order to be convincing. But I *did not write* them, Joanna,' he said, taking a step closer. 'Victoria did. She simply wasn't willing to admit to it in public.'

'But why did *you* become Valentine Lawe? And why admit it to me now? Your sister's first play came out four years ago. Why did it take so long for the truth to come out?'

'To be honest, it wouldn't have come out at all if not for an unfortunate rumour started by a spiteful young woman,' Laurence admitted. 'I won't bore you with the details. Suffice it to say that last year, Victoria and Mr Devlin, then just a friend, encountered one of the actresses from my uncle's troupe with a gentleman she should not have been with at a society event to which they were not invited. When Victoria politely suggested the actress leave, she took offence. Not long after, a rumour began to circulate that Victoria was Valentine Lawe.'

'And a scandal broke out as a result,' Joanna said.

'Yes. Winifred was being courted by Mr Fulton at the time and was furious when his attentions suddenly turned elsewhere. We even began to fear that Mr Devlin's regard for Victoria might be in jeopardy. Naturally, Mama was beside herself. She accused Victoria of ruining the family's name and went on to predict doom and gloom for both my sisters in the marital arena. So the rest of us, my aunt and uncle, my father and myself, decided that the only way to fight the rumour was to maintain it wasn't true. And that's what we did,' Laurence said. 'We didn't think it would hurt anyone, and in hindsight, it wasn't the smartest choice we could have made, but once it was embarked upon, we had no choice but to carry on and hope in time that it would all blow over.'

'But it did not,' Joanna surmised.

'No. Matters came to a most unfortunate head when Sir Michael Loftus appeared at our door one day and asked Victoria point blank if the rumours were true and if she was, in fact, Valentine Lawe. It was particularly awkward given that Devlin was there too, having arrived only a few minutes earlier to speak to Victoria about that very subject. So, in the fleeting moments between Sir Michael asking the question and my sister answering it, I made a decision. I knew no one would question the propriety of a gentleman being a playwright, so I stepped forwards and said I was Valentine Lawe. Once Sir Michael let that be known, the die was cast and, overnight, I became a famous playwright with four wildly successful plays under my belt. Suddenly, I was in demand at literary gatherings and soirées, and while I was able to hold my own, I would be lying if I said I was comfortable in the role.'

'You were very convincing at Mrs Blough-Upton's soirée,' Joanna murmured.

'Yes, and you have no idea how much I regretted that appearance after I saw you there that night.'

She blinked. 'You cared what I thought even then?'

'Good Lord, yes. I wanted you to believe I

was the earnest student of history you'd met in the bookshop,' Laurence said. 'The one eager to learn as much about Egypt as he could. But the next time you saw me, I was Valentine Lawe, the famous playwright, and two more different men I cannot imagine.'

A smile came unbidden to Joanna's lips. 'No, I dare say you cannot. I decided you must have been using the book as an excuse to approach me.'

'I was…but only because I heard you talk about Egypt and realised we had a common interest. From that point on, the situation evolved into what it is now. I wanted to tell you the truth about my not being Valentine Lawe weeks ago, but the timing never seemed right,' Laurence said. 'Then when Winifred came home and told me Mr Fulton had asked her to marry him *because* of what I'd done, I realised I *couldn't* tell you. I didn't know what you would do with the information and I couldn't risk being the cause of Winifred's unhappiness.'

'I wouldn't have said anything,' Joanna said softly. 'It would never have occurred to me to betray you like that.'

'I know that now, but I didn't at the time. I thought you were so angry with me you would have done anything you could to disgrace me. I reminded myself that even had I told you the truth, it wouldn't have mattered. I was neither titled nor wealthy, and I knew you had to marry a rich man so I decided to keep silent, knowing how important it was to my family that I maintain the façade.'

It was a fascinating story and now that she knew it all, Joanna could well understand why Laurence had done what he had. 'So, this latest play. *The Silver Chalice*. Is it really yours?'

'Oh, yes, and I was very pleased when Theo told me it was good.'

'As I recall, the word he used was outstanding.'

'He does tend to overstate things.'

'Not, I suspect, in this case.' Joanna looked at him for a long time, aware that he was baring his soul to her and that no matter what happened now, there would never be any need for lies or deception between them again. 'No wonder you were so angry with me when I accused you of wanting to be famous,' she said. 'I know now that nothing could be further from the truth. But why have you told me all this now?'

'Because if you would admire me, let it be for the man I am rather than the character society *believes* me to be,' Laurence said quietly. 'I could no longer live with the knowledge that I was lying to you. Not given the fact that I—' He broke off, frowning. 'Miss Gavin!'

Joanna spun around to see Jane standing in the doorway, her eyes growing wider by the moment as she glanced from one to the other. 'Mr Bretton! I'm so sorry! Mama didn't tell me you were here.'

'That's because I didn't think he still *would* be here,' Mrs Gavin announced, marching into the room. 'I do believe that was ten minutes, not five, Mr Bretton,' she added with a pointed glance in his direction.

'And I was, in fact, just leaving,' Laurence said, heading for the door. 'I was simply keeping Lady Joanna company until you and Miss Gavin came down.'

It was a flimsy excuse and Joanna knew it. The fact Laurence had been found in her aunt's drawing room raised one set of questions; the fact he had been caught alone with her raised another. But she didn't care. Not after what he'd just told her. 'Mr Bretton—'

'Come along, Joanna,' Mrs Gavin said briskly. 'We have an appointment to keep. Good afternoon, Mr Bretton,' she added, shooing him from the room and closing the door behind him. 'Such a forward young man. I would appreciate you not making any mention of this to Lady Cynthia, Joanna,' she said. 'It is bad enough she is so critical of your behaviour. I really do not need her to be condemning of mine as well.'

* * *

Needless to say, Joanna was on pins and needles by the time she got home. Four hours of shopping for shawls had done nothing to erase the memory of Laurence's words. It had only given her four more hours to think over everything he'd said in an effort to assuage her doubts and to finally clear the air between them.

He was not Valentine Lawe—but his reasons for *pretending* to be were the most admirable in nature. How could she condemn any man for putting the welfare of his family first?

'Ah, Joanna, you're home,' her father said, walking into the room. 'I was hoping we might have a chance to talk. Am I to understand that you have refused Captain Sterne's proposal of marriage?'

The mention of the man's name was unwelcome, but Joanna knew she had to deal with it. In all honesty, she was surprised the subject hadn't come up before. 'I'm sorry, Papa, but I had no choice. I know you were counting on his fortune to pay off our debts, but I could not marry him after finding out what kind of man he was.'

'I take it the two of you argued?'

'He lied to me,' Joanna said. 'He said he would allow me to go to Egypt with him if we were married, but then I found him interviewing someone else for the artist's position and realised he'd never *had* any intention of taking me with him. He expected me to accept his proposal, but would have insisted that I remain at home. So I refused.' Joanna sighed. 'I take it he's spoken to you about what happened?'

'Oh, yes. He told me his own version and demanded that I remind you of what you—and I—stand to lose if you do not reconsider his proposal.'

'I cannot, Papa,' Joanna said, slowly shaking her head. 'I'm sorry, but I will not marry him.'

'Of course you won't marry him,' her father said firmly. 'I told Sterne as much myself. Just as I told him that he is no longer welcome on my expedition to Abu Simbel.'

Joanna raised her eyes in astonishment. 'He isn't?'

'Certainly not. I cannot like a man who goes behind my back, even if he believes his reasons for doing so are commendable. I made it very clear that *I* decide who goes on the expedition and who does not, and said he had no right to interview someone on my behalf. I told him I have no desire to see him again and, given his treatment of you, I feel no regrets about it whatsoever.'

'But what are we to do about the bills? How will we manage?'

'Actually, that is the other matter I wished to discuss with you,' her father said, looking, to

Joanna's surprise, a little embarrassed. 'I'm not sure if you remember, but there was a lady at your aunt's dinner party. A widow by the name of Mrs Taylor.'

'Yes, I remember her,' Joanna said. 'Aunt Florence told me she was very nice.'

'She is. And I have seen her…a number of times since that evening,' her father said, sounding even more embarrassed. 'And while it is still early days, I am hopeful of Mrs Taylor and I becoming even closer in the future.'

'Closer?' Joanna repeated in delight. 'Are you telling me you wish to *marry* Mrs Taylor, Papa?'

'The thought had occurred to me,' her father said, smiling in a way Joanna hadn't seen him smile in a very long time. 'But how would you feel about it, my dear? I know how much you loved and miss your mother, and it would never be my intention to try to replace her—'

'But you wouldn't be replacing her, Papa,' Joanna said gently. 'You would simply be finding someone else with whom to share your life and I am *more* than happy at the idea of you doing that. I *want* to see you happy again.'

He looked both relieved and a little uncertain. 'I must say, this is the first time since your mother died that I've felt any kind of attraction towards another woman,' he acknowledged.

'I know that, Papa, and you must be sure to act upon it,' Joanna said, giving his arm a squeeze. 'Because if you find Mrs Taylor attractive, I guarantee other men will too, especially if she is as wealthy as they say. Oh, dear—' She broke off, gazing at her father. 'That's not why you wish to marry her, is it?'

'Good Lord, no! I've never been motivated by money and even in light of our present circumstances, I would not marry Mrs Taylor if I did not care deeply for her,' her father said. 'I've told her of my circumstances, preferring that she hear it from me, and said that if she wished to put an end to our association I would understand completely. But the lady seems not to mind my pecuniary difficulties and has assured me that she would be happy to make available whatever funds might be necessary…if she were to find herself in the position of being able to do so.'

'Oh, Papa, it sounds as though the lady would be very happy to marry you,' Joanna said, elated by her father's good fortune in having found a lady worthy of his love.

'I sincerely hope that is the case. If it is, it means *you* won't have to worry about finding a wealthy husband, and I know that is the only reason you were considering Captain Sterne,' her father said. 'I was wrong to put the onus for solving the problems of the estate on your shoulders, my dear. As earl, that is my responsibility, and I believe I am blessed in having found such a delightful way of doing so.'

'I couldn't be happier, Papa,' Joanna said, giving him a hug. 'I will be happy to welcome Mrs Taylor as my stepmother.'

'Good, because it also means *you* are free to marry a man you love.' He smiled and gently set her away. 'And if I'm not mistaken, you have already found that man.'

Joanna blushed. 'You knew?'

'I suspected. I remember the night Bretton gave you the amulet. I heard the longing in your voice when you spoke of him even then.'

'But what about the difference in our social positions? Will that not cause problems?'

'Yes, but I have no doubt the two of you will work it out,' her father said. 'Your mother and I certainly did, and I would far rather see you marry a man you love than a man you feel obliged to. Society will have a hay day with it, I've no doubt, but eventually they'll find something else to talk about. They always do.'

It was as though the sun had come out after an extended period of grey. Joanna threw her arms around her father's neck again, hugged him tightly and then started for the door.

'Should I ask where you are going?' he called after her.

'No, but I would have you wish me luck. And please don't start looking for a new expedition artist just yet!'

* * *

'So it's settled,' Theo said, putting his hand on the thick sheaf of papers that was *The Silver Chalice*. 'Sir Michael and I both agree that the play is brilliant, but that there are a few minor revisions to be made before we start into production. Once that's done, all we have to do is decide when and where it should be staged.'

Laurence leaned his back against the door of his uncle's office at the Gryphon and tried to keep his focus on the matter at hand. The fact that his uncle and Sir Michael were working together on the play should have been all that mattered, but as always, thoughts of Joanna took precedence over anything his heart considered of less importance.

Their conversation was interrupted by a knock at the door. 'Come in,' Theo called.

'Pardon me, Mr Templeton,' a stage hand said, opening the door a crack, 'but there's someone to see Mr Bretton. Says her name's Lady Joanna Northrup.'

'Joanna?' Laurence got up and, opening the door, saw her standing a few feet beyond. 'Joanna!'

'Well, I believe that's my cue to leave.' Theo put his hands on his knees and stood up. 'Come along, Mr Belkins, it's time we checked on the progress of that new backdrop.'

Laurence knew it was an excuse, but he

wasn't about to complain. As soon as the two men left, he took Joanna by the hand and drew her into the office. 'What are you doing here?'

'I had to come.' Joanna's voice sounded breathless, as though she'd run all the way from Eaton Place. 'You left my aunt's house before you had time to finish the conversation we were having. The one in which you were about to tell me… how you felt about me.'

'I am sorry,' Laurence said, gazing down at her, hardly able to believe that she was standing right in front of him. 'I would have told you I was in hopelessly love with you if I'd had a few more minutes alone with you, but I didn't think you'd wish to hear something like that in front of Mrs Gavin and her daughter.'

'No, I most certainly would not,' Joanna agreed. 'I would prefer that we be alone, as we are now. But…are you quite sure you love me?'

'There is absolutely no doubt in my mind,' Laurence said. 'I fell in love with you the night of your father's lecture and my feelings have only been growing stronger ever since. But before I show you how much I love you, there is something else I need to say. You are not the only one who knows the truth about Valentine Lawe. I went to see Sir Michael Loftus yesterday and told him the whole story.'

'You *told* a theatre critic who writes for *the Morning Chronicle* that you were *not* Valentine

Lawe?' Joanna said incredulously. 'Oh, Laurence, why ever did you do it?'

'Because I wanted you to know that being honest with you was more important to me than having to deal with what society thinks. And the only way I could prove that was by going to Sir Michael and admitting that what I'd told him that day in the drawing room was a lie.'

'You dear man, what a noble thing to do. But what about your sisters? What will happen to them when society finds out the truth?'

'No one is going to find out, though if they do, we will deal with it,' Laurence said, convinced that the family was strong enough now to deal with anything that came their way. 'Sir Michael assured me he has no intention of making this public. He seems to think theatre lovers don't care who Valentine Lawe is as long as the plays keep coming. He really is quite a decent chap once you get to know him.'

'I am so relieved,' Joanna said. 'And so incredibly touched you would do this for me. That you would put so much at risk for my sake.'

'It was the only way I could convince you of how much I loved you,' Laurence said, wondering how he was managing not to pull her into his arms and kiss her senseless. 'I don't want there to be any secrets between us, Joanna. Because I do want to marry you, even though you haven't given me *any* idea as to how you feel about me.'

The happiness on her face lit up the entire room. 'Darling man, I love you! I was sure I had given myself away countless times over the past few weeks.'

'Not once.' He tipped her face up to his, knowing he would never get tired of seeing those enchanting green eyes. 'I've known talented actresses who weren't half as convincing as you.'

'Obviously they weren't half as motivated.'

'Obviously. But what about Captain Sterne? I thought you were going to marry him in order to save your father's estate.'

'I was, until I found out what a detestable man he is. You were right, Laurence. He never had any intention of allowing me to go to Egypt with him after we were married. He only said that so that I might look more favourably upon his suit. And I did for a while, thinking it was the answer to Papa's problems. But I couldn't have gone through with it. I don't want to settle for a convenient marriage. I want to be passionately in love with my husband, the way I am with you. And I don't want there to be any secrets.'

'Darling Joanna, you know all my secrets now,' Laurence said, before telling her, in the most convincing way possible, that there would never be any secrets between them again.

'Are you sure you won't mind being the wife of a playwright?' he murmured against her lips some time later.

'As long as you don't mind being the husband of an artist.'

'I think I can bear it. But there is one more thing I want to tell you. I've spoken to my uncle and we've agreed that whatever profits we make on the new play will go to you to help cover your father's debts.'

'Oh, Laurence, what an incredibly generous thing to do—'

'Wait, hear me out,' Laurence said. 'Quite some time ago, I came into an inheritance. It was…an unexpected windfall to say the least, but my uncle invested it and it has performed rather well in the intervening years. And while it may not be enough to completely cover your father's debts, it will go a long way towards paying them down.'

'You would do that for me?' Joanna whispered.

'I would do anything and everything I could to make you happy as my wife,' Laurence said. 'You are going to marry me, aren't you, Joanna? In spite of the fact that I don't come with an impressive title or a fancy carriage.'

Joanna laughed, then, drawing his head down to hers, did her very best to banish any lingering doubts he might have had.

Laurence finally groaned and pushed her away. 'I think, my beautiful muse, that if we don't wish to end up doing something that should by all rights be reserved for our wedding night, I had best keep my distance. I cannot vouch for my will-power when you kiss me like that.'

Joanna laughed again and, obviously not caring a wit for his will-power, snuggled back into his arms. 'I have never been anyone's muse before, but perhaps the gift of language has become mine as well.' She gazed up at him and quoted softly, *"My bounty is as boundless as the sea, my love as deep, the more I give to thee."'*

Laurence smiled and drew her close, loving the feeling of her body pressed against him. 'Dearest girl, you can quote the old Bard to me any time you like, but when it comes to loving you, I intend to make sure that nobody—not even Valentine Lawe—does it better!'

* * * * *

A sneaky peek at next month...

HISTORICAL

IGNITE YOUR IMAGINATION, STEP INTO THE PAST...

My wish list for next month's titles...

In stores from 2nd August 2013:

❏ Not Just a Governess – Carole Mortimer

❏ A Lady Dares – Bronwyn Scott

❏ Bought for Revenge – Sarah Mallory

❏ To Sin with a Viking – Michelle Willingham

❏ The Black Sheep's Return – Elizabeth Beacon

❏ Smoke River Bride – Lynna Banning

Available at WHSmith, Tesco, Asda, Eason, Amazon and Apple

Just can't wait?

Visit us Online

You can buy our books online a month before they hit the shops! **www.millsandboon.co.uk**

0713

Special Offers

very month we put together collections and
onger reads written by your favourite authors.

lere are some of next month's highlights—
nd don't miss our fabulous discount online!

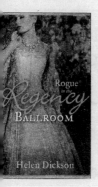

n sale 2nd August   On sale 2nd August   On sale 19th July

 **Save 20%**
on all Special Releases

Find out more at
www.millsandboon.co.uk/specialreleases

*Visit us
Online*

0813/ST/MB428

Join the Mills & Boon Book Club

Subscribe to **Historical** today for 3, 6 or 12 months and you could **save over £50!**

We'll also treat you to these fabulous extras:

- 🌹 **FREE L'Occitane gift set worth £10**

- 🌹 **FREE home delivery**

- 🌹 **Rewards scheme, exclusive offers…and much more!**

Subscribe now and save over £50
www.millsandboon.co.uk/subscribeme

SUBS/OFFER/H1